I0614636

The Pumpkin Butter Murder

by

Meg Benjamin

Luscious Delights Mystery, Book 2

This is a work of fiction. Names, characters, places, and incidents are either the product of the author's imagination or are used fictitiously, and any resemblance to actual persons living or dead, business establishments, events, or locales, is entirely coincidental.

The Pumpkin Butter Murder

COPYRIGHT © 2023 by Meg Benjamin

All rights reserved. No part of this book may be used or reproduced in any manner whatsoever without written permission of the author or The Wild Rose Press, Inc. except in the case of brief quotations embodied in critical articles or reviews.
Contact Information: info@thewildrosepress.com

Cover Art by *Tina Lynn Stout*

The Wild Rose Press, Inc.
PO Box 708
Adams Basin, NY 14410-0708
Visit us at www.thewildrosepress.com

Publishing History
First Edition, 2023
Trade Paperback ISBN 978-1-5092-5059-2
Digital ISBN 978-1-5092-5060-8

Luscious Delights Mystery, Book 2
Published in the United States of America

Fowler was the last person I expected to see on Tera's doorstep. I threw open the door, then stood blinking at him. "What are you doing here?"

Fowler raised his eyebrows. "I might ask you the same thing."

"We fixed dinner. Nate and I. We were just putting our stuff together so we could drive down to Shavano."

Fowler stepped inside. "You cooked dinner, the two of you?"

I nodded. "Yeah. We'd just finished. And then people got sick." All of a sudden my heart beat sped up alarmingly. "Why are you here? What's happened?"

Fowler ignored my questions in favor of his own. "Where's your partner?"

"You mean me?" Nate asked from behind me. "I'm right here. I agree with Roxy. We need to know what's happened."

Fowler gave us a long look, as if he was weighing a lot of different possibilities before he answered. Then he sighed. "Ms. Bloomfield passed away about a half hour ago. I'm here to secure the scene."

I felt as if my stomach had dropped to my knees. My heart was hammering, and I wasn't sure I could stand up on my own. I propped one hand on the wall until I felt Nate's arm around me, bracing me against him.

Praise for Meg Benjamin

"Readers will be hooked from the very first paragraph."
–*RT Book Reviews*

"It's the characters in Meg Benjamin's books who create the warm, intimate, irresistible atmosphere."
– Long and Short Reviews

"Tight writing and a fantastic narrative make this story not only enjoyable, but something I'd recommend to others who love a good, solid romance."
– Long and Short Reviews

"A wonderful story that readers will be sorry to see end."
– RT Book Reviews

"Benjamin is an extraordinary storyteller who melds sizzling spice, flirty fun and lively laughter to entertain the reader with every word."
– RT Book Reviews

"Every time I read a book by Meg Benjamin, it flat out makes me happy"
– Simply Love Books

Awards: Romantic Times Reviewers Choice Award, Holt Medallion, EPIC Award, Prism Award, Beanpot Award

Dedication

To my hubs and Pancho and Letty, who put up with me.

Prologue

The kitchen door swung open and Alex, the waiter, stepped through with the last of the dirty dishes. "Tera wants to know if you'd like to join them for port."

Nate rolled his eyes. "Nope. We need to get finished in here and then start loading up. I had a glass of wine at the table, and that's about all I can handle when I've got to drive down that road."

"I hear you." Alex raised an eyebrow. "But you're going to tell her that yourself, right?"

Nate sighed. "Yeah, sure." He pushed through the kitchen door.

I felt like sighing myself. It was already late, and given the way everything had been going so far, he'd probably be stuck out there for another hour.

"Are all the guests still there?"

Alex shook his head. "The couples left. It's just four guys, Tera, and the blonde."

"Susa?" I raised my eyebrows. The men I'd seen at the dinner table hadn't seemed like Susa's type. But maybe Tera wanted her to stick around to keep from being the only woman in the room. Of course, that didn't strike me as something Tera would worry about.

"Yeah, I guess that's Susa. It looks like they're settling in for the evening."

I started toward the boxes I was packing up when I heard an odd sound from the direction of the dining

1

room. Like someone had screamed, but not exactly. More like someone had groaned.

Alex and I both turned toward the door, both of us frowning, when it flew open and Siggi, the bartender, ran in, her face the color of rice paper. "Help. Get help now. She's sick. Call a doctor. Get an ambulance."

"What the hell?" I muttered and hurried through the kitchen door myself.

In the dining room, I saw a circle of leather chairs and a sofa, with a group of people gathered there. Tera was bent over a footstool at the front, retching. She wasn't the only one. One of the men was grasping his middle and groaning, while another was on his knees throwing up. Two more had staggered backward from the group, but it wasn't clear whether they were sick themselves or just trying to get away from the others. Nate was bent over his phone, talking fast to someone on the other end about medical emergencies and the need for urgent help, while Susa stood at the side of the room, hugging herself.

She looked more terrified than I'd ever seen her, and I'd known her since we were both seven.

I grabbed her arm. "Susa, what happened? What's going on?"

"I don't know. I don't…they all started throwing up and groaning. Maybe it was something they ate?" She gave me an anguished look as a stream of ice promptly slithered down my backbone.

It looked like we were in deep, deep trouble.

Chapter One

"Well, that looks like crap."

Herman glanced at me from across the room. He'd been banned from my cabin during the jam busy season, which extended from July through September and into the beginning of October. But it was late October now, and he was back in his doggie bed in the living room corner. He was used to hearing me cuss about my jams, so he didn't do much beyond giving me a soulful look before replacing his chin on his extended paws.

"What's the matter with it?" Uncle Mike arched an eyebrow in my direction. He was almost as accustomed to my cussing as Herman was.

"This is supposed to be paste, like a very firm jelly. And look at it." I spooned up a sample of what was supposed to be membrillo, Spanish quince paste, and let it drip off the spoon into the pan. "It's more like syrup."

Uncle Mike turned from the kitchen table to study the mess on my sheet pan. "Don't know much about quinces myself. Not much interest in them around here since you can't eat them out of hand."

"Luann doesn't know what to do with them either." Luann Sylvester and her husband Terry had purchased an orchard down the road from our place. It was mostly apples and pears, but there were also two quince trees.

Uncle Mike pushed himself to his feet and ambled

toward me. "Is it like apple jelly? Or pear conserve?"

"Quinces are related to apples and pears, but they don't behave the same way when you turn them into jam." I ran my spoon through what was supposed to be quince paste again. "Maybe I didn't let it dehydrate in the oven long enough. Or maybe it wasn't cooked down as much as I thought before I put it in there."

"Sounds like a lot of trouble." Uncle Mike narrowed his eyes at the pan of pink syrup.

"I guess I'll keep looking for something else to do for Winter Market. This still isn't right."

The Winter Market was the last hurrah for the farmers market until spring. The regular outdoor market closed down in mid-October when snow started being a real possibility, but Winter Market usually took place during November. It was great for Christmas sales.

"Can't you just go with your usual stock?" Uncle Mike leaned over to pick up his cup before pouring himself more coffee.

"I will go with my usual stock. I've got around ten cases of last summer's stuff. But I want to have something exotic, too. Winter jam, sort of."

Uncle Mike snorted. "Winter jam. What's that? Snow with chopped icicles?"

I picked up the pan, ready to transfer the contents to the refrigerator while I tried to decide what to do with the syrup. "You laugh, but Bianca Jordan always has a crowd for her gingerbread snowmen." Of course, she had a crowd because she was a sensational baker. But the snowmen helped.

Uncle Mike sighed. "Why not use seasonal fruit? Apples and pears. Lord knows there's enough of them around this time of year." He nodded toward the quince paste. "What does that stuff taste like?"

"It's pretty good, actually." I paused to scoop up a spoonful of pink quince syrup which I handed to him.

He tasted a little gingerly, then shrugged. "Probably be okay on ice cream."

"Probably. And I can put some on that leftover crumb cake Madge sent home with you."

Uncle Mike's ears turned slightly pink. References to Madge Robicheaux always seemed to fluster him a little. Maybe he was embarrassed to be dating at his age. "Yeah. That was good. Madge has got the touch."

Actually, the crumb cake had probably been baked by Madge's daughter, Coco, who did desserts for Robicheaux's Café, but I didn't bother to correct him. It was good crumb cake, and Uncle Mike and Madge made a great couple. I'd do what I could to encourage them.

Uncle Mike watched me put the quince sauce into the refrigerator. "Nate coming over tonight?"

I shrugged. "Maybe. He's working breakfast tomorrow, but he said he had some stuff he wanted to talk to me about."

Nate Robicheaux is my Significant Other, my main squeeze, all of that. He's also the guy who got me over my own Intimacy Issues after an attempted sexual assault in my restaurant days. I'm taken with Nate, although I'm still a little nervous about using the *L* word.

Uncle Mike frowned. "Is this like a 'We have to talk' situation?"

"I don't think so. He said he had a couple of ideas he wanted to run by me." Which could mean anything from menu selections to redecorating hints for Nate's apartment over Madge's garage. But I didn't think it had anything to do with us.

I was pretty sure, anyway.

"So you want me to get my own dinner?" Uncle Mike asked innocently.

"Only if you're not in the mood for pot pie. Susa's coming by, too, and Nate may be here in time to eat." My pot pie recipe was designed for family suppers, the kind where you just throw in an extra potato and a handful of carrots if someone shows up unexpectedly.

"Okay, I'll be back at dinner time." Uncle Mike put his coffee cup next to the sink. "I need to go check on some stuff with Donnie. Dolce still helping you out?"

Donnie was Uncle Mike's long-time next-in-command, and Donnie's daughter, Dolce, was my sales assistant at the farmers market during the summer. She was also one of the students I was mentoring at the high school. "She's working on some projects at school right now. I don't have anything for her to do in the kitchen." And I wouldn't have anything until I decided what I was going to do for my special Winter Market jam.

"Apple jelly," Uncle Mike said sagely. "Pear conserve. Maybe crabapple jam. See you later." He closed the front door before I had a chance to point out the problems with all of those possibilities. But all those problems boiled down to one: they were boring.

Well, not boring exactly. They were all tasty and they all sold well when I made them. But they didn't get my creative juices going. I needed something unique and tasty, something to catch people's attention and maybe get them to spend a little extra for a hostess gift.

It took me the rest of the afternoon to clean up after

my membrillo debacle and get the pot pie ready to go. I'd just put the pie in the oven when someone knocked on the door. *Nate.* He was a little early, but we could have a glass of wine and a chance to talk. Or a chance to cuddle. Either would work for me. I turned toward the door with my best welcoming smile.

But when the door swung open, it wasn't Nate at all. It was Susa, my other dinner guest.

Susa Sondergaard has been my best friend since second grade. She knows every lousy decision I've ever made, and I know most of hers. And neither of us has ever told anybody else about them, which shows you what kind of friends we are. Susa is smallish, maybe five foot two or so, and I'm close to six feet. Plus she looks like her Norwegian ancestors, all blonde hair and blue eyes, while I'm a very brunette Greek. We've always looked like improbable friends. But it never bothered us much. If Susa ever needed a kidney, I'd be first in line.

"Hey. I just put dinner in the oven. You want some chips and salsa? I've even got some margaritas in the freezer."

Susa shook her head, running a hand through her hair. She looked a little more harried than usual—she had dark circles beneath her eyes, and her smile seemed forced. "Thanks, that sounds great, but I can't stay. That's what I came out to tell you. Tera's got a new idea she wants me to try out online. I need to go over there and get to work."

My eyebrows went up. "Now?" It was five o'clock, after all.

"Yep. I'm pretty much on call twenty-four seven these days. Tera's paying me a ton of money to keep her site up to date, so I can't complain if she wants me to be available when she gets a new idea." Susa gave me another of those forced smiles. "Sorry, Rox. Maybe we can get together next week sometime."

"Sure." I worked hard at keeping my own smile in place. "Don't worry about it."

"Okay, call me." She turned and was gone almost before I could say anything. Unfortunately, the first thing that popped into my head to say was, *Why don't you call me? You're the one who's cancelling on dinner.*

Oh, grow up. That was my more realistic side kicking my inner seven-year-old to the curb. Susa was a freelance electronics guru who took care of practically every computer in town, or at least she used to. Now she was reducing the number of clients she was handling personally, although she still took care of my website and Uncle Mike's business software.

Lately it seemed she'd been spending most of her time working for Tera Bloomfield.

Tera was relatively new in town. She'd moved to Shavano a few months ago after selling her investment company in Denver and buying one of the fancy houses up toward Lost Horse Pass. I'd never heard of her, but other people told me she was famous as a hotshot financial guru.

Now she was starting up a new company here in our little backwater town. Nobody in Shavano knew just what she was up to, but something big was going on, given the fancy office space she'd leased in one of the buildings downtown. There was also a lot of traffic driving up the road to Tera's estate, expensive cars and SUVs we didn't normally see in our part of the mountains.

Most people in Shavano were excited about Tera moving her business here. The town might never be Aspen, but some of the citizens thought we could give Telluride or Crested Butte a run for their money. Having someone like Tera Bloomfield attracting the rich and richer to our city might help at least put Shavano on the map.

That idea assumed all the citizens of Shavano wanted to be Telluride or Crested Butte. Some of us liked the town just the way it was—quirky, unpredictable, and beautiful. And yes, I counted myself among the people who felt that way.

Tera and I hadn't exactly hit it off. She was one of those women who looked like she survived on filet of air with a spring water chaser, and nobody has ever accused me of being under-nourished. The jeans Tera wore cost more than my best week of summer profits, while my jeans are the kind you can wear to muck out a barn. We were not natural soulmates, to put it mildly.

When Susa introduced us at Dirty Pete's, Tera looked me over and said, "Oh, you're the jam woman." I am, in fact, a woman, and I do, in fact, make jam. However, something about the way she said it put my back up. Like jam was the sum total of who I was and everything I'd ever be. Susa gave me an embarrassed smile, but she didn't say anything. Of course, by then Tera was her major client, so I understood why she kept quiet. I understood, but I didn't like it.

These days, Tera was taking up more and more of Susa's time. I was happy for my friend because it was a high-paying gig with all sorts of possibilities for the future. But at the same time I was annoyed. Susa never seemed to have time anymore.

Herman stood in the entry way, staring disconsolately at the closed door after Susa left. She was one of his favorite people, and she hadn't even scratched his ears. I knelt down to give him a quick hug. "It's all right, Herm. She still loves you. She's just a little rushed right now. Anyway, you've got me and Uncle Mike."

Herman didn't look like that was much of a consolation, but it was the best I could do. "Come on, boy, I'll put on *Great British Baking Show* and you can snarl at Paul."

I was just setting the table when I heard the door open again. By now I'd reduced my expectations, so I assumed it was Uncle Mike. I didn't bother to turn around. "There's some beer in the refrigerator or we can have wine with dinner if you want. I've got a bottle of chenin blanc that might work."

"A bottle of chenin blanc would definitely work for me." A pair of strong arms looped around my waist from behind and Nate pulled me against him, kissing my cheek. "Hello, gorgeous. How's it going?"

And just like that, everything felt a lot better. Well, not everything—I'm not that far gone. But having Nate's arms around me helped me toss my gloom away. I turned around to kiss him properly, then rubbed my nose against his collarbone. One of the great things about Nate—one of many—is that he's over six feet himself. Which means I don't have to contort myself to fit in his arms.

"Dinner's almost ready. Uncle Mike should be on his way down from the main house."

"Which gives us another five minutes or so," Nate

said. And he took advantage of our time.

Having Nate and pot pie and Herman and Uncle Mike all together made up for a lot. But I still missed my best friend. I hoped sometime we'd be able to hang out again.

Without any interruptions from Tera Freaking Bloomfield.

Chapter Two

Uncle Mike was disappointed Susa wasn't coming to dinner. "What kind of work is she doing for that Bloomfield woman, anyway? Seems like she's never around these days."

I had to stand up for Susa even though I secretly agreed with him. "Tera Bloomfield's paying Susa a lot of money to take care of her website. And Susa's hired on a couple of full-time assistants to do the work for all her regular clients. She's trying to make sure everybody gets taken care of, but it's running her a little ragged."

"One of her assistants has been taking care of the café's website," Nate said. "She looks like she's barely out of high school, but Coco vouched for her. She's doing okay. No complaints."

"But not as good as Susa, right?" Uncle Mike speared a pearl onion from his serving of pot pie.

"Nope. I'm just glad Susa got us somebody. I was afraid we'd have to figure out how to run the website ourselves."

"I keep hearing that Bloomfield woman's supposed to be cooking up some big deal for the town. Don Friedrich said she'd put us on the map. Hell, we're already on the map as I see it." Uncle Mike shared my lack of enthusiasm for the upgrade Shavano was supposed to get from Tera.

"Could be good," Nate said. "Right now we're

depending on summer tourists. Then things drop off in the fall. If we could build up our appeal with winter visitors, it would help the bottom line at Robicheaux's and a lot of people like us."

I shook my head. "I don't know how Tera could increase our winter tourist numbers. Right now the people who pass through town are all coming up to see her presentations. I don't know what their interest is in Shavano, assuming they have any."

"Maybe not," Nate said, "but maybe her project would get more people to invest here. I heard some big real estate developer from Ft. Worth has been looking around. Maybe he's interested in building some condos or a limited development. If more people bought vacation houses in Shavano or Geary, they'd probably come up in the winter, too."

I felt like groaning. Real estate development is a major hot button issue around here. Along with the usual environmental concerns and worries about things like roads and schools, farmers and ranchers like Uncle Mike oppose turning good pasture and orchard land into condos. That could lead to increased property taxes on already pricey land.

Uncle Mike folded his arms across his chest. "Real estate developers? Hell, why doesn't she bring in some timber companies and mine drillers at the same time. Might as well screw up the whole area while she's at it."

"I don't know that for sure," Nate said hastily. "Just one of the rumors floating around. For the moment nobody knows what Bloomfield's up to."

"She's not interested in helping us out," Uncle Mike said darkly. "Why should she? She's not from around here."

That was his ultimate put-down, of course. Fortunately, both Nate and I had grown up within the city limits.

"Time for dessert." And a change of subject, assuming I could get Uncle Mike to stop making dire predictions.

Fortunately, the quince syrup was a natural conversation topic, along with Madge's crumb cake. Nate seconded my conclusion that membrillo wouldn't work for a Winter Market showpiece.

"What about something like chokecherry jam?" he suggested. "Yours is spectacular."

"Thanks, but I've got less than a case of that left. I'll sell what I've got, but I'm nearly out by now." And had no chance of finding more berries since I buy them in spring.

"Apple jelly," Uncle Mike pronounced. "Or crabapple. I told you."

He had. Repeatedly. "I'll make some. But I'm still looking for something to make people stop and grab a jar just for the novelty. But then it also has to taste good."

Uncle Mike pushed himself to his feet. "Guess I'll get up to the house. Want me to take Herman?"

That wasn't a particularly subtle way of asking if Nate was staying over. "If you want him. He's okay here if you'd rather be on your own." In other words, I didn't know if Nate was staying or not.

Uncle Mike turned toward the hall, where Herman was currently sprawled. "Come on, Herm. I'll find you a Lassie movie to watch."

Herman scrambled to his feet, his claws clicking on

the wooden floor, and Uncle Mike turned to us. "Night all. See you tomorrow."

Nate watched man and dog disappear up the walk toward the main house. "I didn't mean to piss him off. I've just been thinking a lot about how to increase profits at the café lately. Getting some of our summer visitors to become year-round visitors seemed like a good idea."

"It *is* a good idea. Hell, if we had more winter tourists, I'd sell more jam, too. But development's tricky. Nobody wants half-built deserted housing projects like they had over on the Western Slope. It's up to the county commissioners to make sure things don't go to hell."

"Terrific." Nate looked glum. "Somebody said Tera's thinking of running for the commission."

"Well, damn. There's a bad idea." I picked up my glass of wine. "You want to move to the living room?" Specifically, the living room couch, which was a lot more comfortable, not to mention a lot better for a little cuddling.

"Sure." Nate grabbed his wine and followed me down the hall.

"What did you want to tell me about?" We needed to take care of any discussion before the *cuddling* part of the evening started.

Nate settled on the couch beside me, placing his wine on the coffee table so he could put his arm around my shoulders. "It's an idea I had. I want to run it by you before I discuss it with anybody else, to get your feedback."

"Okay, what's up?"

Nate took a deep breath, like he was ordering his

15

thoughts. "You know that empty building next door to the café?"

"It's always been empty, hasn't it? I don't think I've ever seen anybody inside."

"We own it. I guess Dad was going to expand into it, but he never got around to drawing up any plans. We use it for storage, mostly. But at one point it was also a restaurant. There's a small kitchen separated off from the main room—sink, refrigerator, stove. No flattop, though, and not a lot of prep space."

I wondered where he was going with this. Robicheaux's Café had a great kitchen and lots of prep space. "Do you use the kitchen as an extra prep area?"

Nate shook his head. "Everything in that building is strictly overflow right now. We've got cases of canned goods and extra dishes and flatware over there. And we store stuff in the refrigerator, too. Like if we get a good deal on sweet corn or something, we can stack it over there."

"So what do you want to do with it?"

Nate leaned back a little, staring up at the ceiling. "You know we don't serve dinner."

"Right." Robicheaux's did a big business at breakfast and lunch, and it was a family-run restaurant. No outside help beyond the guy who cleaned up and ran the dishwasher, along with the wait staff. They must have decided that dinner would be too much for the Robicheaux family to handle on its own.

"I've been thinking maybe doing dinner would be a way to increase our reach."

"What does your mom think?"

"I haven't talked to her about it yet. I wanted to get everything worked out before I brought it up."

"What are you thinking about?"

"I want to turn the storage space into a bistro. Only a few tables, room for twenty or thirty customers, tops. Open maybe three or four evenings a week." Nate said it all in a rush, as if he'd been keeping this to himself for so long he needed to let it out fast.

"Wow." I took a breath. "You've been working on this idea for a while, haven't you?"

He nodded. "Ever since the contest last summer."

Nate had won the Best In Shavano contest in the dessert category with a crepes dish including my special rose petal jam. And one of the judges—a chef in Aspen—had said he should have won the whole thing. I agreed with him. Nate had been a chef in Las Vegas before he'd had some health problems that sent him to Shavano. He was very good at his job.

"What kind of menu are you thinking of?"

"Bistro food. Soups and paninis, salads, frittatas or soufflés, one or two entrées at most. I figure we could buy the desserts from Bianca, or maybe get Coco to make them. And I'd want to get a beer and wine liquor license. What do you think?" He looked little tense, like he was afraid I might try to discourage him.

As if. "I think it sounds great. It would be unique in Shavano. You're a terrific chef, and it would give you a chance to work on new menu stuff. Can I get inside the building sometime to see what you can do with it?"

He nodded, breaking into a grin. "Sure. Come over after lunch service someday."

I was definitely grinning back. The thought of having a bistro to work on during the winter slow season was exciting. "Can I help? Paint a few walls? Look for secondhand furniture?"

Nate's grin widened, then he pulled me into a very enthusiastic kiss. "Thanks, Rox. I was worried about what you'd say. Thanks for saying just the right thing."

"Why would you be worried? It's a great idea. You've got the space and the clientele. And if you keep the menu within bounds, you should turn a profit. I've always thought the town was lacking when it came to dinner restaurants. Most of them are old fashioned or so high priced they're mainly special occasion places."

Nate nodded. "I agree. We've got a lot of great specialty places and taverns like Dirty Pete's, but we don't have many small dinner places for couples and singles who just want a light meal. I'm thinking most of our sales will be paninis and frittatas, along with some good hearty soups."

"Right." My own enthusiasm kept building, although the fact it was slow season and I hadn't had anything to concentrate on since September might have had something to do with it. "When can I get a look at the place? Monday?"

Nate blew out a long breath. "That's the rub. I need to discuss it with Mom first, and probably Bobby, before I go any further. If they're against it, I'm stuck."

"Madge will be on board, I'm sure."

Nate's smile was dry. "But Bobby?"

"I'm not so sure about Bobby." In fact, I was pretty sure Bobby would be firmly against it. Bobby was firmly against anything that changed the way the café had always been run. "How are you going to persuade him?"

"I'll give him breakfast. He really wants to cook it every day instead of just three days a week like now. If I'm cooking dinner three days a week, I'll tell him I can't do both. Then I can help with lunch."

There was a certain logic in that. Bobby hated to share the cooking. He'd relented enough to divide it up with Nate once he'd returned from Las Vegas, but we both knew Bobby was dying to get his hands on things again.

"When are you going to tell them?"

"I'll try to talk to Mom tomorrow. If she doesn't buy in, there's no point in talking to Bobby. But if she's willing to give it a try, I'll bring it up with him next week."

"And then I can take a look at the place?"

"Sure. You can see it any time, but I'd rather wait until after Mom buys in at least."

"Next week," I said firmly. "What are you going to call it?" Because, to me, that was the most important question.

Nate stared down at his hands for a moment, then shrugged. "Bob's Place. Or Robert's Place. I can't decide. Probably Bob's because it's a little more informal, although most people called my dad Robert."

Robert Robicheaux had founded Robicheaux's Café. People like my uncle still talked about him and his food. He'd died of a heart attack in his own kitchen a few years ago. "I'd go with Robert's. Just Robert's. No Place."

Nate gave me a slow smile. "Robert's. Yeah. I like the sound of that."

"Robert's it is. And like I said, if you need help cleaning or painting or finding tables and fixtures—I'm available." Until I geared up for Winter Market, I had a lot of time on my hands.

"I'll be glad of the help. And your eye for

decorating. I suck at it."

"Sadly, so do I." I was living proof that not all women are natural born designers.

"Coco's the designer in the family. Assuming she'd be willing to help." Nate looked doubtful. His sister Coco was unpredictable.

I snuggled down closer so I could rest my head on his shoulder. "This is exciting, Nate. I can't wait to get started."

"You may feel different after you've seen the place." Nate tightened his arm around my shoulders. "I probably should go home. I have to cook breakfast tomorrow."

I turned to look up at him. "It's only seven thirty."

He paused. "And it's only a fifteen-minute drive."

"And if you're in bed by nine, you should be able to make it out by five."

He stared down at me, the corners of his mouth edging up. "I was thinking of maybe being in bed a little before that. If it's okay with you."

I looped my arms around his neck. "That can be arranged."

For the first time since Susa had cancelled out, I was feeling happy about life. Just shows you should never get ahead of yourself.

Chapter Three

I spent most of the next morning researching jam recipes that might work for the Winter Market. There was a sort of Christmas-colored cranberry pear thing, but I was trying to avoid using ingredients not found in Colorado, and we definitely lacked cranberries. Persimmons offered some possibilities, but they had the same problem.

In the end, I spent the rest of the afternoon making more of my perennials—peach, raspberry, and apricot. I had to use frozen fruit I'd put by from the growing season, but it would still be good, and I'd still sell a bunch. And, of course, Uncle Mike was right. Apple and crabapple would be popular. So would apple butter, which was easy enough to make, along with pear butter.

But thinking about apple and pear butter got my creative juices flowing again. I'd seen a recipe for pumpkin butter once upon a time. It made sense— pumpkins had a lot of natural sugar and if you added pumpkin spice along with some sugar or other sweetening, it would probably taste good. And Colorado grew pumpkins. Hell, everybody grew pumpkins.

The next morning I was digging through the internet and not finding what I needed (no, people, adding butter to pumpkins does not produce pumpkin butter—it produces pumpkins *with* butter) when my cell phone rang with a call from Nate.

"Hey, what's going on?"

"I talked to Mom. We're going over to take a look at the storage building this afternoon. Want to come?"

"Absolutely." I could do some pepper peach jam during the rest of the morning and let it set up while I went into town.

A couple of hours later, I pulled into the parking lot next to Robicheaux's. Several cars still sat in the lot, which meant the lunch crowd hadn't departed yet.

I paused to study the building next door, the future site of Robert's. It looked as if it had been a one-story bungalow once upon a time, but the front had been built out a bit, probably to accommodate more seating. It had large windows that could probably let in a lot of light when they weren't covered by plywood. It didn't look awful, just not stunning. But then, it didn't need to look stunning in its current incarnation. I turned toward Robicheaux's.

Madge was at the hostess stand, stacking menus. She gave me a quick grin when she saw me. "Hey, Roxy, how are you?"

"Fine, thanks. Is Nate still in the kitchen?"

Madge nodded. "They're just finishing up. You might as well go on back."

I walked through the swinging doors to the kitchen, careful to stay out of the way of the four very hard-working waitresses. Nate's brother Bobby was out front, probably checking the number of remaining customers. He acknowledged my presence with raised eyebrows, and I gave him a smile. Bobby and I weren't exactly friends, but our relationship was civil.

In the kitchen, Nate was working the flattop, where

most of the lunchtime cooking took place. He had a couple of burgers almost ready to go, with a grilled cheese already plated. He dropped the burgers into their plastic baskets along with a scoop of French fries each and placed the three orders at the pass-through window, ringing the bell to let the waitresses know an order was ready.

He glanced over and saw me, breaking into a grin. "Hey, babe."

"Hey, yourself." I gave him a quick kiss on the cheek, avoiding the hand with the spatula.

"Canoodling in the kitchen. I'm gonna tell Bobby." Coco peeked around the corner of her prep area, her dark feathery bangs pushed beneath a ball cap. "When are you going to make some jam for my doughnuts?"

I frowned. "Are you actually making doughnuts? I thought you bought your breakfast pastries from City Market."

Coco gave me a slightly sour look. "We do. But a girl can dream."

Coco already made most of Robicheaux's desserts, and they were prime. I hadn't realized she also wanted to do breakfast pastries. Maybe another sore point with Bobby since fresh pastries cost more.

Just then the kitchen door swung open and Bobby himself stepped in. "That's it. Door's closed. You can shut it down."

He glanced at me again, a little more critically, then at Nate. "You sticking around to do prep?"

Nate nodded, his smile flattening. "Yeah, I'll get to it. I've got a couple of things to do first. We'll be back in a half hour or so." He put his hand on my elbow, ushering me out the door into the dining room.

I wondered if Nate had told Bobby about his plans. I was guessing not, since Bobby hadn't made any comments. I was pretty sure he wouldn't have stayed quiet if he'd known Nate was going to be showing Madge and me around the storage building.

Madge was waiting for us by the front door. "I can't take too long. I've got to go over the website with Carly. We need to update the menu."

"It shouldn't take more than twenty minutes. It's a small building." Nate gave her a quick smile, but I noticed the tension around his mouth.

Apparently, so did Madge. She put her hand on his arm. "We can take as long as we need to. Don't worry."

"Okay, good. Let's check it out." Nate pulled a key out of his pocket and headed for the front door of the storage building.

Up close, it was a little more interesting. You could see the bones of the old bungalow underneath the weight of renovations probably done in the fifties or sixties. Nate unlocked the door and stepped through, reaching along the side wall for the light switch.

The space inside looked…okay. At the moment it was strictly storage. Cases of canned tomatoes and pinto beans rested against the walls, along with other boxes where the contents weren't quite as obvious. Our footsteps stirred up a little dust.

It was dark, cluttered, and depressing.

Madge waved a hand in front of her face. "I didn't realize how dirty this place had gotten. We should hire a cleaning service to come in and do a deep clean."

They'd definitely want to do that if they turned the place into a restaurant. I tried to picture the room without the boxes, but it was hard. Nate clicked on more lights and the overhead fluorescents blinked into life.

Madge folded her arms across her chest. "Okay, you're thinking of this as the dining room?"

Nate nodded. "I measured the dimensions. We could fit five four tops in here and still have enough space for wait staff to move. If the windows were uncovered, there'd be a lot of natural light. With the right decoration, it would be a warm space."

Madge narrowed her eyes, taking in the room. "Okay, I believe you. But the room would have to be repainted as a start."

"Right. No question. The floor is hardwood, what you can see of it. It might need to be refinished, but we wouldn't need anything new. And the windows and door frames are hardwood, too. The room would set up nicely."

I felt like knocking wood, but he'd clearly given it a lot of thought.

"How's the kitchen?" Madge asked. "I don't remember much about it."

"Through here." Nate pushed open a swinging door and switched on the light.

The kitchen was small, but it had a prep table in the center. I could see a utility sink at one side and a double refrigerator. The stove was somewhere behind Nate.

Madge frowned. "This needs work, too. More deep cleaning for one thing. And I'm betting the floor would need to be replaced to bring it up to code."

I glanced down and saw cracked linoleum. Madge had a point.

"Right," Nate said. "I think it's hardwood underneath, but we might want to cover it with tile."

"What about the stove?" Madge moved beside Nate, hands on her hips.

"Needs to be replaced. I'd worry about the safety of turning those burners on as it is. And it's too small for a restaurant."

Madge sighed, doing a quick survey of the kitchen as a whole. There was a closet pantry on one side and several open shelves containing a couple of ancient frying pans. They'd probably need to buy new pots and pans, too, unless there were some in the boxes in the other room. After a moment, she looked at Nate again. "It needs a lot of work, Nathan."

He nodded. "Agreed. Some of it I can do on my own, but some of it will take professionals. And an upgraded stove will run a couple thousand at least. Then there's the fixtures in the dining room. And one of the windows looks like it needs to be replaced."

I had to admire Nate for being honest. Then again, it wasn't like Madge wouldn't notice those details on her own.

She pressed her lips together, staring down at the ugly floor again, then at Nate. "I don't know if we can afford it, Nathan. We're clearing a nice profit at the café, as you know. But I'm not sure I'm ready to take on more debt. And this would involve a large loan to begin with."

Nate nodded. "I understand. But there's an alternative—finding some backers to advance us the initial investment."

Madge frowned. "How would using backers differ from getting a loan at the bank? We'd still have to pay them."

"We would. But we could get the amount of money

we need, not just the amount the bank would be willing to lend. Plus backers would be more involved with the place. They'd have a vested interest in making sure we succeeded. They might send us some customers. At the very least, they'd help us get the word out."

"Where would you find these backers?" I asked, although I had an uncomfortable feeling I already knew the answer.

"I could talk to Tera Bloomfield. It's the kind of thing she does. I've got a business plan already drawn up, and I could show her what we wanted to do."

I tried not to look as dubious as I felt. "I thought Tera just did stock market stuff. Would she know anything about setting up a restaurant?"

"I talked to Susa about it. She says yes."

Madge and I must have both looked unhappy he'd gone to Susa before he'd talked to us.

Nate held up his hands. "I just talked to her in a general way. I didn't spell anything out. But she said Tera's looking to invest locally as well as regionally. And we'd be local."

Madge leaned her hip against the prep table, still frowning. "I want you to show your business plan to Morris before you go any further. He may have some suggestions—and he might have some ideas about loans around here." Morris Logan was the accountant for Robicheaux's and a lot of other people in town, including Uncle Mike. He was good at his job, although he could also be a pain in the ass. I happened to know this because I'd run my own business plan by Morris before Luscious Delights got off the ground.

Nate didn't look happy, but Madge shook her head. "We need to think of all the contingencies, all the things that might not occur to us but would occur to Morris. For one thing, I want the café to be kept separate from the bistro. I don't want any of your backers to come after Robicheaux's if they decide their payout isn't as generous as they'd anticipated."

Nate paused. "You're saying you're okay with me going ahead?"

"Of course, you can keep going. You need to put together a budget for me and Morris to look over. Then we'll see how much money this would take."

"I've already got a budget," Nate said quickly. "It's pretty barebones right now. I wanted to see if Coco had any ideas for decorating the place."

Madge gave him a dry smile. "I'm sure your sister will have ideas. Whether they'll be affordable ideas is another question." She paused again. "We'll have to tell Bobby."

"Right." Nate blew out a breath. "I wanted to have the budget and business plan ready before I did that."

"He's likely to be more annoyed if he thinks you went ahead without considering his opinion. You should talk to him now. Before you start working with Morris or talking to Tera Bloomfield."

Nate nodded. "Okay. I'll do it today."

"Good." Madge's smile was a little warmer this time. "This is an interesting idea, Nathan. Your father always wanted to expand into this place, but he was concerned about the amount of time and money it would take, particularly if we had to close down Robicheaux's for a while. Making it a separate restaurant takes care of that. And it lets us expand our customer base."

"I thought so." Nate returned her smile.

"I've got to get over there and meet Carly. Let me know what happens with Bobby." Madge paused. "But you probably won't have to. I'll probably hear directly from him." She kissed her son on the cheek, gave my shoulder a quick hug, and turned toward the front door.

Nate blew out a long breath. "Okay, one obstacle down. Now I take on the next one."

"Would you like me to stay?"

"No, you can get back to your own kitchen." He put his arms around my waist, pulling me close, then rested his forehead on mine. "So what do you really think?"

"I think you've got your work cut out for you, but I still think it's an exciting idea. And I still want to help."

The next five minutes were pleasant, and I would have liked to have spent the rest of the afternoon there. But I had to work, and so did he. "Call and tell me what happens. Or you can come for dinner."

"I can't. I've got to go over my budget and business plan again, and I told Mom I'd have dinner with her."

We walked to the door together, his arm around my waist. "Want to get together this weekend? Saturday at my place?"

"Right. Then Sunday at mine." The café did a Sunday brunch, but they were closed on Monday, which meant Nate got to sleep in. We spent most weekends together.

"Yep, works for me. I'll call you."

As I drove to the farm, I considered the Tera Bloomfield question. Susa had vouched for her, or at least agreed Nate's bistro was the kind of investment opportunity Tera was open to. I wasn't convinced Tera was going to take Nate's ideas seriously, though. Judging from the things I'd heard about her, she dealt in million-dollar projects—real estate and industrial development. Nate's expenses wouldn't be major. The family already owned the property, after all. And if he used local contractors, as well as doing a lot of the work himself, the renovations shouldn't run much. From what I could see, the building looked sound, and I didn't think Nate's plans were too ambitious.

But what did I know about building costs? My last project had been a commercial stove for my cabin, and installation had been part of the price. I had no idea how much it would cost to get the bistro up to code. The most I'd be able to do would be to help out with painting.

I was better off sticking to my pumpkin butter. Assuming I could make it work.

Chapter Four

Bobby reacted more or less the way I expected him to, according to Nate. He grumbled about the expense and argued the restaurant was doing just fine as it was. But Madge refused to let him kill the idea.

The next few days were a blur of activity. Morris had some suggestions, which Nate incorporated. Madge checked both budget and business plan and had a few more suggestions of her own. I helped him rephrase a little, but I wasn't much help on the budget since I'd never done anything as ambitious as what Nate was proposing.

Meanwhile, I was still chugging along with my pumpkin butter. Most of the recipes seemed to be for refrigerator versions, which were great for home cooks but lousy if you wanted to sell the stuff. I'd have to have a cooler with frozen jars and put something on the label about keeping the butter in the refrigerator. One small batch turned out way too sweet. I substituted brown sugar for granulated sugar and tried it again. This time it was a little too bland. I tried cinnamon, allspice, cloves, ginger—all the sweet spices in various combinations. Finally I gave in and went with pumpkin spice.

Uncle Mike isn't much of a pumpkin fan in the best of times, and he burned out early on in the tasting. Nate tried, but he had too much on his mind. I gave it to

Dolce, but she was grossed out at the idea of making jam out of pumpkins. I put her to work sticking labels on jars of the other jams I'd be selling at the Winter Market and drove into town.

I wanted to talk to Susa about the pumpkin butter, but also about whether Tera would be able to help Nate. I had my doubts, but I wondered if they were a result of my not liking Tera much.

Susa worked out of a converted miner's cottage near the county courthouse. At one point she'd also lived there, but now she had a house of her own. I had no idea if she was actually at her office. Yes, I could have called her, but I had a feeling it might be better for me to just show up. That way she couldn't tell me she was busy, assuming she was there.

Susa's assistant, Carly, was sitting at the front desk when I came in. That didn't necessarily mean Susa wasn't around, but it wasn't a good sign. She broke into a grin when she saw the cooler. "A snack. Just what I need."

I could have used Carly and her co-workers as tasters, but I had a feeling they ate anything that crossed their plates since they were all in their early twenties and living on shoestrings. I needed Susa. "Maybe later. Is Susa here?"

Carly's grin faded to a grimace. "She's in her office, but you might want to call her first. She's breathing fire."

I thought about it for around a micro-second, then trotted up the hall. It seemed silly to call from the front of her own place. Besides, I told myself, I did this all the time. Which was true in the days before Tera. Lately, though, I hadn't been around her office much.

I knocked on the door frame and stepped into Susa's office as she swiveled toward me, snarling, "What the hell do you want?" Her expression reminded me of the little girl in *The Exorcist* when she was high on the devil.

I froze, the cooler dangling from my fingers. "Um…your opinion on some pumpkin butter. But maybe some other time."

I started to back out as quickly as I could, but Susa jumped to her feet. "Aw, Rox, I'm sorry. I didn't know it was you. Why didn't you call?" She grabbed my arm and pulled me into the office, closing the door behind me. "I've got all this work to do, and people keep interrupting me. It's making me nuts."

That made me feel even worse, of course. "I'm sorry, Suz, I can come when you're not so busy."

"These days I'm never not busy." Susa shook her head and I saw dark circles under her eyes again. She's always been a happy-go-lucky girl, knocking off early on Friday so she could go have a margarita and chips at Dirty Pete's, moving through boyfriends at the speed of sound. She was tops at her job, and everybody in town knew it, but she'd found a way to have both a business and a life. And to enjoy both.

Now it looked like her balance was gone.

"Suz, I'm sorry. I didn't mean to bother you. I'll get out of your way."

She shook her head so hard her blonde hair flew out in a cloud. "No, no, I'm sick of what I'm doing. Whatever you brought, I want to try it. What is it?"

I dropped into a chair opposite her desk. "Pumpkin butter. I'm going to try it for Winter Market, but I still need to get the recipe right. You want a taste?"

"Hell, yes, I want a taste." She massaged the back of her neck. "Sounds yummy."

I pulled out the jars and lined them up on her desk. "Here," I said, handing her a spoon as I opened the tops. "I'm not telling you what the differences are. Just tell me which one you like best."

We spent a pleasant thirty minutes tasting pumpkin butter. Susa called in Carly and a guy apparently named Kip. He and Carly both looked a little undernourished. Everybody tasted. Everybody had opinions. Nobody was grossed out by the idea of pumpkin butter, and Kip even said it was the best thing he'd tasted in at least a month. I gave him the jar—he looked like he needed food.

But at the end of a half hour, I knew it was time to go. Susa was beginning to look panicky again, and Carly was edging toward the door. Susa had always gotten along well with the people who worked for her. The fact they were wary of her struck me as another bad sign.

"Okay," I said. "Thanks for the input. I'll go home and make some more butter."

"Sure, any time. Let's have lunch or something." Susa paused for a moment, leaning on her desk. "How long has it been since we've had a meal together anyway?"

"A couple of weeks." It was more like four, but she already looked miserable.

"I keep thinking I'll be done with this stuff for Tera. And then something else pops up. I'm pretty much wrung dry."

I bit my lip to keep from suggesting she tell Tera to take a hike. "Any end in sight?"

She shrugged. "Your guess is as good as mine. She's supposed to launch in a few weeks, but I don't know how on target she is. Oh, by the way, tell Nate I put in a good word."

"About what?"

"About making his pitch to Tera. Tell him to call me." She started to turn to her computer, then paused. "You know about that, right? About the whole bistro thing?"

"Yeah, I've even been inside the building. I knew he was thinking of asking Tera for advice."

"Right. Sounds interesting."

"I guess he's going to talk to her, try to get her advice about finding investors. I hope she'll have time to help him out." That was as close as I could come to asking Susa if Tera would help Nate or just blow him off.

"I'm sure she'll find time." Something flickered in her eyes, so subtle I almost missed it.

"What?" I asked.

Susa stared down at her keyboard for a moment, but then she shrugged. "Tera always likes talking to good-looking guys. And Nate falls into that category. I brought Sean to one of her parties and she ended up talking to him for most of the evening."

Sean was one of Susa's parade of boyfriends, but he'd been at the top of her list for a while. "Did you talk to him about it later?"

"Haven't had a chance. I've been busy, and he's been…otherwise occupied." She gave me a very lame smile.

"With Tera?"

She nodded. "Easy come, easy go. She's paying me

enough. I guess she can poach one of my formers."

My shoulders tightened. But I trusted Nate. Absolutely.

Susa's eyes darted toward her computer, and I grabbed my cooler. "Call me when you've got a spare nanosecond. Or come out some evening. Uncle Mike and I can provide food and drink."

"That sounds wonderful." Susa closed her eyes for a moment. "I'll do that as soon as I can."

I had a feeling she wouldn't be by any time soon. I made my way toward the street, leaving another jar of pumpkin butter with Carly as I passed her desk.

I wondered if I should swing by Nate's place on my way home but decided against it. I'd already interrupted one super busy person today. I didn't need the guilt of interrupting somebody else.

And I did trust him.

I called him when I got home, though, just to tell him what Susa had said about recommending him to Tera. And to give him a chance to tell me what was up.

"Remind me to thank her. I've got an appointment to see Tera Bloomfield on Friday." He sounded a little distracted, and I had a slight pinch of guilt for bothering him. Not much, mind you, but a slight one.

Which didn't stop me from keeping him on the phone. "What are you going to ask her? Do you want her to invest with you, or do you want her to suggest other people?"

"I'm just going to ask her for advice. I figure she knows more about finding backers than I do. Maybe she can steer me in the right direction."

"Do you want to get together with me afterward so you can tell me what happened? I'll want to hear." All of a sudden it seemed important to talk to him after he met Tera.

"Sure. I'm meeting her at four. We should be done by five at least."

"Okay, I'll go to Dirty Pete's at five fifteen or so. You can tell me about it over margaritas."

During the rest of the week I nailed down the pumpkin butter, including adding a secret ingredient—chili flakes. It gave the butter a great zing of flavor.

By Friday, I was more than ready for a margarita and something made without chopped pie pumpkins. Dirty Pete's is a bar on Second Street, where most of the restaurants in Shavano are located. It's not actually dirty, and they serve a terrific plate of enchiladas along with first-rate margaritas, courtesy of their bartender, Harry Potter. Yes, that is his real name and no, he doesn't want to hear any clever remarks about it. By now, he's heard them all.

I took a quick survey of the room, but I didn't see Nate yet, just a lot of Shavano office workers taking a TGIF lap with Harry's specials. I slouched over to the bar, trying not to feel conspicuous as one of the few unaccompanied people in the room. "Hi, Harry. Seen Nate?"

Harry shook his head. "Nope. Want your usual?"

I nodded. Having a usual meant I'd been spending a lot of time at Dirty Pete's. Maybe I needed to regroup. I took my margarita in hand and found myself a table.

Pete's was fairly full for a Friday in fall, but lots of people who worked downtown hiked over after work. I found a two-top at the side and sat down to await Nate's arrival.

I wasn't worried. Well, not much. I didn't think

Tera had abducted him to her lair. But I didn't like knowing their meeting had run long. After what Susa had told me about Tera and Sean, I was uneasy about extended conversations.

After a few minutes, the front door swung open and I craned my neck to see who'd come in, but it wasn't Nate. It was Ethan Fowler, Chief of Police and once upon a time my nemesis when he thought I'd murdered another chef. Fowler still made me a bit nervous. He didn't smile much, and he had a way of looking at me that gave the impression he had X-ray vision. But we'd had a few normal conversations over the past couple of months, and we were cautiously moving toward being friends.

He paused when he saw me, then turned in my direction. "Mind if I join you?"

I couldn't very well say no, and I actually didn't want to. It felt a little weird sitting by myself when everybody else seemed to be in pairs. "Sure, have a seat."

Fowler waved to Caroline, the main waitress at Dirty Pete's, and then pulled out the chair opposite me. "Where's the boyfriend?"

"Nate's meeting me later." I hoped mightily that was true. Otherwise I was going to be sitting here with my sad margarita, trying to decide if I should drive to the farm.

Don't be ridiculous. He's just late. Not missing.

Caroline brought Fowler a bottle of beer and a glass. Apparently, he was also a regular at Dirty Pete's by now. "So," he said as he poured his beer, "what are you going to do with your business during the winter? Make jam for the summer?"

"Pretty much. The farmers market runs from May to October, and I spend the rest of the winter trying to get everything ready for next spring, along with selling some around town. What about you?"

He raised an eyebrow. "What about me?"

"Does crime go down in the winter when people can't get around as easily?"

He shrugged. "No idea. This is my first winter here. Based on past experience, I'd say no. People can be idiots any time of the year. And cabin fever can make idiots of the best of us."

"True enough. But a few feet of snow usually slows us all down. Unless they're on snowmobiles. Some of those guys go like maniacs, no matter how deep the snow is."

"Who goes hell for leather on a snowmobile? Sounds like a crappy ride."

"It probably is, but they've usually been imbibing."

"The beginning of every excuse I hear on Friday and Saturday nights. 'We were imbibing…' Although that's not usually the word they use."

He gave me one of his rare grins, and I was reminded that Fowler is actually a good-looking man. His eyes are an unsettling shade of ice blue, but his hair is the color of river sand, and it looked like it might have some curl if he hadn't kept it so short. If I hadn't been involved with somebody, I might have been attracted to him.

But then I *was* very much involved with somebody. And even noticing that Fowler wasn't bad looking seemed a little disloyal.

"Your boyfriend's late."

"A little," I admitted.

"You want to grab some dinner while you wait?" He raised an eyebrow, and I realized this was close to asking me out.

"No, I'll wait for Nate. He's at a meeting with Tera Bloomfield, and it may have run long."

He shrugged. "A lot of interest in Ms. Bloomfield these days."

"A lot of people in Shavano have projects they'd like to get backing for. Right now, she's the only one in town who's looking for investments."

"So I hear." Fowler gave me one of those X-ray looks, and I felt like squirming.

"Hey." Nate stepped beside the table. He glanced between me and Fowler, looking a little confused.

"Hi. I didn't see you come in." But I hadn't seen him come in because I'd been talking to Fowler. I wasn't sure why that made me feel guilty, but it did. I pushed myself to my feet and kissed his cheek.

Act out much, Roxy?

Fowler stood up, too, extending his hand to Nate. "Robicheaux."

Nate shook his hand. His expression seemed a little wary.

Fowler turned to me. "Good talking to you, Roxy. Have a nice evening."

"Thanks. You, too."

Fowler picked up his empty glass and his beer, heading toward the bar to settle up with Harry. Nate gave me another of those vaguely confused looks. "What was that all about?"

"Nothing. Let's get some enchiladas." And talk about Tera Bloomfield. Which seemed a lot less dangerous than talking about Ethan Fowler.

Chapter Five

After we'd ordered our enchiladas and settled at the table with our margaritas, Nate gave me a quick kiss. "I'm sorry I'm late. Tera and I were talking about all the ins and outs of starting a restaurant and we just lost track of time."

I was a little put off by the *Tera and I,* but I told myself to grow up. "Did she have any advice?"

"It turns out she's actually been involved in some restaurant launches. It was one of her specialties in Denver."

I tried to work up some enthusiasm. "That's handy."

"Right. It was. She had a lot of questions about the budget and the business plan, things I hadn't thought of. Of course, all her experience was in big city restaurants, so some aspects may be different in Shavano."

"Right." My guess was aspects would be very different in Shavano.

"Anyway, she's interested in checking us out. She wants to see the building. And maybe meet Mom, too."

He looked so happy I smiled a little more warmly. "That's great. Is this so she can recommend you to some of her clients who might want to invest in the bistro?"

"She may be interested in investing in the bistro herself. That's the feeling I got."

Maybe she was interested in the restaurant. Maybe she was interested in Nate. Maybe she was interested in both.

Just because she went after Sean, that doesn't mean she'll go after Nate.

I was trying my best, but my spider sense was into hyperdrive. "That's great. Maybe Susa can ask her about it. Find out what she's thinking."

"I don't want to get Susa involved any more than she already is. I got the feeling Tera was a little annoyed with her, maybe because she stepped in for me. I don't want to make anything worse."

"Did Tera say something nasty about Suz?" I gave up any pretense of being positive.

"She didn't say much, but when I mentioned Susa, she rolled her eyes. I figured it was time to back off."

"She rolled her eyes? Susa's working herself to exhaustion for her." And she'd stolen Susa's number one boyfriend. I was righteously pissed on Susa's behalf.

Nate held up a placating hand. "You know how it is when people work together. Sometimes they can get on each other's nerves, even if they don't mean to."

All of a sudden, I noticed the shadows around his eyes, the deepening grooves around his mouth. He'd been working pretty hard himself, and I wasn't making things any easier.

Still, I didn't like Tera Bloomfield, and I wasn't likely to change my opinion of her no matter what she did for Nate. I couldn't shake the feeling she saw Shavano people as a bunch of easy marks.

"So when is she going to inspect the building?"

"Tomorrow evening, after we finish lunch service

and brunch prep. She's going to come by the café so she can see what we do. I told her I'd cook dinner for her, to show her what kind of dishes I'm thinking of for the bistro. Coco's going to stick around and help."

He looked tense again, and I could see why. He was going to have to come up with something on the fly, using the ingredients they had around at the café. And it needed to be good, maybe even a showpiece.

"Could you do the meal you cooked for Best In Shavano?"

He shook his head. "Don't have the ingredients. I ordered those pork chops special. I don't have time to get more."

I wondered if the short notice was deliberate, to see how Nate functioned under pressure. But Nate usually functioned just fine. "You could do something simple. Your burgers are fantastic, and I love your mac and cheese with mushrooms."

"I want to move away from what we do at the café to what we could do at the bistro. Right now I'm thinking a two-cheese frittata with some kind of salad. I'll have to talk to Coco about it."

"That sounds great," I said loyally. Actually, it sounded a little lean, but Tera was from Denver. Maybe she was into minimalism. I, on the other hand, was enjoying my enchiladas. A lot.

"So anyway." He stared down at his plate, and all of a sudden I had a feeling bad news was coming.

"Anyway?" I prompted.

"Anyway, if I'm cooking and cleaning and serving and answering questions and so on, we probably can't get together tomorrow night," he said in a rush. "I probably won't have time."

I paused, absorbing what he'd just said. Saturday was usually the day I stayed with Nate at his apartment and then got up to help with Sunday brunch at the café. It wasn't set in stone or anything, but we'd been doing it for several weeks. It was pretty much my weekend routine.

I took a breath, calming my ever-active spider sense. "That's okay. You can come out after brunch on Sunday and tell me how it went."

"Sure," Nate said quickly. "That works. And if I have any leftovers I'll bring them along."

I wasn't excited about eating Tera's leftovers, but at least we'd be getting together. "Sure. Whatever you've got is fine."

Nate gave me a relieved smile and dug into his enchiladas. Meanwhile, I tried to decide if I needed to be worried about this or if I was being nutsy. I'd been encouraging Nate to move ahead with his plans for the bistro. And he needed investors to make those plans happen. And Tera Bloomfield was the kind of investment guru people listened to. All of it made sense. It wasn't necessarily a threat. I was probably just overreacting.

Across the room, somebody dropped a coin into the antique jukebox that was one of Dirty Pete's charms, and what to my wondering ears should start playing but Dolly Parton's "Jolene."

I gritted my teeth. It wasn't my favorite song under the best of circumstances, and this was far from the best. I was not some trembling damsel trying to convince the evil femme fatale to keep her hands off my man, and I wasn't—*was not*—going to fall into that hole. When push came to shove, I trusted Nate. And I'd go on trusting him until he gave me a reason not to.

Still, I might trust Nate, but the same didn't go for Tera. I'd keep an eye on her, even from a distance.

I spent Saturday making pumpkin butter. I'd decided I'd do a couple of cases for the Winter Market, but probably not much more. It was a kind of hit or miss thing—people might love it, but they also might hate it. And the refrigeration made it a pain.

Uncle Mike came down for dinner, which was chicken paprikash. I'd planned to serve it to Nate so there was a little more than the two of us could eat, but I could always freeze the leftovers.

"Where's your boyfriend?" Uncle Mike asked.

Normally, I might have challenged him on the word *boyfriend,* but I didn't feel up to it. "Nate had to work. He's trying to line up investors for his new place."

"New place?" Uncle Mike frowned. "He's leaving his family's café?"

"No, no." I dropped a scoop of noodles on his plate, then went to the stove to get the paprikash. "He wants to renovate the building next door to the café so they can start serving dinner a few nights a week. Didn't Madge mention it?" I figured he'd been out with Madge at least once since last weekend.

"She didn't say anything. How long has he been working on this?"

"He floated the idea to the family last week. Madge liked it, but she said they couldn't handle the expense. So Nate's looking for investors." I took a breath. "He's been talking to Tera Bloomfield."

Uncle Mike's expression turned stormy. "He'd be better off just going to the bank and taking out a loan

45

than depending on anything he could get from Bloomfield. I don't trust her any farther than I can throw Herman."

Herman looked up at him hopefully, his tail thumping on the floor. Sometimes when we mentioned his name, food was involved.

"Apparently, Tera's done restaurant openings before. Nate said she had some good advice." I wasn't about to let Uncle Mike know I shared his opinion of Tera.

"So what's he doing tonight?"

"He's cooking a sample dinner for Tera at the café so she can see the kind of food he wants to serve. Coco's helping," I added, just to make it clear Nate wasn't on his own with Tera Bloomfield.

"Sounds shady to me." Uncle Mike folded his arms.

I closed my eyes and counted to ten. "It's fine. He'll probably be doing this a lot for different people so they can see what he has in mind. The only problem this time around is that she didn't give him much time to plan. He's got Coco doing salad and dessert. He can concentrate on the frittata."

Uncle Mike stayed quiet this time, fortunately. I didn't want to get into a situation where I was defending Tera Bloomfield, particularly since I thought her motives were suspect.

After supper was over, I packed up the leftovers and brought out the remains of a pumpkin pie I'd baked the day before. I had lots of pumpkins around and not much to do with them after I'd made my two cases of pumpkin butter.

Uncle Mike accepted a piece of pie once I'd

adorned it with maximum squirts of whipped cream, and he ate it happily enough. He should have. It was a helluva good pie. "You want me to take Herman?"

Herm did his tail wagging thing again, but he was pretty involved with the rawhide chew I'd bought him downtown. "Nah, he can stay with me." Since I didn't have Nate's company, I'd settle for Herman's.

"Okay." Uncle Mike pushed himself to his feet, then frowned at me from the door. "There's no trouble between you and Nate, is there?"

I shook my head. "Like I said, he's working. He's probably going to be spending a lot of time on his bistro from now on. I've got things I should be doing, too. I need to get my online store in better shape."

Uncle Mike sighed. "Yeah, you do. Once they run that episode of *Sweet Thing* with your farmers market stand, you'll probably have more orders than you know what to do with."

I'd been featured on a television show about desserts, but the episode probably wouldn't air until after the first of the year. I needed to have a functioning website by then. Which meant I needed Susa's help. Assuming she had any to give. If she didn't, I'd end up with Carly, or even Kip. That possibility made me glum.

"Take care of Herman," Uncle Mike said and headed up to the main house.

I settled down to brood. Between her demands on Susa and her possible designs on Nate, Tera Bloomfield was messing with my life in a big way. And as far as I could see, there wasn't a thing I could do about it.

Normally I ate brunch at the café on Sundays, which meant I usually had a great meal. Nate and

Bobby had an informal competition going to see who could make the fluffiest omelet, and the breakfast pastries Coco only made for brunch were terrific.

But this Sunday, I was on my own. I thought about making pancakes, but decided it was too much trouble. I had an English muffin instead. With pumpkin butter. Then I spent the rest of the day leafing through my antique cookbooks looking for interesting jams.

Nate showed up around three, after he'd finished with brunch and cleanup and prep for Tuesday breakfast. He looked exhausted, not surprisingly. He'd been looking exhausted for the past week or so, ever since he'd started moving forward with the bistro idea.

I gave him a kiss and then sank down on the couch beside him. He handed me a grocery sack. "Leftover peach cobbler. We ate everything else last night."

That meant he'd had dinner with Tera. Which made perfect sense, although it didn't make me happy. "How'd it go?"

Nate rubbed his eyes. "I guess it went okay. She liked the frittata. And Coco's stuff. God, I'm tired." He leaned his head against the back of the couch.

"Would you like a drink? I could make ranch water." That's a margarita without the sweet stuff and with a slug of Topo Chico, one of my favorites.

Nate reached out and took my hand. "Just sit here beside me for a little, okay? I missed you."

That melted my heart and convinced me I'd been an idiot. I slid down to rest my head on his shoulder. "You've had a week, haven't you? Any chance things will settle down next week?"

"Nope." He slid his arm around my shoulder, bringing me closer.

I could happily stay on the couch for the rest of the afternoon, but maybe he had other ideas. "What's coming up?"

"It's kind of complicated, but roll with me. Tera's got this dinner club thing."

"Dinner club?" I pictured something like Studio 54 out in the hills. "You mean like a nightclub?"

He shook his head. "Not that kind of club. She invites people to her house and then she has local chefs come in and cook dinner. Apparently, she started it in Denver. And now she's doing it here, too. I know Spence has done it, and Tal Nguyen from Jade Garden. And now she wants me to do one, too."

Spence was the chef at High Country, and a hound where ladies were concerned. It made sense Tera would invite him to her lair if she was interested in more than cooking. My good mood promptly soured. "Well, I guess that means she likes your stuff."

"Yeah, apparently. But it's a big dinner. She usually invites around ten people. It's going to be a lot of work."

That probably meant next weekend would be another no-show. My opinion of Tera was hitting record lows. "Do you come up with the menu or does she?"

"I do. She pays for the food."

But not, I assumed, for the labor, which would likely be considerable. "Are there going to be potential investors there?"

He nodded. "That's the idea. I show my stuff to people who might be willing to buy in on the bistro. Which means I need to come up with a menu featuring the kind of stuff we'll serve."

"Well, you've sort of got one. You've been working on the bistro concept for a while, and you know the dishes you want to fix."

"Right. And now it's put up or shut up time."

"Sure you wouldn't like some ranch water?" He looked like he could use some tequila.

"Maybe in a minute. Let me finish first."

That sounded ominous. I frowned. "What else is there?"

He took my hand, staring at me intensely, and I wondered if he was going to break up with me. *Why on earth would you think that?*

"I need help," he said.

"What kind of help?"

"The expert kind. I need a sous chef."

He kept hold of my hand, and I bit my lip. "Maybe Coco…"

He sighed. "Coco doesn't have the right kind of experience for this. She's a terrific baker, and her salads are great. But she's never worked as a line cook."

My heart began to thump hard. I knew what was coming.

"I know you haven't done any line cooking since you left Denver. And I can see how you might not be too excited about doing it now."

That was putting it mildly, of course. My Denver experiences had been disastrous on a whole lot of levels, including interpersonal since my boss had attempted to rape me and I'd slugged him with a can of tomatoes. I hadn't been in a restaurant kitchen since then, not counting Robicheaux's brunch.

"I don't know if I still have the chops." I took a deep breath. "When is this supposed to happen?"

"Next weekend. Saturday night. Tera wanted it this Wednesday, but I needed more time to put together a menu."

"No kidding." Tera might have helped open restaurants, but she didn't have a clear idea of how long it took to put together a decent dinner for ten.

Nate gave my hand a squeeze. "So what do you think? I need someone in the kitchen with me, and I can't think of anyone I'd rather have there than you."

I took another in a series of deep breaths. I cooked all the time, but not at peak level, the kind of adrenaline rush food prep I'd done as a line cook. And on one level returning to restaurant cooking could give me a panic attack.

Still, I'd invested a lot of money in culinary school. And I had my chef's coat. And I didn't back down from a challenge. "Okay. If you think I can do it."

"I know you can do it." Nate pulled me into an enthusiastic embrace. "This is going to be great."

I hoped he was right, but I still felt a niggling pinch of doubt. Could anything be great if it involved Tera Bloomfield?

Chapter Six

We spent most of that Sunday afternoon and evening running through possibilities for Tera's menu. I was pushing for roast chicken myself, since it's about as bistro a meal as I could think of.

Nate was afraid roast chicken would be too simple to impress the investors. Which was probably true but also crazy since roast chicken is tough to get right, as I knew only too well from childhood dinners featuring dried out, flabby-skinned birds.

Still, he had a point. We ran through other possibilities: cassoulet (too complicated with too many things that could go wrong), paella (not classic bistro, plus seafood is always pricey in the mountains), and spaghetti Bolognese (in the ballpark, but still less impressive).

Finally, we settled on beef bourguignon, a very upscale beef stew. Nate thought he could do it with either short ribs or chuck roast, whichever Casey Swain, the café's meat supplier, had on hand. The root vegetables—carrots, potatoes, maybe some turnips or parsnips—wouldn't cost much. And he could gussy it up with herbs and mushrooms. And of course pearl onions for a little wow factor. It was classic bistro stuff, so classic he might put it on the actual bistro menu.

Which still left open the question of the other dishes. We needed a soup or a salad, possibly both. And an appetizer. And dessert, but maybe we could leave the dessert to Coco.

"Has she bought in on the whole idea?" I asked. Coco was hard to read. She was exempted from most of the battles with Bobby, but I knew some sore points still existed between them.

"I think so. She's willing to bake some tarts and galettes for desserts."

I pulled out the leftover paprikash along with some garlic sausage I'd gotten in trade from Marcus Jordan's artisan butcher place. He was my friend Bianca's boy and crazy about my raspberry preserves. I, in turn, was crazy about his sausages. Serendipity at work.

I also had some goat cheese I'd grabbed at Bianca's bakery, along with a loaf of her focaccia. I found bread-and-butter pickles from Annabelle Dorsey and routine olives from City Market. I also had a block of cheddar from a dairy over in Geary.

Nate was creating sausage, cheese, and focaccia sandwiches with pickles on the side, while I warmed up the paprikash. "What about a bistro appetizer? Do we need more than one?"

Nate paused for a moment, then made a sweeping gesture taking in the table with all its goodies. "Charcuterie. Classic bistro appetizer. Throw in a little cheese and some of Bianca's bread and it should be terrific."

"Cool. I assume you're thinking of using commercial stuff rather than making your own sausage given the time."

"Right, but maybe I could make some for the bistro. Some ground pork and veal, good bacon." He got the kind of dreamy look I recognized as a cook working out how to make something tasty.

"Charcuterie I can probably find since I know the local suppliers. If we want bread from Bianca, we might want to order something. And soon, since she runs out regularly."

Nate nodded. "Right. Baguettes. Maybe six or eight for the whole dinner. Perfect for sopping up bourguignon juice." He handed me a sandwich. "This is great sausage. Whose is it?"

"Marcus Jordan's. He's Bianca's son."

Nate gave me a rueful smile. "And already I understand why you should be the one to do the charcuterie sourcing. I didn't know Bianca had a son, much less one with a butcher shop."

"He just opened his shop recently. I'll introduce you. He'd be a good source for the bistro. Bianca, too."

"Assuming I can work out deals with them both. As long as Tera's paying, sky's the limit. But when I'm paying, it's a different story."

"Bianca already supplies about half the restaurants in town. You can work with her. My guess is Marcus would love to pick up more restaurant customers. He's just starting out."

The rest of the meal was spent throwing out possibilities for the menu. Maybe vichyssoise for the soup, doubly good because we could make it in advance. And a simple salad with lettuce and maybe some of Annabelle's pickled mushrooms.

Uncle Mike wandered in around seven, helping himself to sausage and cheese, although I was pretty sure he'd already had dinner up at the main house. He grimaced at our conversation. "What's wrong with good old American food?"

"This is good old American food. Marcus's sausage, Annabelle's pickles, Bianca's bread, cheese from Geary." I wasn't going to let him bring me down. I was having too much fun menu planning.

"What's all the rest of the stuff you're talking about, then?" He settled into a chair at the table, munching on his sausage sandwich.

"I'm catering a dinner party next weekend," Nate explained. "Roxy's going to help."

"Didn't know the café did catering." Uncle Mike speared a pickle from the Mason jar.

"This is more of a special deal. A demonstration of some possible menu stuff from the bistro. For potential investors." I wasn't going to mention Tera's name unless I had to.

Uncle Mike gave me a sour look. "Suppose Tera Bloomfield's involved."

"It's at her house," Nate said. "She's got some kind of dinner club where chefs cook for her guests."

I steeled myself for the inevitable snide remark, but Uncle Mike helped himself to a plateful of noodles and paprikash. "Guess not many people get their meals prepared by a personal chef." He gave me a quick smile. "I'm luckier than most."

And that was one of the things I loved about my uncle. Just when he was annoying the heck out of me, he did a one eighty and made me blush.

"You're a very lucky man," Nate said slowly. "And at the moment, so am I."

I took a deep breath. They were both making me verklempt. "Glad to do it. Now who wants pumpkin pie?"

Having just praised my cooking, they were both

obligated to take a piece of the pie, but I had no regrets. After all, like I said, it was a helluva good pie. If you liked pumpkin.

We had five days to assemble all the ingredients for the meal at Tera's, and some of the dishes could be prepared in advance. Coco agreed to make fruit tarts for dessert, which we'd serve with some artisan ice cream from the same place in Geary that produced the cheddar. Nate figured we'd fix the vichyssoise on Friday to give it plenty of time to chill.

I was doing a lot of the ordering and picking up because Nate was still cooking breakfast and lunch at the café. I got the bread order in with Bianca early in the week so we'd be sure of having it ready on Saturday morning. Since she was a friend, I gave her a little more information about Nate's plans for the bistro. "It's all hypothetical right now. But Nate's excited about the possibilities."

"Interesting idea," Bianca said. "His dad talked a lot about expanding the café into the building next door, but he never got around to it. A bistro would give them access to some new customers. Expensive, though."

I nodded. "The renovations won't be cheap, but Nate's looking for investors."

Bianca narrowed her eyes. "Around here? I suppose there might be a few business types willing to put some money in. Particularly since it's associated with Robicheaux's. That's pretty much a Shavano institution."

"He's working with Tera Bloomfield. She's got access to outside investors, along with the locals."

"True enough. She might be able to come up with some people for him. It's probably a good idea to look for money outside of Shavano. I don't know much about her, though."

I knew a bit more about her than I wanted to. "I guess she's got some major connections in finance. Susa's working with her, doing her website and some business software."

Bianca's expression soured. "Susa needs to get her ducks in a row. That assistant of hers made some 'improvements' to my website and sent it straight to hell. It took them two days to get it on track again."

That sounded worrying since Carly or Kip might be working on my site. "She keeps thinking she's finished, and then Tera finds something else for her to do."

"Maybe she should send her assistant out to work on Bloomfield's stuff. She'd probably stop asking for help pretty quick."

Poor Susa. Tera was running her ragged while rolling her eyes, and her old customers were losing their patience. "Susa's bound to be on her game soon. She's always been the best."

Bianca nodded. "She's definitely been the best around here, but things change quickly these days. Somebody else could undercut her with her current customers if she can't get her act together."

I left the bakery chewing on my lip. Susa's business wasn't my problem, but I was still concerned for her. She'd worked hard to build everything up, and it seemed worse than unfair for things to go to hell just because she'd gotten a big client.

I walked a couple of streets over toward Marcus Jordan's place. We'd need sausage for the charcuterie platter. Marcus's shop was located toward the industrial end of First Street. The rents were probably a little cheaper there, and he was just getting started. Plus a lot of stores in classier locations might not be too happy about having a butcher next door.

Marcus was in the front of the shop when I got there. Usually his wife, Sara, ran the counter while Marcus and his apprentice did the meat cutting in the rear. But this time they were both up front. "Hey, Roxy," he called. "Got any more jam to trade? We're just about through our last jar of raspberry."

Sara frowned. "We've got three more jars, Marc. You never look in the pantry."

"Actually, I've got an order this time. For money instead of jam," I said.

Marcus and Sara both moved a little closer. "What do you need?"

"It's for a catered meal Nate Robicheaux is doing. He needs some sausage for a charcuterie plate." I didn't feel like explaining the whole bistro thing again. Among other things, I wasn't sure Nate was ready for the story to be spread around town.

Marcus nodded. "Okay. We've got some garlic salami and soppressata. And if you want to go a little crazy, we've got some capicola. Are you buying Mom's bread?"

I nodded. "Baguettes. We'll put some out with the charcuterie."

"Then the capicola's a great choice. The texture's a little rougher than the soppressata. You put it on a slice of baguette with a little mustard and you've got heaven." He kissed his fingers, grinning.

"Okay, I'll take all three. Have you got any whole grain mustard?"

"Sure." He leaned around the counter to fumble at a display of jars. "This one's good."

"Add it in." I looked at the meat in the display case. It was too bad we were getting the beef from Swain. Marcus had some gorgeous chuck. "Do you have any bacon?"

Marcus paused. "We've got guancale and pancetta. Right now that's as close as we get."

"Heaven forbid we should have anything normal," Sara muttered.

"Pancetta's normal." Marcus sounded aggrieved. "Pancetta's Italian bacon. It's delicious."

Sara gave him a flat look. "You know that, and I know that. How many other people in Shavano know that?"

"I'll take a pound of the pancetta," I said hastily. If Nate didn't want pancetta, I'd pay for it myself and make some carbonara for dinner.

"Great," Marcus said. "Let me wrap this for you. Sara can ring you up."

As it turned out, Nate was perfectly fine with pancetta, in fact he thought it might work better with bourguignon than more heavily smoked bacon. He glanced through the three sausages and grinned. "I can already smell the garlic from the salami. We'll need to wrap it up tight or we'll end up with a garlic flavored refrigerator."

We were using storage space in the walk-in cooler at the café to keep our purchases together. Bobby wasn't happy, but I had the feeling Bobby wasn't happy about anything we were doing. He mostly stayed away from us, like we might be contagious.

"What more do we need?" I asked as Nate

surveyed the pile of ingredients we'd assembled.

"Salad greens, root vegetables, pickles." He counted off on his fingers. "I'll get the greens the day before, and I can pick up the root vegetables then, too. Can you take care of the pickles?" I paused for a microsecond, and he shook his head. "If you don't want to talk to Annabelle, that's okay. I understand."

Annabelle Dorsey was the local pickle guru. She and I had been keeping each other at arm's length ever since last summer. Her daughter had gotten involved with a chef who'd been murdered in his kitchen. I'd gotten hurt in the fallout, and my feelings had been bruised in the process. Annabelle had apologized, but we still weren't best buds.

"Annabelle's selling her stuff at the Made In Colorado store downtown. I'm due to take them a case of jam—I can pick up some pickles while I'm at it."

Buying Annabelle's pickles at Made In Colorado had other advantages, chief among them the fact she might not be there since the store sold on consignment. That afternoon I put together a mixed case of jam and drove downtown.

The new manager of Made In Colorado met me at the door. Her name was Larraine Pearson, and she was one of the most enthusiastic people I knew.

"Roxy! How great to see you! And you brought jam! Whoa, terrific!" Larraine usually spoke in exclamation points.

"Good to see you, too, Larraine. Where do you want the jam?"

"Maybe just in the storeroom for now." She frowned, studying one of the display tables. "I'll have to rearrange some of the stock. We want to make sure your jam is featured. It's always so popular!"

I did sell a decent amount of jam at Made In Colorado. Not as much as I sold at Bianca's bakery, but decent. I put the case in the storeroom, then returned to Larraine again. "Do you have any of Annabelle Dorsey's pickles?"

"Her pickles are so scrumptious! And she's right over there restocking. Isn't that lucky?"

I glanced at the table where Larraine was pointing. Annabelle was pulling some jars out of a carton on the floor.

"Thanks, Larraine." I walked over to Annabelle's table.

She glanced up when I got closer, frowning slightly. "Hi, Roxy. Making a delivery?"

I'd guess Annabelle is in her early forties. She's a part-time pickler, serving as a court reporter during the week. "Right. And I need some of your pickles while I'm here."

Annabelle's frown became more pronounced. "My pickles? Why?"

"Nate Robicheaux's catering a private party and he's doing a charcuterie tray. He thought your pickles would be great." I'd thought so, too, but all of a sudden I didn't feel like telling Annabelle that. She was being sort of pissy.

"Oh." Annabelle paused, looking down at the jars on the table. "What kind did he want?"

"Some of the gherkins. And some pickled mushrooms."

Annabelle bent down to rummage through the carton on the floor. After a moment, she handed me a couple of jars. "Here you go."

"Thanks." I set the jars on the table and grabbed my purse. "What do I owe you?"

Annabelle paused again, folding her arms across her chest. "On the house."

I shook my head. "No, really, Annabelle. Nate's got a customer who's paying for everything. Let me give you some money for this."

Annabelle's spine was ramrod straight all of a sudden. "I owe you. So does Dorothy. A couple of jars of pickles are the least I can do."

I took a breath to argue again, then decided to let it go. I could let her spring for some pickles. "Thanks."

"Okay." Annabelle gave me a quick nod. "Tell Nate good luck."

"I will. And I'll make sure people know the pickles are yours."

That seemed like a good way to advertise Annabelle's stuff. Of course, that assumed people liked her pickles. But I couldn't see why they wouldn't. Not then, anyway.

Chapter Seven

Saturday dawned with a bright blue sky, what we call a bluebird day around here. I fixed myself and Uncle Mike some pancakes for breakfast because I was feeling energized. I had a whole day of food prep ahead of me, and I was raring to go.

Nate had said he'd get started on the bourguignon as soon as the breakfast rush was over. It needed to braise for at least four hours, but letting it go longer wouldn't do any damage and might actually make the flavors deepen a little.

I was going to finish up on the vichyssoise at the café after breakfast. Nate had done the initial cooking yesterday, and he'd left it to cool in the refrigerator overnight. Now I'd run the vegetables through a food mill to puree them before adding the cream and sour cream and then chilling everything down again. Tonight we'd let it come to a little below room temperature before serving it so all the flavors would pop.

That was my stated reason for going to the café around ten: to do some work on the meal for tonight. But in reality I was too nervous to stay around the farm any longer. I had a feeling if I tried to make jam, I'd jinx it. Better to get to work on the food for Tera's party.

The kitchen at the café was in the usual holding pattern between breakfast and lunch. Nate's prep bowls were lined up on the counter beside him as he worked on the meat for the bourguignon.

"What did you get?" I asked. "Chuck or short ribs?"

"Chuck. Swain didn't have any short ribs. This is okay—not as nice as I would have liked but decent."

I thought of the chuck at Marcus's, which was a lot better than okay. Oh well, maybe next time. Assuming there was a next time.

While Nate set about browning the pancetta, I started chopping vegetables. Traditionally, beef bourguignon contains only onions, carrots, and mushrooms, but that could seem a little lean for people who were used to beef stew. Nate was adding baby turnips along with the pearl onions he'd throw in toward the end of the cooking. Everything would braise happily in a low oven for the rest of the afternoon. We'd cool it off before we headed up to Tera's place, then reheat it carefully before we served it. Speaking of which…

"Did Tera hire waiters for this gig?" I asked Nate. "We won't have to also bring the stuff out of the kitchen, will we?"

Nate shook his head. "She said she had a waiter who'd worked for her before. All we'll have to do is make sure the food's ready to go on time."

"What about wine?" I hadn't even thought of that, but now I was guessing Tera might expect us to supply some.

"Way ahead of you." Nate gestured toward a case of red wine sitting just inside the pantry. "It's the same stuff I'll be using in the bourguignon, so it ties together."

We worked for the rest of the afternoon, although Nate had to take a break to run the flattop at lunch. Bobby didn't say anything about the things we were doing in his kitchen for Tera's dinner, but he made his feelings known through the occasional side eye he threw my way and his complaints about not being able to use the oven where Nate was braising the bourguignon. Nate seemed to take the whole thing with Zen forbearance, maybe because he put up with Bobby regularly. I considered going outside to wait until lunch was finished, but I had to run the leeks and potatoes through the food mill for the vichyssoise. I tried for some Zen of my own.

I'd finished all I could finish by the end of the lunch service. The vichyssoise was chilling and ready to get its garnishes and warm up a bit before serving. The bourguignon was braising away happily. Coco had finished the two fruit tarts and they rested on a shelf in the cooler she reserved for her desserts and salads. Bianca's baguettes were stacked in a corner.

That left the charcuterie and the lettuce and vinaigrette for the salad, both of which we'd fix at Tera's place.

I folded my arms across my middle, trying to get my heart to stop hammering. If I was this nervous in the middle of the afternoon, I'd be a basket case by the time we drove up to Tera's place around five. Nate stepped behind me, wrapping his arms around my waist. "Okay?"

I blew out a long breath. "Getting there."

He pulled me against him. "We're good. We've gotten everything done we needed to get done, and the rest of it will fall into place as soon as we get set up in

Tera's kitchen."

"Right." I was still concentrating on breathing evenly.

"Do you want to go to your place and grab your stuff? I can pick you up around four thirty." He turned me slightly so we were looking at each other, nose-to-nose.

"That'll work, I guess. Should I bring my knife roll?" Calling it a *knife roll* sounded a lot more imposing than my beat-up nylon case probably deserved, but it was one of the few relics of culinary school I still had.

Nate rested his forehead against mine. "Only if you want to. You can use my knives if you need one."

That was a truly generous offer since most chefs, including Nate, are protective of their knives.

"Okay, I'll leave it. But I want to bring my mandoline slicer for the charcuterie." I stopped, suddenly panicked. "Oh man, do we need cheese? I didn't even think of it." I knew I'd forgotten something.

Nate gave me a quick smile. "I thought of it. I picked up a chunk of cheddar and some goat cheese. It's not artisan, but we've got enough other artisan stuff to prove our cred."

I nodded. "More than enough. I guess I'll go home and get changed." My heart gave another thump, but I'd learned to ignore it by then.

"Okay." Nate leaned forward and kissed the tip of my nose. "See you at four thirty."

"Four thirty. Yeah. Four thirty it is." I trotted out to the parking lot, practicing my deep breathing.

Uncle Mike had given me my chef's coat when I'd graduated from culinary school, when my future as a restaurant chef still looked rosy. I hadn't worn it at the restaurant where I'd worked because it seemed pretentious for a line cook. Most of us stuck to canvas aprons over T-shirts and jeans, along with baseball caps to hold back our hair.

But tonight was a perfect situation for my coat. I wasn't a line cook; I was a sous chef. And I had a feeling I needed to strut my stuff in front of Tera Bloomfield—she might have her doubts about letting me in her kitchen otherwise. When Nate pulled up in his SUV at four thirty, I was wearing my black chef pants and a T-shirt under my cardigan with my coat on a hanger over my shoulder. I had Annabelle's pickles and a carton of olives in my string bag, along with my industrial-strength mandoline slicer in a box, trusting Nate to have everything else.

He trotted up the porch stairs, holding out his hand before I could close the door. "Have you got any jam you can spare?"

I shrugged. "Sure. Always."

"Grab a couple of jars. We can put it out with the charcuterie. I'll make sure people know it's yours." He grinned. "It's as close as I can come to paying you."

I stepped inside and picked up jars of raspberry and apricot. They were some of my best sellers and ones most people liked. I'd save the pumpkin butter for the market.

As we drove up the winding road leading to Lost Horse Pass, I tried to remember if I'd ever been to any of the houses scattered along the hillsides. Once upon a time, Lost Horse Pass had been strictly for miners and prospectors, but now the area was popular with the wealthier citizens of Shavano and Denver. The architecture ran to massive pine logs and lots of fieldstone along the Roaring Branch River. I'd been told the average price of one these Paul Bunyan mansions started at several million, and I could believe it.

Nate pulled into a parking area below one of the more imposing houses in the neighborhood. It was more Mountain Modern than Nineteenth Century Logging Camp—lots of glass and stone and oxidized metal. A flight of stairs led up to what I assumed was the entrance. "Is there a back door?" I asked. "Preferably without stairs?"

Nate shrugged. "I don't know. I've never been here before. Let me grab the case of wine—that's something that could come through the front door."

We hiked up the stairs, panting a bit when we came to the top. The altitude had to be north of eight thousand feet, and even people like us who live at seven thousand can get winded with exercise.

I rang the bell, then waited until we finally heard footsteps. Tera opened the door, her face lighting up when she saw Nate. "Oh, hi! I was hoping you'd come early enough for us to have a drink before everyone else shows up."

She glanced to the side then and saw me for the first time. Her smile dimmed considerably. "Hello, there," she said in a tone approaching subzero.

Nate's affable grin didn't waver. "We need to bring in the food and get started on the charcuterie tray. Is there a kitchen entrance where we can carry everything?"

"Around the side." Tera gestured, losing all remnants of her smile. "I'll tell Alex to let you in. He's the waiter for the evening."

"Thanks. Maybe I can leave this here." Nate lifted the case of wine a little to show her what he meant.

Tera let herself smile again, although it didn't seem to reach her eyes. "Just set it here, and I'll have Alex carry it up."

"Great." He put the case down, then started down the stairs.

Apparently, Tera had assumed Nate would be on his own. I hoped my presence wouldn't make any difference in her support for the bistro.

It took us three trips to get everything into the kitchen, with the help of Alex, the waiter. Normally, he worked at High Country, and Saturday was his day off. But he said Tera's salary was worth it. "You need to get it up front, though," he told Nate, which sounded a little ominous.

"I got most of it already. She only owes us for a couple of things."

Alex said he'd have help when it came to actually serving—a bartender from town who'd serve drinks and then help get the food from the kitchen to the table.

Once we were set up, I pulled my mandoline slicer out of the cardboard box and began slicing the sausage for the charcuterie. Nate put the bourguignon into a slow oven and then started helping me with the appetizers. We'd brought along some utilitarian trays, but we found some nice wooden platters in the cupboard that looked a lot more striking.

It was a good kitchen, but I expected no less from a house as expensive as this one. Tera had a high-end stove and refrigerator, so I was properly impressed. I was just slicing the cheese when our hostess appeared in the kitchen doorway.

She was wearing silken pants that clung to her thighs and then widened to swish around her calves. Her sweater looked like cashmere and her "statement necklace" was telling me it cost an unholy amount of money. She'd pulled her hair back severely so her earrings could make a statement of their own. Her lipstick was bright red and it contrasted with her jet-black hair and pale skin. To me, she looked like a high-class vampire.

I had my chef's coat on, but it hung unbuttoned over my T-shirt. I was in uniform, but mostly not. Tera looked me over with a critical eye, eyebrows elevating. "I suppose that'll be all right as a serving outfit," she said finally. "Usually I expect something more formal."

I froze, staring at her, as a full range of responses flicked through my brain, starting with *What the hell?* and ending with *Go fuck yourself.*

"Roxy's my sous chef," Nate said at my elbow. "I can't spare her to serve. I need her help in the kitchen."

I straightened a little, grateful for his support but still longing to tell Tera just what I thought of her.

Oh yeah, such *a good idea. She's in charge of investors for the bistro, remember?*

Tera shrugged, looking slightly bored. "Oh, all right. I suppose Alex and Sigrid can manage. Are these the apps?" She gestured toward the platters of charcuterie we were setting up.

"Yep," Nate said, his voice warming. "Most of this comes from local sources. It's a chance for your guests to see what Shavano has to offer in the way of artisan food."

Tera nodded a little absently, as if artisan food was

no big deal. "The apps need to be ready by five thirty. Is that doable?"

Nate nodded, turning to the island where I was slicing the cheese. "We'll be ready."

Tera gave me another critical glance, and I turned to the sink, making myself as inconspicuous as it's possible for a six-feet-tall Amazon to be.

"Fine. We'll start serving around five forty-five or so." She glanced at Alex. "You know the drill."

He nodded. "I do."

"Excellent." Tera turned her full attention to Nate again. "I'm looking forward to seeing what you've brought for tonight. I've been mentioning your concept to some interested people. There's a lot of anticipation."

He gave her what I thought of as his professional smile. "I think you'll be pleased. It's a bistro meal, but an upscale bistro."

Tera gave him the kind of look that usually required a certain amount of privacy. "Great. You should come out when dinner's over to take a bow. And meet the guests. You can talk to some of the investors."

"Sure. Glad to." Somehow Nate didn't sound glad, but he was doing his best to play the game.

I'd buttoned my coat and pulled on my Constantine Farms ball cap while Tera was concentrating on Nate, and I was keeping my focus on the mandoline. I suppose I should have been feeling jealous since Tera was coming on to my boyfriend pretty blatantly. But I mostly felt sorry for Nate. He looked uncomfortable, although I might have been the only one who noticed the stiffness in his shoulders and his automatic smile.

Tera wasn't being subtle in her approach. I didn't know if she realized Nate and I were involved, but if she did, she clearly didn't care. I hoped she wasn't using her introductions to the potential investors as a springboard to anything more intimate that night. Among other things, Nate was my ride home, and I'd have to wait around while he resisted her advances.

After a few more murmured comments and a full complement of seductive smiles, Tera left the kitchen. Nate's shoulders relaxed fractionally, and he returned to arranging small bowls of pickles and olives, along with my jam.

"Is she always like that?" he asked Alex.

Alex paused in lifting down the china and silver. "Depends. She usually spends a little time charming the chef just as part of the evening. But she was coming on a little stronger than usual with you." He gave Nate a dry smile. "She doesn't bother with anyone below the chef level, though. My virtue's still intact."

I snickered before I could stop myself. Nate glanced up, his smile rueful. I figured he could take care of himself.

We got the charcuterie boards ready to go a little before five thirty. I'd been aware of the doorbell sounding periodically as guests arrived. Alex was busy getting the dining room table set, so I moved on to getting the first course ready. I pulled the vichyssoise out of the refrigerator to warm it a little. Then I started washing lettuce for the salad.

I had dropped the lettuce into the salad spinner to whirl it dry when the kitchen door swung open again. I steeled myself, ready for Tera, returning for another round of innuendo. But when I looked up, I saw familiar golden curls and bright blue eyes.

"Roxy," Susa blurted. "I didn't know you were

here. I thought this was Nate's show."

"It is Nate's show. I'm being a sous chef for the evening."

Susa gave me a quick hug, then turned to Nate. "There's a lot of interest up there. I keep hearing the word *bistro.* I can't wait to see what you're serving."

Nate stood away from the stove. "Great. More pressure. Thanks, Suz."

Susa laughed, punching him in the shoulder. "You'll be great. Everybody's pumped. Go for it!"

"Right. Have you been to these before? What's the vibe usually like?"

Susa shook her head. "This is my first. I think somebody cancelled out—Tera called me last night to invite me over."

That seemed like a scuzzy thing to do, but by then I was inclined to think the worst of Tera. Maybe she thought Susa would be glad to come to a dinner cooked by a friend.

"I've got to get out there." Susa glanced at her watch. "I'm supposed to be answering questions from people who want to know about our web capabilities. I just wanted to step in and say hi." She leaned up to kiss Nate's cheek and then gave me another hug. "Knock 'em dead, kids. Is that what you're supposed to say in situations like this? Or is it break a leg?"

"We prefer not to injure our guests. And we definitely try not to kill them." I grinned as Alex came in again.

His eyes widened slightly. "Did I miss something?"

"No, just pre-dinner banter."

Show time!

Chapter Eight

We served dinner around seven, which gave us plenty of time to get everything done after we'd sent off the charcuterie platters. Nate worked on the bourguignon while I dished up the vichyssoise and got the salad dressed. We'd go one plate at a time, soup first followed by salad, but we weren't going to be fussy about the sequencing. So what if both courses were on the table a little close together? The two of us dropped salad greens on the plates and then sprinkled hand-torn croutons and cherry tomatoes on top. The plates looked simultaneously casual and gorgeous.

Alex and the bartender, Sigrid aka Siggi, flashed in, carrying the empty vichyssoise bowls which they piled next to the dishwasher. "Lots of lip-smacking," Alex said. "I heard some 'yums'." He started loading Siggi up with salad plates.

"Okay." Nate wiped his hands on his apron. "We'll start dishing up the bourguignon as soon as you guys get the salad on the table. That should get us enough time to get it to the people while it's still warm."

Alex nodded. "Right. Off we go." He pushed the kitchen door open with his shoulder, then stood, his arms laden with salad plates, while Siggi stepped through. He followed her, letting the door swing closed behind him. A competent waiter is a joy to watch, believe me.

We'd gone back and forth over how the bourguignon should be served, in bowls or on plates. As it turned out, Tera had some shallow soup bowls that were a cross between the two. Nate and I lined the soup plates up on the island at the center of the kitchen. He grabbed the Dutch oven and a ladle, then placed it on the island with a trivet underneath. "The chopped parsley's on the counter. Give each bowl a sprinkle after I dish."

"Right." I was in the groove by then, dishing and sprinkling with a practiced eye.

Nate was careful with the ladle, moving the Dutch oven along the island and wiping any stray drops off the bowls with his kitchen towel. I tried to sprinkle the parsley artistically, keeping it centered so it looked neat.

"Now for the bread," he murmured as he reached the last bowl.

We'd saved five baguettes for dinner, and Nate broke them into quarters. The diners could tear off chunks if they wanted smaller portions. I was putting the last of the bread into baskets with napkins when Alex appeared again, carrying empty salad plates. "Moving right along," he said. "Siggi's refilling wine glasses, so I need to pick up the last of the plates."

"Right," Nate said. "Everything's ready here. More or less."

He pulled the butter crocks off the counter. That had been another discussion point—how to serve the butter. Coco had suggested the crocks, which the café used at brunch. They were just rustic enough to look like something out of a bistro.

Alex brought in the last of the salad plates,

followed by Siggi. They used a tray to serve the bourguignon since balancing hot bowls on their arms would be an invitation to disaster. When they'd gotten the tray loaded, Alex hoisted it to his shoulder and Siggi opened the door for him. A few minutes later, she returned to grab the bread.

Nate and I stood watching the kitchen door swing closed as they left again. He put an arm around my shoulders. "How are you doing?"

I let myself rest my head on his shoulder for a moment. "Okay, I think. And you?"

"Still running on adrenaline. Let's get dessert dished up, then maybe we can take a minute to eat something ourselves." My stomach chose that moment to growl, and he grinned at me. "Not a moment too soon, either."

Coco's fruit tarts were easy to slice. We'd put a small scoop of vanilla ice cream next to each serving just before Alex took them out, but the guests might take their time over the bourguignon. We hoped so, anyway. That meant we just had to serve up the slices for now.

After we finished, Nate handed me a piece of bread and some of Marcus's soppressata. I dipped it in the bowl of mustard. It was, as predicted, sensational. I hoped Tera had mentioned Marcus's name to her guests. Nate had made a point of telling her about his suppliers, but I had a feeling Tera would ignore anything as mundane as local producers.

I'd just loaded up another piece of bread with some cheese and a little salami when Alex leaned in the kitchen door. "She wants you to come out and meet the guests," he said to Nate.

Nate looked down at his bread and sausage sandwich a little regretfully, then shrugged. "Okay. Should Roxy start scooping ice cream?"

Alex gave both of us his dry smile. "I wouldn't. Chances are you're going to be out there talking a while. I can slip back and let Roxy know when to start dishing."

Nate's shoulders stiffened again. He wasn't much for schmoozing. But if he wanted investors, he'd need to play the game. Even if it included making nice with Tera Bloomfield and her rich guests. He fastened the top buttons of his chef's coat, but I noticed he didn't take off his Robicheaux's baseball cap. It made him look a little edgy and definitely hot.

I thought about peeking through the kitchen door to see what Nate had to say, but I decided against it. If anyone saw me, I'd look like an idiot. Besides, being alone in the kitchen gave me another chance to sample Marcus's sausages. I'd just taken a good bite of salami when Alex leaned through the kitchen door and gave me another of his dry smiles. "Nate wants you to step out and take a bow."

"Hell," I muttered, swallowing fast. I jammed my own ball cap on my head, then stepped through the door and across a hall to the dining room.

Twelve people were seated around the table, but I only recognized three of them: Susa, Tera, and Phil Duncan, who owned several office buildings downtown, along with a car dealership. The other nine, three women and six men, were total strangers.

"Here she is," Nate called. "My sous chef, Roxanne Constantine."

The people around the table gave me a perfunctory

round of applause, and I managed a smile.

"Roxy made the jam, too." Susa grinned up at me and my smile got a little more genuine. Until I caught sight of Tera giving Susa some major side eye. Apparently shout-outs for the jam woman were discouraged.

I nodded again, and then stepped toward the kitchen. Let Nate finish answering questions and charming the diners. I'd get the ice cream out of the freezer and start warming up the scoop. I started a pot of coffee brewing in Tera's fancy coffee maker on the assumption some people might like coffee before driving down the road to Shavano, and I found the serving pot to go with it. Getting the sugar bowl and cream pitcher ready to go took another five minutes or so.

And still Nate wasn't back.

I was almost ready to crack the kitchen door so I could try to listen to what was being said when Alex pushed it open from the other side. "They're still talking. But Nate signaled me to start getting the dessert service going."

"Right. Let me put the ice cream on the plates."

Siggi came in just as I finished the dishing and set up the coffee tray with cups. She disappeared into the dining room as I helped Alex load up his own serving tray with desserts.

After he pushed his way through the door again, I was on my own and wondering what to do next. The dirty dishes were stacked beside Tera's dishwasher, but I was reasonably certain they weren't our problem. Either Tera would have hired someone to come in and clean up tomorrow or maybe Alex and Siggi took care of it as part of their night's duties.

On the other hand, the cooking implements and pans were mostly Nate's from the café. Those we needed to clean up and pack away. I washed my mandoline slicer and put it into its box. Then I started on the containers associated with the salad and the vichyssoise. There was maybe a serving or so left of the bourguignon, so I didn't do anything with the Dutch oven.

Alex brought the dessert plates in as I went on working. Apparently, dinner was over, but Nate was still MIA.

Like most people who've worked in restaurants, I'd learned to clean up after myself most of the time, so there wasn't a lot of chaos to take care of. Mainly I needed to pack up, so we could take off whenever Nate appeared again.

I rinsed out the small dishes we'd brought for the charcuterie, the ones for pickles and jam. I wrapped the ends of the sausages and cheese in plastic wrap and fastened the lids on Annabelle's pickle jars and my jam pots. The boxes and tote bags we'd used to bring the food were still off at the side, along with the two industrial size coolers. I wasn't sure whether I should pack away the leftover bits of charcuterie or leave them for Tera. She'd paid for them, after all. Or at least she'd paid for some of them. The jam was still mine. I packed the butter crocks in the cooler since they still had small amounts of butter inside. Knowing Bobby, he'd find some way to use it.

Alex loaded the dishwasher while Siggi saw to the coffee. The dishwasher was big enough to handle almost everything, but I'd expected Tera to want the china and crystal washed by hand. If she did, she was out of luck, and I couldn't blame Alex for loading everything up. The dishwasher had enough settings to take care of just about any kind of dish.

The kitchen was looking more and more put together, and I was still missing the chef, who'd have the final say on what went where.

Finally, when I was wondering if I should actually clean out the Dutch oven and get everything packed away, Nate pushed his way through the kitchen door. He stopped to lean on the island, closing his eyes for a moment. "Sheesh."

"Everything okay?" He looked worn out.

"Fine. I think I sprained my mouth from smiling, though."

"How'd they like the dinner?" Which was, after all, the main point.

"Everybody seemed happy. The bourguignon went over well. People loved Bianca's bread, so I got to give her a plug. Marcus, too. And I didn't see any leftovers on the dessert plates."

"Of course not. It's a fruit tart with blueberries and kiwis on top. People can tell themselves they're eating healthy." I grinned at him, hoping he'd grin back.

He did, slinging an arm around my shoulders. "We did good, kid. The food was a hit."

"You did good. You came up with the menu. Looks like it worked."

He grinned again, hugging my shoulders. "It did. Definitely."

"Did you meet any of the potential investors Tera promised?"

"Who knows? Everybody looked rich, but that

doesn't mean anything. Nobody pulled out a checkbook and offered me a stake."

"Not that you expected them to, right?"

He gave me a tired smile. "No. I didn't expect them to. We'll see what happens over the next couple of weeks."

The kitchen door swung open, and Alex stepped through with the last of the dirty dishes. "Tera wants to know if you'd like to join them for port."

Nate rolled his eyes. "Nope. We need to get finished in here and then start loading up. I had a glass of wine at the table, and that's about all I can handle when I've got to drive down that road."

"I hear you." Alex raised an eyebrow. "But you're going to tell her yourself, right?"

Nate sighed. "Yeah, sure." He pushed through the kitchen door.

I felt like sighing myself. It was already late, and given the way everything had been going so far, he'd probably be stuck out there for another hour.

"Are all the guests still there?"

Alex shook his head. "The couples left. It's just four guys, along with Tera and the blonde."

"Susa?" I narrowed my eyes. The men I'd seen at the dinner table hadn't seemed like Susa's type. But maybe Tera wanted her to stick around to keep from being the only woman in the room. Then again, that didn't strike me as something Tera would worry about.

"Yeah, I guess that's Susa. It looks like they're settling in for the evening."

I started toward the boxes I was packing up when I heard an odd sound from the direction of the dining room. Like someone had screamed, but not exactly.

More like someone had groaned.

Alex and I both turned toward the door, both of us frowning, when it flew open and Siggi ran in, her face the color of rice paper. "Help. Get help now. She's sick. Call a doctor. Get an ambulance."

"What the hell?" I muttered and hurried through the kitchen door myself.

At the side of the dining room, I saw a circle of leather chairs and a sofa with a group of people. Tera was bent over a footstool at the front, retching. She wasn't the only one. One of the men was grasping his middle and groaning, while another was on his knees throwing up. Two more had staggered backward from the group, but it wasn't clear whether they were sick themselves or just trying to get away from the others. Nate was bent over his phone, talking fast about medical emergencies and the need for urgent help, while Susa stood at the side of the room, hugging herself.

She looked more terrified than I'd ever seen her, and I'd known her since we were seven.

I grabbed her arm. "Susa, what happened? What's going on?"

"I don't know. I don't…they all started throwing up and groaning. Maybe it was something they ate?" She gave me an anguished look as a stream of ice promptly slithered down my backbone.

Nate looked up at me, tossing his phone in his pocket. "Aid car's on its way. Let's see what we can do to help these people." He knelt beside Tera, turning her gently onto her back. She turned to her side, doubling up again, bringing her knees to her chest and moaning.

I turned and ran to the kitchen. I knew nothing

about treating what looked like food poisoning, but I knew people who vomited needed water and I'd seen a case of bottled water in Tera's pantry. I grabbed four or five bottles and ran toward the dining room again.

Siggi stood just inside the door, looking almost as terrified as Susa had. I pressed a bottle of water into her hands. "Give this to one of those men and help them lie down."

I knelt beside the nearest guy, who looked to be around Uncle Mike's age. "Here." I propped him up a little. "Drink some water. Let's get you away from all this." *All this* was, of course, the now disgusting circle of furniture where the sick people were huddled.

Alex grabbed another of the bottles of water and gave it to the guy who was still clutching his middle and groaning. After a moment, Susa took the other bottle of water away from me and tended to a guy propped against the wall.

Nate was still bending over Tera. I pushed a bottle of water into his hands, and he unscrewed the top quickly. Tera was still doubled up on the floor. I wasn't sure she was conscious. She didn't seem aware of anything Nate was doing or saying.

The man I was helping stared up at me blearily. "What happened?"

"I don't know. I was off in the kitchen. I guess something made you sick." I helped him drink a little more water.

He stared at me again, his eyes a little sharper. "What did you put in the food?"

"In the food?" I shook my head. "Nothing. It was food. That's all."

He took another sip of water. "Doesn't look that

way."

My heart thumped hard. Until that moment, I hadn't actually taken in the level of disaster we were facing. "We didn't poison you. I don't know what happened, but it wasn't us."

Just then I heard a siren coming from outside the house. I don't think I was ever so glad to hear anything in my life. "Hang on. Sounds like the medics are here." I handed him the water bottle and ran to the front door as someone outside rang the bell repeatedly.

I threw the door open. "They're in the dining room. A bunch of people got sick all at once, vomiting sick."

The medics rushed past me, but someone grasped my arm before I could return to the dining room. I turned to see Jean Bancroft, dressed in a dark blue uniform with a patch on the sleeve, giving me a very concerned look. "What's going on here?"

Jean was a medic who was also a part time cop, and I had a feeling it wasn't an idle question. "This is Tera Bloomfield's place. She had a dinner party. Nate Robicheaux and I cooked. We were cleaning up. Some of the people left, but the ones who stayed were having after-dinner drinks. All of a sudden they started throwing up. That's all I know."

Jean narrowed her eyes. "Was it food poisoning?"

Please God, no. "I don't know. I don't think so. We didn't serve anything tricky. No eggs, no fish, no chicken. All the perishables were kept under refrigeration. The food was served at the right temperature."

Jean nodded slowly. "Are there any leftovers?"

"Some. Not much." And Alex had washed the dishes. So had I.

"Keep what there is. I'm pretty sure there'll be questions."

I nodded. All of a sudden I was pretty sure, too.

One of the medics rushed through the room and out the door. Moments later he returned, pushing a gurney.

"Shit," Jean murmured and followed him toward the dining room.

I stood staring after them, more ice dripping down my backbone. It looked like we were in big, big trouble.

Chapter Nine

The aid car took off quickly with Tera, siren blasting. Another car arrived minutes later and took three more men down the mountain, including the man I'd helped with the water. The fourth man said he felt okay, well enough to drive himself to town anyway. That left Susa, Alex, Siggi, Nate, and me.

None of us had any idea what we were supposed to do next.

We gathered in the kitchen. "Maybe we should clean up," Siggi said doubtfully.

All four of us gave her horrified looks. "Not happening," Alex mumbled.

"No, no, not in there. I meant the kitchen. Like we usually do. There's still some dishes we need to load in the dishwasher."

"We could do that." Alex sounded relieved.

"No," I said. "Don't. Jean Bancroft said we should preserve everything the way it is. There's bound to be an investigation."

"Jean who?" Alex raised an eyebrow. "Who's going to investigate what and why?"

"Jean Bancroft. She's one of the medics. She's also a cop, part time." I gave him a level look. "At the very least, the health department is going to want to investigate this. Since five people got sick from ingesting something."

I hoped it was only five. If everybody got sick after eating our food, we were screwed. On the other hand, Alex didn't look like he believed me.

Nate raised his hand. "Roxy's right. Don't wash anything more. Leave it. The health department will want to see it. If we're lucky, they're the only ones who will."

He stepped into Tera's pantry and grabbed a box of zipper lock bags and a couple of containers. "I'm going to put all the leftovers into these and date them. I'll tape them closed so that they'll know they haven't been tampered with. This is a serious situation. Potentially anyway."

"No shit," Susa mumbled.

Alex folded his arms across his chest. "Siggi and I didn't do anything. We carried the food out and brought the plates back. That's it. We didn't touch the food."

"I made drinks," Siggi said. "I poured wine."

"From sealed bottles. There was nothing wrong with the wine." Nate gave Alex a long look. "And there was nothing wrong with the food. But I can't prove that until they've examined the leftovers and checked the dirty plates."

Alex threw his hands up. "Okay, whatever. I'm going home. I'm done, completely done with this evening."

He strode through the kitchen door, leaving the four of us staring after him. "I guess he's right. There's nothing more we can do here," Siggi said. "I'm going home, too." She pulled on her jacket and followed Alex out the kitchen door.

Susa stood watching us for a moment, her lower lip trembling. "I guess I should go home," she said finally.

I put my hand on her shoulder, worried all over again. "Are you sure you feel up to driving? We can give you a lift."

"I can do it. I just want to get out of here. And I don't want to have to come back tomorrow to get my car."

Nate studied her for a moment. "How do you feel? Any nausea?"

Susa shook her head. "I'm not sick. I'm just upset about Tera. I want to go now."

"Go ahead." I was still worried about Susa driving herself, but she looked so shaken up I decided it was better for her to go home.

"Okay." She gave me a kind of wobbly smile. "Thanks, Rox. I'll call you tomorrow. It's all going to work out. I'm sure."

I wished I was, but right then wasn't the time to talk about our problems. "I hope so. Drive carefully."

We watched her leave the kitchen, then Nate turned to me. "Is she okay?"

"I'm not sure. But I didn't want to keep her here. We need to go down the mountain ourselves."

"Right. As soon as we get everything taken care of here, we will."

I wasn't sure what we were taking care of, but I watched Nate put the sausage and cheese into zipper lock bags and date them on the outside. He took a roll of freezer tape and signed his name on a piece, then put the piece crosswise over the bag seal. "This isn't foolproof by any means. But it's the best I can think of. We need to show nothing was tampered with."

"Right." I pulled the dutch oven out of the refrigerator and emptied the last of the bourguignon into one of the freezer containers. Nate wrote the date on top and put another signed piece of tape all the way around it. "Do we have anything else left?" he asked.

I checked the refrigerator. "Salad's all gone," I said. "But there's a little vichyssoise." I scraped the last bits into another freezer container and watched Nate do his thing.

"We could take it all home with us. That way we wouldn't need to worry about anyone getting into this stuff." I gestured toward the last of the dirty dishes piled next to the dishwasher. All of a sudden I felt nervous about leaving evidence in Tera's refrigerator and on her counters.

Nate shook his head. "I don't want to do anything to make people think we were acting suspicious. Let's leave it all here and tell the health department what we did."

"Yeah, but maybe we need a little more insurance." I pulled my phone out of my purse and took pictures of the food before we put it in the refrigerator, along with the pile of dishes. "At least if anything fishy happens we'll have evidence we tried to preserve what was left."

Nate sighed, rubbing a hand over his tired eyes. "I hate to think something fishy might happen, but at this point, I'm not arguing with you."

"I guess we'd better leave the containers, too." I gestured at the dutch oven and the food storage container we'd used to transport the vichyssoise. I'd already washed out the salad bowl.

"I guess so," Nate said. He did the thing with the freezer tape again, sealing the dutch oven and the storage container.

I took a couple more photos, then put the pans in

the refrigerator with the leftovers. We were covered, sort of.

"Let's get loaded up and go home," Nate said. "We can figure out who to contact tomorrow, assuming they don't contact us first."

Considering the number of people in the hospital, I was guessing the health department would be contacting us at first light.

I was helping load the clean containers and implements into the boxes we'd used to transport them when I heard the doorbell ring again.

Nate frowned at me. "You think somebody forgot something?"

"Possibly." Or maybe it was the health department getting a head start on things. "I'll go see who's there."

I made my way to the front door, avoiding the unspeakable dining room. Then I peered through the peep hole.

And saw Chief Ethan Fowler staring at me.

Fowler was the last person I expected to see on Tera's doorstep. I threw open the door, then stood blinking at him. "What are you doing here?"

Fowler raised his eyebrows. "I might ask you the same thing."

"We fixed dinner. Nate and I. We were just putting our stuff together so we could drive down to Shavano."

Fowler stepped inside. "You cooked dinner, the two of you?"

I nodded. "Yeah. We'd just finished. And then people got sick." All of a sudden my heart beat sped up alarmingly. "Why are you here? What's happened?"

Fowler ignored my questions in favor of his own. "Where's your partner?"

"You mean me?" Nate asked from behind me. "I'm right here. I agree with Roxy. We need to know what's happened."

Fowler gave us a long look, as if he was weighing a lot of different possibilities before he answered. Then he sighed. "Ms. Bloomfield passed away about a half hour ago. I'm here to secure the scene."

I felt as if my stomach had dropped to my knees. My heart was hammering, and I wasn't sure I could stand up on my own. I propped one hand on the wall until I felt Nate's arm around me, bracing me against him.

"What was the cause of death?" he asked.

"Undetermined at the moment." Fowler glanced around the foyer. "Is there someplace we can sit down?"

"Let's go to the kitchen," Nate said. "You can see what we've done with the leftovers."

The kitchen was better for a meeting than the dining room and probably any of the other rooms nearby. Nate pulled up a couple of chairs to the island and we all sat down.

I was still feeling a little shaky, but having a very calm Nate nearby helped. "What about the other people, the men who went to the hospital along with Tera?"

"All recovering," Fowler said. "What happened here tonight?"

Nate and I glanced at each other, then Nate leaned forward, propping his arms on the island. "Okay, I had this idea for a bistro."

He told the whole story, from the beginning, how he'd gone to Tera for advice, how he'd cooked her a sample meal, how she'd hired him to cook a meal for her dinner group. Fowler took notes, watching Nate but not asking him many questions.

After Nate explained about asking me to help him as sous chef, Fowler glanced at me. "So you cooked some of the meal?"

I nodded. "And I ordered a lot of the food from people around town. Like Bianca Jordan and her son Marcus. And Annabelle Dorsey."

Fowler frowned. "All the food was local?"

Nate shook his head. "I ordered meat and vegetables from the café's suppliers. They've all been in the restaurant business for years." Which didn't rule out their selling us stuff that had nasty microbes aboard but did reduce the possibility quite a bit.

Fowler nodded and took down the names. "When did people get sick?"

"After we finished serving dinner. Alex, the waiter, had brought all the dessert plates back." I gestured toward the counter. "They're still there. We told him not to wash them so the health department could examine them. There are also a few plates left from the rest of the meal."

Fowler nodded. "Okay, that should help. I'll make sure the forensics guys check them."

"We have forensics?" I was amazed.

Fowler grimaced. "Of course, we have forensics. But we're also pulling in the Colorado Bureau of Investigation on this. They've got more resources than we do. Back to when people started getting sick…"

"Alex said Tera was having port and wanted me to join them. I went out to thank her and tell her I didn't have time to do that. She and her guests were sitting on a sofa and chairs at the side of the dining room." Nate paused. "She didn't look good. Her face was sweaty, and she was grimacing. Then all of a sudden one of the guys started vomiting. And then Tera did, too. And…" He paused again, and I had a feeling he was pulling himself together. "Then I saw all these people being sick. So I pulled out my cell and called 911 to tell them we had a medical emergency."

"I came out to the dining room around then," I said. "Siggi, the bartender, came into the kitchen and said people needed help. The four guys and Tera were sick, two of them vomiting. Susa seemed to be okay. She was standing at the side."

Fowler stopped writing notes. "Susa Sondergaard?"

I nodded. "She was one of the guests. And I think Tera asked her to stay after the others left."

"These weren't all of the guests?" Fowler asked. "The six people drinking port?"

I shook my head. "The other guests had already left." For the first time, I felt a glimmer of hope. If those guests were okay, we might be off the hook.

Fowler turned to Nate. "Do you have a list of the dinner guests?"

He shrugged. "Nope. I just knew we were feeding twelve, not who the twelve were. I met a few of them—Phil Duncan, Tony Aldo, Tom Everett."

"Everett and Aldo are two of the ones in the hospital." He turned to me. "Did you know any of them?"

"I know Phil Duncan by sight, but none of the others. Susa might know. She worked for Tera." And she was actually sitting at the table rather than coming and going at Tera's command like us.

"Okay," Fowler said. "What were you saying about the leftovers?"

"They're in the refrigerator." Nate opened the refrigerator door to show Fowler his neatly labeled bags. "We don't have samples of everything. Roxy washed up the salad bowl and the salad plates were in the dishwasher. The fruit tart we had for dessert was finished off, but the dessert plates have remnants and we didn't wash the tart pan."

Fowler frowned as he examined the bag of charcuterie. "Very thorough. Whose idea was the piece of freezer tape?"

"Mine." Nate gave him a level look. "I saw a bunch of people being violently sick after eating food I cooked. I want to make sure the leftovers get a full analysis. I'm as certain as I can be we didn't feed those people anything that would make them throw up, but I know nobody's going to take my word for it."

The corners of Fowler's mouth edged up marginally. "No, I'm guessing they won't. I'll make sure the lab guys treat these with respect. Did anybody clean up the dining room?"

I shook my head. "Alex and Siggi, the wait staff, brought in the dirty dishes before people started getting sick, but we didn't do anything beyond that. The…remains are still up there." And he was welcome to them. I was doubly glad I wasn't in charge of investigating all this.

"Right." Fowler sighed, then turned to Nate. "I hate to make you do this, but I need you to show me where Tera Bloomfield was sitting when she took sick."

Nate's jaw tensed, but he nodded. "I can do that."

The two of them stepped through the kitchen door.

I stayed where I was. Unless my presence was specifically requested, there was no way I was going into that dining room again.

Nate returned a few minutes later, his face pale. "The forensics people have arrived. Fowler says we can go home now, but he told me to leave everything here until their lab people can get their samples."

I nodded as I grabbed my jacket. "Okay, let's go then."

"Right." Nate blew out a long breath. "I guess there's nothing more for us to do here anyway."

I wanted to tell him everything would be all right, nobody could believe our food had made people sick, but I knew better. I was as sure as Nate was that we hadn't poisoned those people, but I also knew people who heard the story of Tera's dinner party and its aftermath would probably assume our food was to blame. And unless we could prove it wasn't, they'd probably go on believing it no matter what we said.

The ride down the mountain was quiet since neither of us had much to say. I wondered if I ought to call Bianca and Annabelle to give them a heads up. The chance of anybody getting sick from eating Bianca's baguettes was remote, unless we had a cluster of people suffering from undiagnosed celiac disease. I guessed Annabelle's pickles would be similar—fermented food could go bad, but it usually smelled like it. Annabelle's stuff had smelled like pickles. The same went for Marcus's sausages: cured meats kept under refrigeration didn't usually go bad.

Which left the dishes we'd prepared: the bourguignon, the vichyssoise, the salad, Coco's fruit tart with ice cream.

It was remotely possible we'd gotten tainted lettuce for the salad. There had been cases of salmonella contracted from salad greens, some sold by big national grocery chains. But I thought salmonella poisoning took longer to develop than the relatively short time between the guests eating their salad and those same guests becoming violently ill.

The bourguignon had been thoroughly cooked and served hot. It was an unlikely source of illness, particularly since it didn't contain any of the usual suspects, like dairy products or shellfish.

Which left the vichyssoise. The vichyssoise I'd prepared. The vichyssoise that was served chilled and included cream and sour cream. Of all the dishes we'd served, the vichyssoise was the most likely to have contained something nasty. And I'd been responsible for it.

I sat very still as Nate turned down the road to the farm. I didn't want to be the culprit, the one who'd made a mistake that had ended up killing a woman. But I thought I was more likely to have been at fault than Nate.

There was a sealed sample of vichyssoise in the refrigerator. If I'd screwed up, we'd know soon enough.

"Okay, what's wrong?" Nate asked as he pulled up next to my cabin. "Besides the obvious."

I went on staring straight ahead. "I'm just wondering about the vichyssoise. If I screwed up somehow. It's the only thing we served chilled, except for the dessert, and it contained dairy. Maybe I let it sit outside the refrigerator too long to take off the chill."

Nate sighed. "I thought of that. And the tart. And the salad. And even the bourguignon. Hell, for all we know Marcus's sausage had E. coli or something, although I thought curing was supposed to take care of stuff like that. On the one hand, I'm as certain as I can be everything we served was fixed right and kept at the right temperature. We both know all the rules about avoiding contamination, and we both stuck with them. But something happened. And until we know for sure what it was, we'll be driving ourselves nuts trying to figure it out."

I leaned against the car seat, so tired I could barely keep my eyes open. "You want to stay over? It's pretty late."

He shook his head. "I'd like to, but I need to go to town so I can tell Mom and Bobby what happened tomorrow. In case there's blowback for the café."

I started to ask him why the café would be involved, but that was obvious. He was a Robicheaux, part of the Robicheaux Café dynasty. And he'd cooked a lot of the dinner in the café's kitchen. People might assume the café itself was the source of the problem.

"Shit," I murmured. "This just gets worse and worse."

Nate nodded. "It does. We have to hang on until we know for sure what went wrong."

Assuming we ever do. But neither of us needed to say that. We both knew it already. I walked inside for a sleepless night.

Chapter Ten

The next morning I described the whole situation to Uncle Mike. He'd hear about it soon enough, and he needed to know the details in case anyone asked him about it.

"That's bull," he said after I'd given him a complete rundown. "You've been cooking most of your life and you never made anybody sick. Well, other than that time when you put too much sugar in the lemon pie, but that was more a matter of taste than poison."

He gave me a grin meant to tease me out of my misery. I appreciated the effort, but it wasn't happening. "We'll see what happens when the cops complete their investigation. I imagine the health department will be involved, too. They may want to inspect my kitchen again."

"But your jam wasn't involved. And you didn't cook that dinner here—you were up at Bloomfield's place. God only knows what might have been going on in her kitchen."

"Actually, my jam *was* involved. Nate had me bring up a couple of jars to add to the charcuterie tray. But I doubt anybody ate enough of it to make them sick." At least I hoped so.

Uncle Mike laid his hand on mine. "We'll get through this, kid. It wasn't your fault, and they'll prove it. You just need to hang on until they do."

I felt like knocking on the wood table just to keep his words from backfiring, but I wanted him to be right. "Thanks, Uncle Mike. I guess we'll see."

After breakfast, I called Bianca. She'd already heard some rumors about trouble at Tera Bloomfield's place. I gave her an abbreviated version of the story, emphasizing things were being investigated and we felt confident about our innocence. I wasn't really that confident. But it was my story, and I was definitely sticking to it.

Bianca made sympathetic noises and promised to call Marcus. I tried to call Annabelle Dorsey, but she wasn't home. I left her a long voice mail, and she could call me if she wanted more details.

And then I sat in my kitchen and tried to decide what else I could do. I itched to call Fowler and ask if he'd discovered anything else about what killed Tera, but I knew that would be useless. He wouldn't tell me even if I got through, which I doubted I would. I thought about calling Nate, but I didn't want to make things more difficult for him if he was trying to explain to his family.

Susa was another call I longed to make. I was willing to bet Fowler had gotten in touch with her by now. I wanted to find out what he'd told her, assuming he'd told her anything at all. If we pooled our knowledge, maybe we could figure out some of the details about Tera's death. Such as what caused it, the major question currently confronting us.

I ended up doing what I usually do when I don't know what to do with myself. I made jam—peach and pepper peach, two of my big sellers. I was pulling the jars out of the hot water bath when I heard someone knock on the door.

"Come on in. It's open," I called since I was just about done pulling the jars out of the boiling water and I didn't want to lose my place, so to speak.

Nate stepped inside. "I wasn't sure you were home."

Where else would I be? But that wasn't kind. We were in this together, and we needed to take care of each other.

He looked exhausted. His complexion was gray and his eyes more deep-set than usual. I should have told him to go home and get some rest, but I knew he wouldn't. And anyway, I didn't want him to.

Realistically, I probably looked as bad as he did.

"Have a seat. I'm almost done." I placed the last jars at the end of the row I'd created on the counter. At least I'd accomplished something, unimpressive though it was. "How was brunch?"

"The meal or the drama?" He settled onto one of the bar stools next to my kitchen island and rubbed his hand across his face.

"Both, I guess." I pushed the canning pot to the rear of the stove so the water could cool down a little before I dumped it out.

He sighed. "Bobby thinks I've probably destroyed the café because everyone will assume I poisoned four people even if I didn't. Mom doesn't go that far, but she's worried about what the fallout will be. Coco's making jokes about her 'killer fruit tart,' but underneath it she's scared too." He pinched the bridge of his nose. "I'm trying to be the big brave chef, but the truth is I'm pretty nervous myself."

I leaned on the counter for a moment, trying to

gather myself together, but it wasn't happening. I'd been stuffing my feelings down ever since we'd left Tera's place last night, and I couldn't do it anymore. "So am I," I murmured, and my voice broke on the last word.

Nate was on his feet in an instant, catching me in an embrace as he rubbed my back. "I'm sorry," he whispered. "I'm so sorry I got you into this. You wouldn't have been there if it hadn't been for me."

I held onto him for a moment, but then I pulled away. "I'm not letting you take the blame for this. It's not your fault, and it's not my fault. We don't know whose fault it is yet, but I know that for a fact."

"Okay, damn straight. We didn't do anything wrong, and pretty soon everybody will know we didn't. We'll get through this. I know *that* for a fact."

We leaned together for a long moment, holding onto each other and trying to draw on our joint strength. After a little while, I stepped away again.

"You know what I keep thinking? It was a damn fine dinner we cooked. Maybe nobody will believe it after what happened, but it was. I was proud of what we did."

Nate nodded. "So was I. I felt like we hit every note. It was a hell of a meal, pretty close to a career high."

I paused, my mind suddenly clicking to a new perspective. "Which we, both of us, knew because we, both of us, tasted everything. We tasted as we worked along making everything and we tasted again before we plated everything. You don't send something out until you're sure it tastes okay. Both of us ate the dishes we cooked."

Nate stared at me for a long moment. "Okay, we did eat some. But we didn't eat much."

"No, we didn't. But if the food had something like salmonella or botulism or E. coli, even eating a little should have made us sick. Maybe not fall down vomiting sick, but queasy at least." I took a deep breath. "I'm tired and upset and ready to tear my hair out, but I'm not sick. Not that way, anyway. And I haven't felt sick since I left Tera's place." I straightened, feeling a little more confident than I had five minutes ago.

Nate shook his head. "I haven't felt sick either, but that doesn't mean the food was okay. It's suggestive, but it's not enough to clear us."

"But it's enough to make me believe something else *will* be enough to clear us."

Nate put his arms around me again, pulling me close. "Here's hoping, sweetheart. Here's hoping. Let me fix you some dinner. I wasn't hungry before, but I've got a little appetite now."

Neither of us was ravenous, but I had enough lettuce sitting around to put together a salad, and Nate whipped up a kind of low-rent cacio e pepe spaghetti sauce with the last of a jar of grated parmesan. And there was wine, two or three glasses at least. After what we'd been through, we'd earned it.

We were just finishing up the spaghetti when I heard a car drive up outside. Nate frowned. "You expecting anyone?"

"Nope. Maybe it's Fowler. I keep hoping he'll give us an update if he finds out what killed Tera."

Nate gave me a sour smile. "I know Fowler's a fan of yours, but I don't expect him to keep us up to date on his investigation."

I started to ask him what he meant by saying Fowler was my fan, but just then my front door flew open and Susa rushed in. "Oh my God, oh my God, oh my God. I'm so glad you're home. I can't even…"

She flopped down on the sofa, rubbing her eyes with the heels of her hands. "I'm sorry I didn't call first. It's been a day since I spoke to anybody except the cops. I'm going sort of crazy."

I sat down beside her on the couch. Nate had looked exhausted when he'd driven up, but Susa looked beyond exhaustion, into some state where the only things keeping her upright were nerves. "Are you okay? Did you get sick after you left?"

She shook her head. "No, I mean not beyond just being queasy about what happened to Tera. But the food didn't make me sick. No. On the other hand, I haven't slept for twenty-four hours or so. I don't exactly know what I feel at this point." Her eyes seemed unnaturally bright. I hoped she wasn't headed for a meltdown.

Nate sat down opposite us. "Have you talked to Fowler yet?"

"No. I went straight home last night, but I couldn't go to sleep. I spent most of the night catching up on work. A couple of uniformed cops showed up at my front door around seven in the morning. They said it was a welfare check. I guess they were visiting everyone who was at the dinner to make sure we were okay."

I glanced at Nate. "They must have found the guest list after we left."

Susa blinked up at me. "There were fancy place cards. If they wanted to know who was there, all they had to do was look at the table."

I half-remembered the place cards, but last night I'd been so frantic they'd slipped my mind.

"Did the police tell you if anyone else was sick, besides the people who went to the hospital?" Nate asked.

"No. I asked them about a couple of people, but they said they hadn't talked to them. I guess Fowler had several people out checking."

"So you're okay, right? What about the guy you were helping?"

"So far as I know, he's okay. I just met him last night—Tony something or other."

"Did you eat everything we served?" Nate leaned forward, folding his hands on his knees.

"Absolutely." Susa nodded emphatically. "I was starving, and it was delicious."

"Even the charcuterie?" A lot of the charcuterie went early. All we had left in the kitchen were the sausage ends.

"The sausage and Bianca's bread? Yeah, it was great." She gave me a slightly confused look. "You don't think that made people sick, do you? The sausage?"

"I don't know what happened, and I'm still trying to find out. I'm sorry. We've been grilling you, and I haven't even asked you how you're feeling now. Do you want some wine?"

Susa sighed, leaning against the couch. "I would love a glass of wine. And I don't know how I'm feeling exactly. I don't understand what happened any more than you do. I'm running on adrenaline."

I went to the kitchen to grab the wine bottle and

another glass. "I know the police are investigating and they've called in the CBI. But I don't know if that means anything other than an unexplained death. Fowler came to Tera's house last night after you left. We told him what happened, but he didn't tell us anything more."

Susa shivered as she sipped her wine. "Fowler scares the hell out of me normally."

"You think Fowler's scary?"

"Lord, yes. He looks straight through you, and he never smiles. He gives me chills."

I wasn't sure why Fowler would give Susa chills in the present situation. She hadn't been in the kitchen. Except she had been, now that I thought about it. She'd come in to wish us well.

"He can look as scary as he wants as long as he clears this up," Nate said. "The longer things go on without a solution, the worse it'll be for everybody. Well, not everybody. The worse it'll be for us. And the people who sold us food." He leaned back in his chair, and I passed him the wine bottle.

"Oh Lord, Nate, I'm sorry. Of course, this needs to be settled. It's not your fault, and you're getting screwed." Susa glanced at me. "Both of you."

"So far I think we're okay, but once the news gets out tomorrow, we'll be doing damage control." I paused. "Do you want something to eat? Nate fixed spaghetti."

Susa stared up at me, and the pause felt like a million years rather than a few seconds. I could sense the tension in Nate's shoulders all the way across the room. "I don't know. I'm trying to remember the last time I had something to eat. I think I had breakfast, but

I'm not sure. I guess I should be hungry. I'm trying to decide if I am."

"Come on, Suz, this isn't like you. We were just sitting down to dinner ourselves. You can join us." The panicked look in her eyes was beginning to scare me a little.

"I guess I want something to eat. I shouldn't just sit here and swill wine. That wouldn't be good."

"No, it wouldn't. I'll get the spaghetti on the table."

"I'll help," Nate said.

I didn't need any help, but maybe he wanted to talk to me away from Susa. I didn't blame him.

In the kitchen, I grabbed a platter and dumped spaghetti onto it. I hoped there was enough for three. After a moment I grabbed a loaf of Bianca's bread and some butter.

"Is she okay?" Nate sounded worried.

"I don't know." I felt worried myself. Susa had always been a little ditzy—it was part of her charm. But she was way beyond ditzy now. I'd never seen her so scattered and disoriented. Of course, she'd seen her employer become violently ill, and if she hadn't seen Tera die, she knew it had happened. The cumulative effect might be enough to make anyone a little wild.

Nate picked up the salad bowl while I carried the spaghetti to the dining nook, only to find Susa up on her feet again. "I'm so sorry. I shouldn't have come over and interrupted your evening. You all have enough to worry about without me making it worse."

Worry made me snappish. "Susa, come over here and sit down right now. You need to eat. You need to drink. You need to relax. You're going to burn out if you don't calm down. Eat some of Nate's spaghetti and some of Bianca's bread, and if you want anything more I'll make you a peanut butter and jelly sandwich. And if you annoy me, I'll make it with pumpkin butter."

Susa stared at me for a moment, the corners of her mouth trembling. "Oh. Okay." She took her place at the table.

Nate joined us a moment later with the salad and the three of us helped ourselves to some minimalist dinner. Nate took a notably small helping. So did Susa. I took more spaghetti than I thought I'd eat, but somebody had to set an example.

Susa took one bite and then another. And then she started eating more systematically, quickly demolishing all the food on her plate. "Oh my God, this is delicious. I was so hungry, and I didn't even know it."

Nate dug into his own spaghetti, nodding after a moment. "You're right. I didn't know I needed to eat until I tasted it."

"Anybody need a sandwich?" I watched the dinner disappear in record time.

Susa shook her head. "Just more of Bianca's bread if there is any."

"There is." I went into the kitchen and grabbed the rest of the loaf.

Nate and Susa divided the bread between them. Then he glanced at me. "Okay?"

"Maybe. Getting there."

After we'd finished silently demolishing the food, I slumped in my chair, blowing out a long breath as I studied Susa. "So how do you feel now?"

"Getting there, like you said. What about you?"

"I don't know. I cycle between feeling okay and

feeling like I'm on the verge of hysterics. One minute I've talked myself into being in control, and the next I'm howling at the moon."

Susa closed her eyes for a moment. When she looked up at me again, I saw tears. "Damn straight. Except my in-control moments seem more few and far between. I'm sort of falling apart."

"Okay, you're staying here tonight. You are not driving around like this. We're going to watch several episodes of *Friends* and finish another bottle of wine."

"Nate wants to watch *Friends*?" Susa asked.

"Sure." I carefully did not look at Nate. I didn't know how he felt about *Friends*, but this constituted a crisis. My best friend was having a meltdown, and I wasn't doing well myself. If Nate didn't want to watch *Friends*, he could go up and visit with Uncle Mike.

Nate sighed. "Could we sneak in a couple of episodes of *Parks and Rec*?"

"Yep. All points of view will be honored. We might even try some of *The Office*."

Susa closed her eyes for a moment. "Okay. I can do that. It's certainly better than anything else I can think of."

I gave her my most reassuring smile, although I had to strain to do it. Nothing about this situation was reassuring, but hanging out together and watching TV was better than being on our own. And that went for all of us right then.

Chapter Eleven

In the end, Nate and Susa both stayed over, which was fine with me. More than fine, in fact. Essential. I was still reasonably certain we'd be cleared after Fowler finished his investigation, but I wasn't so certain I wanted to be alone. And I didn't think Susa or Nate should be alone either.

Uncle Mike and Herman came down for breakfast, causing cries of delight from both Herman and Susa. Herm probably thought I'd arranged for her to be there as a special treat. Susa looked equally ecstatic to have Herman pressing his head against her hip.

Nate made one of his spectacular fluffy omelets and I scrounged up some very nice country sausage from Marcus Jordan's shop I'd had in the freezer. I will admit to a momentary qualm as I brought it out, but I promptly squelched it. Marcus's sausage was fine. I knew it. And I needed to support other people if I expected them to support me.

In any event, Marcus's sausage was terrific. So was Nate's omelet. Even the toast I made with some supermarket bread was a winner because I served it with peach jam and pumpkin butter.

"This is actually tasty," Nate said. "A little like pumpkin pie." I ignored his slight tone of surprise.

"Is this what you're doing for the Winter Market?" Susa asked.

"Sure. I brought it in for you to taste a couple of weeks ago, remember?"

"That's right, I remember. You gave some to Carly and Kip." Susa paused. "Geez, that seems so long ago. Like another lifetime. I was working on Tera's site then."

It was the first time Tera's name had been mentioned, and it put an immediate damper on everyone's mood.

"Sorry," Susa mumbled. "I didn't mean to bring y'all down."

"We're okay. Don't worry about it." Nate took hold of my hand under the table. "What will you do now about her website? Does it stay up or come down?"

Susa shrugged. "I don't know. I guess that's for her company to decide. It'll have to be revised if they leave it up. Right now it's focused on Tera."

"Who else is in this company of hers?" Uncle Mike asked. "People here in town?"

"I don't know. I never met anyone from the company except Tera. I mean, the board of directors is on the website, but I didn't recognize any of the names."

"Probably all from Denver. Out of towners." Uncle Mike sold his produce all over the state, but he didn't have much patience with people from the Front Range. Unless they were Constantine arugula fans.

"Tera made it sound like a great investment opportunity," Susa said. "She told me she was drawing investors from all around the state. And some from out of state, too."

"Did you give her any money?" Uncle Mike raised

a suspicious eyebrow.

Susa flushed. "No. She gave me a chance to invest, but I didn't understand what she was doing. And I felt nervous about putting money into something I didn't understand."

Uncle Mike gave her a crooked smile. "You're smarter than ninety percent of the investors I've known, honey. If more people thought that way, we'd have a lot fewer bankruptcies in this country."

Susa's cheeks stayed flushed, but she smiled back. "Thanks."

"Did Tera give you any trouble about it?" She hadn't struck me as the sort of woman who took kindly to people who turned her down.

"She didn't say any more about it. She claimed she already had more investors than she could handle. She said she'd had to turn down a lot of people who wanted in."

That sounded like hype to me. "Well, I'm glad you got a high-paying job out of this. I know that sounds kind of callous, given everything, but I'm glad you got something."

All three of them stared at me, and my cheeks flushed. Okay, it *was* callous, but it was also true. Tera had jerked Suz around like she'd tried to jerk Nate around, but in the end, Susa had prevailed.

Or so I thought.

"Theoretically, it was a high-paying job," Susa said. "But I haven't gotten all the money she owed me yet. That's another thing I'll have to talk to her company about. I've got the invoices to show what I did for her."

"She didn't pay her bills?" Nate looked grim all of

a sudden. Not a good sign.

"She paid the invoices I sent her initially. But she kept needing changes. Finally she told me to just invoice her when we were through instead of billing her as we went. She wanted to handle the cost all at once."

Uncle Mike looked like he'd tasted something sour. "Sounds like horseshit to me. I wonder if she'd have paid you at the end."

"We'd slowed down over the last couple of weeks. I was getting ready to send her a bill, but I wanted to wait until the end of the month. Now I guess I'll have to find out who's handling her estate and send them my invoice."

"What about you?" Uncle Mike turned to Nate. "Did she leave you holding the bag on the expenses for this dinner?"

"Not entirely. I billed her for the advance orders I put in with Swain since they had to be paid when we ordered, and she gave me the money. But I was going to send her a bill at the end for the stuff we bought locally. She'd agreed when I said I'd cook the dinner for her."

"So I guess you'll have to submit a bill to her estate, too," Susa said.

Nate and I looked at each other, then looked away. The idea of submitting a bill for the dinner that might have killed Tera obviously struck both of us as a nonstarter.

Nate sighed. "Tell me what you paid Marcus and Bianca and Annabelle. I'll make it right."

"It wasn't expensive. And Annabelle gave me the pickles for free. Chalk it up to experience." Actually, Marcus's sausage had been pricey, but I was the one who decided to buy it all so I should be the one who had to eat the cost, so to speak.

"You didn't do anything wrong." Uncle Mike glanced between us. "Neither one of you. No reason you should have to pay for stuff she ordered."

Except neither of us felt like submitting an invoice when people might think we'd poisoned her. The conversation died off as we finished eating.

I'd started to gather the dirty dishes to load in the dishwasher, while Susa and Nate were both making noises about going home, when I heard another car drive up outside.

"Who the hell's that?" Uncle Mike turned toward the door.

"Since just about everyone who might drop by is already here, I don't know." I carried the dishes into the kitchen as Uncle Mike opened the door. I heard his exclamation of surprise as I set the dishes on the counter.

When I came to the dining room, Chief Fowler was standing in the middle of the living room.

Most times when I saw the chief he looked like he starched his underwear. Now, though, his uniform looked decidedly less crisp than usual, as if he'd been wearing it for a while. Even his Stetson looked less than dapper. All in all, he looked like he hadn't slept for a couple of days, which was probably true.

"Morning, Chief. Would you like some coffee?"

He gave me one of his half-smiles. "If it's not too much trouble."

"No trouble at all," Uncle Mike said flatly. "I'll get you a cup." He headed toward the kitchen as I came farther into the room.

Herman approached the chief a little cautiously, his tail wagging low. He and the chief had met before, but it hadn't been under the best of circumstances. Still, Herman tended to remember people who'd been good to me, and since the chief had saved me from serious injury once upon a time, he fell into that category.

The chief reached down to rub Herman's ears, and Herman gave him one of his soulful looks.

Nate and Susa were still standing at the dining room table. Nate looked faintly annoyed and faintly apprehensive at the same time. The apprehension made sense, but I wasn't sure why Fowler's presence would annoy him. Then again, there was the crack he'd made about Fowler being my "fan."

Susa, on the other hand, looked terrified, which made even less sense than Nate being annoyed.

"Are you off duty?" I asked.

Fowler nodded. "CBI has sent people in to work on the investigation. I'm going home to get some sleep. But I wanted to talk to you before I did." He glanced at Nate. "Both of you, actually. Lucky I found you together."

Nate's expression stayed bland, but I thought his shoulders tensed. "We've been hoping for some news."

"Figured as much." Fowler paused when Uncle Mike returned with his coffee.

"Let's sit." I wanted Nate and Susa to both settle down and sitting around the table seemed like one way to make that happen.

Fowler pulled out a chair, pausing to sip his coffee. "We talked to all the other guests, the ones who left before Ms. Bloomfield took sick."

Took sick was a polite way to describe what

happened, but it worked for me. "Were they okay?"

He nodded. "None of them had had any kind of indigestion, although the ones who'd heard about Ms. Bloomfield were understandably concerned."

Nate sighed. "Great. I take it the news has already spread around town."

"Probably inevitable. But the fact all the other guests were fine is a point in your favor, I'd say. Seems to mean your food wasn't necessarily involved in what happened. Unless you got a group of people who were all allergic to the same things and another group of people who weren't. That stretches credibility a little far."

"What about the other people who were sick besides Tera, the three men?" Susa looked a little less frightened, but still pretty tense. "Are they okay?"

"Two of them have gone home from the hospital. The third is recovering. He'll probably head home later today. Whatever affected Ms. Bloomfield didn't affect them as much." He raised his eyebrows at Susa. "Actually, I wanted to ask you about that since you were in the group that stayed behind after dinner. Was there anything your group consumed the rest of the guests didn't?"

Susa blew out a long breath. Her expression had shifted from frightened to resigned. "The port. Tera let the other people leave, but she asked us to stay around and have some port with her. She said it was special stuff."

"When did she tell you this?" Fowler was listening to her carefully.

"Early in the evening." Susa's forehead furrowed as she thought. "I got there around six because she asked me to come early to help her get set up. I stopped in the kitchen to say hi to Rox and Nate, and then I went into the living room where they were putting out the charcuterie. Tera pulled me aside as the other people were coming in and told me to stick around after dinner. She said she had bottle of something special someone special had given her, and she wanted to share it with some of the high rollers."

Fowler frowned. "She called those four guys 'high rollers'?"

Susa nodded. "I guess they were investors. Or maybe she wanted them to be. Anyway, that's what she said."

" 'Someone special.' Did she tell you who that was?"

"Nope. She acted like it was a big secret. And then a lot of people came in, and she went over to say hello to them. She didn't mention it again."

Fowler turned to Nate. "Did Ms. Bloomfield say anything to you about the port?"

"No. I bought the dinner wine for her, but that was all." His jaw tightened, and I wondered if Tera had paid for the wine. With our luck, probably not.

"I understand she asked you to join them when she served the port?"

"She told Alex, the waiter, to ask me. I went out to tell her thanks but no thanks, and that's when everybody started getting sick."

"Not a port fan?" Fowler gave him one of those half-smiles.

"I just wanted to clean up and go home," Nate said a little stiffly. "It sounded like she wanted to extend the evening, and we'd been working full tilt all day."

Besides, his girlfriend was in the kitchen. If Tera had had a little seduction in mind, she was even more insensitive than I thought.

Fowler nodded, as if he was making some kind of mental note. He turned to Susa. "So was the port good?"

"I don't know. I didn't drink it."

"All the port glasses were empty when I saw them."

"I know." Susa closed her eyes for a moment. Then she shrugged. "I poured it into a ficus plant when she was talking to Alex about Nate. I was standing by the side—Tera and the guys were sitting on the couch. She didn't notice me doing it."

There was a long moment of silence as we all stared at her blankly. "Into a plant?" Fowler said. "Why did you do that?"

"I hate port. I hate sweet wine in general. I mean, I can handle sherry, sort of. But port tastes like cough syrup to me. It makes me feel sick."

Uncle Mike gave her a dry smile. "Is this a holdover from the time you two got into my port on New Year's Eve?"

"Oh, good grief, we were fifteen," I said through gritted teeth. Uncle Mike has a photographic memory for embarrassing information.

"That was probably part of it." Susa gave him a rueful grin. "I never got much into it after that one experience. Too many bad memories."

Fowler cleared his throat, bringing the attention back to him. "So why didn't you just tell Ms. Bloomfield you didn't want any port?"

He looked genuinely mystified, but I wasn't. Tera

never struck me as the kind of woman who reacted well to the word *no.*

Susa stared down at the table, biting her lip. "She made such a big deal out of it. I didn't want to tell her I didn't like it. She was my boss. I mean, I was doing a lot of work for her…" Her voice trailed off, and she gave me a stricken look.

Tera also owed her a lot of money, according to what Susa had said this morning. It was in her best interests to stay on Tera's good side, even if it involved drinking something she hated.

"What about the other guy?" I asked. "The one who didn't end up in the hospital. Did he drink the port?"

Fowler looked like that wasn't information he wanted to share, but then he shrugged. "He drank some of it, but not the whole glass. He said it was syrupy."

"I guess port can be heavy. I don't think I've actually had any that seemed thick, though."

Fowler raised an eyebrow at Uncle Mike. "How about you? Are you still a port drinker?"

"I have it now and then—I'm not a big fan. Lousy port can be sweet. Wino wine. Quality port has more depth. But I wouldn't call it syrupy, no."

"What was the brand?" Nate asked curiously.

"I don't remember. It's being analyzed, though."

"You could conceal something in port," Uncle Mike mused. "The high alcohol content could cover up any off taste, and some of it's pretty strong."

There was another long silence then as we stared at him and then looked away. I guess none of us had made the leap from thinking the problem was something naturally occurring in our food, like botulism or salmonella, to thinking the problem was a poison someone had introduced deliberately.

Well, none of us had made that leap except for Fowler, whose expression promptly became opaque. "Like I said, the port's being analyzed."

"But if the port was poisoned, why was Tera affected so much more than the others? We all had the same amount." Susa paused for a moment. "Well, *they* all had the same amounts. I didn't have any, and I guess the guy who was standing next to me didn't have much either."

"That's something we'll investigate. If there was anything in the port. Which hasn't been proven one way or the other. Yet." Fowler's ice blue eyes were boring into Susa as if he were looking for clues. I began to understand why she thought he was scary.

Nate shook his head, rubbing his hand across the back of his neck. "Jesus, this is a mess. You're saying this was deliberate? That someone set out to poison Tera Bloomfield? Or maybe to poison somebody else and she just got in the way?"

"I'm not saying anything. We aren't drawing any conclusions until we have more facts to deal with, mostly the results from the analysis."

Nate seemed to slump in his chair, and I wasn't feeling too chipper myself. We might be off the hook on food poisoning, but if this was murder we'd be neck deep in a big scandal. "Any chance the news our food wasn't the cause of Tera Bloomfield's death could get around town? Sort of officially unofficial?"

Fowler gave me a long look, then shook his head. "We can't make any announcements until we have something concrete to go on. I know this is doing your business some potential damage, but I can't help until we know more."

"But if we pointed out the other guests at the dinner didn't get sick?" I said. "If we let people know about that? Would that be a problem for you?"

"As long as you didn't attribute it to me or my office, no. The fact the other people didn't get sick is going to be well known, probably by tomorrow. If you want to draw the obvious conclusion for some of the slower types around town, be my guest."

"And the port?" Uncle Mike asked, eyes sharp all of a sudden.

Fowler drew himself up. "There's nothing to say about the port. There's no evidence it was poisoned, and saying it was would mean trouble if it turned out later it was something else."

"But it *was* poison," Nate said. "You're sure of that."

Fowler's jaw firmed. "I'm sure of nothing except we've got one person dead and three others who had acute indigestion. I'm not making any claims about any of it." And, he seemed to imply, neither should we.

Nate sighed, resting his elbows on the table. Susa rubbed her fingers across her forehead, as if she had the beginnings of a headache. Uncle Mike took a large swallow of his coffee, then apparently discovered it was cold.

Fowler pushed himself to his feet, then turned to me. "Thanks for the coffee. And the information."

I nodded. "Thanks for telling us about the other guests."

"No problem. Y'all have a good day, now." He slouched out the front door.

I took a quick survey of the table. Nobody looked happy. But why should we? We knew more now than we had before, but some of that knowledge was likely to cause us no end of trouble.

Not that we weren't in trouble already.

Chapter Twelve

After Nate and Susa took off for their respective businesses—he to report to Bobby and his mom and she to try to catch up on work for her other clients—I decided to go into town myself. The news about the other guests who hadn't gotten sick would brighten up Marcus and Bianca's day, and Annabelle's, too, if I could find her.

And, of course, I had an ulterior motive. I love Bianca, but she's also one of the biggest gossips in Shavano. If I told her, and maybe Harry Potter over at Dirty Pete's, the news would be all around Shavano by tomorrow. Fowler had given us permission to spread the word—or anyway he hadn't told us not to—and I intended to take advantage of it before he changed his mind.

I decided to visit Marcus's shop before Bianca's just because I found a parking spot closer to his end of town. I didn't see him when I walked inside, but his wife, Sara, was behind the counter, dressed in jeans and a Jordan's Meat Market T-shirt. "Hi, Sara. Is Marcus around?"

Sara gave me a look that chilled me to the bone. Her eyes were like black ice. "Why do you want to know?"

"I've got some news for him." I put my hands on my hips, doing my best not to be intimidated. "Good news, actually. Is he here?"

Sara gave me another frigid glance and stepped to the door leading to the butcher part of the shop. "Marcus. Somebody to see you."

I was still trying to figure out why Sara was pissed at me, since she obviously was, when Marcus stepped into the shop, drying his hands on a kitchen towel. He paused when he saw me, frowning a little. "Hi, Roxy, what can we do for you?"

"I've got some news to pass on. You heard about what happened at Tera's, right?"

Marcus nodded, grimacing. "Oh, yeah."

"Us and everybody else in this damn town," Sara muttered. "Thanks so much for dragging us into this."

At least now the source of her irritation was clear. Marcus gave her an annoyed glance then turned to me. "What's up?"

"I talked to the chief this morning. Over half the guests left right after dinner was over. The cops have been checking up on them. They're all okay. None of them got sick."

Marcus blinked. "So what does that mean?"

I remembered Fowler's crack about spelling things out for the slower people in town. "It means whatever made those people sick, it probably wasn't our food. The people who got sick had after-dinner drinks, so it may have been that." I didn't mention the port, but I could still point people in that direction.

Marcus gave me a tentative grin. "So we're off the hook?"

"Not entirely. Not until all the results from the lab analysis come in. But it's looking much better than it did."

Marcus leaned forward, resting his hands on the counter. "Thank God. I've been worried about all kinds of stuff, mostly listeria. I mean I buy my meat from locals, from people I know. But stuff can always creep in. Even with people who know what they're doing. Thanks for telling us, Roxy."

"That's okay. I figured you'd want to know. If I hear anything else, I'll pass it along." I glanced at Sara. She wasn't smiling, but at least she wasn't looking daggers at me anymore.

"When will they get the lab results?" she asked.

"I don't know exactly." It wouldn't take long to test the food or the leftovers on the dishes and in the glasses. But I had no idea how long it took to test the contents of a murder victim's stomach.

"Tell us when you do," Sara snapped. "We need to get this news before other people find out."

Marcus gave her another annoyed glance. "We'd appreciate hearing whatever you find out, Rox. Thanks for telling us this much."

"Sure. No problem." Sara struck me as a problem for Marcus, though.

I strolled up Main toward Bianca's shop. The sky was bright blue, another bluebird day, but there was a little bite to the air. We'd had our first frost not long ago and most of the flower beds had withered. The town had taken down the baskets of petunias hanging from the streetlights in summer, substituting some potted mums in the planters.

Bianca's bakeshop did a flourishing business year round, which meant I'd go on selling jam year round. Locals and tourists alike swung in to grab a couple of loaves of bread or a cinnamon roll. I stepped inside, inhaling the most wonderful smell known to humankind: baking bread. One of Bianca's constantly changing cast of assistants, a bored-looking teenager, was standing behind the counter frowning down at his phone.

"Hi. Is Bianca in the bakery?"

He gave me a token smile and a nod, then returned to checking his phone. I stepped through the swinging doors to Bianca's working area.

She glanced up as I came in. Then she came around the corner of her work table, wiping her hands on her white canvas apron. "Hey, Roxy, just the kind of person I wanted to see. Try this." She handed me a small slice of bread from one of her baguettes. "Tell me what you think."

I took a bite, and then stood staring down at the counter, trying to analyze the tastes. Garlic certainly. And some kind of herb, maybe rosemary, but very faint.

Bianca gave me a dry smile. "That bad, eh?"

I shook my head. "It's terrific. Like all your bread. I was just trying to analyze what I was tasting. Garlic and rosemary?"

"Thyme. I need to add more. Or maybe try a different type." Bianca leaned against the side of her table, folding her arms. "It's not coming through the way it should."

Bianca's failures would count as spectacular successes for anybody else. "I repeat, it's terrific. At least from my nonbaker point of view."

Bianca grinned, brushing flour from the work table. "Glad to hear it, since most of my customers are nonbakers. What else can I do for you? I've got a couple of overdone croissants from this morning if you're interested."

My mouth immediately began to water. "Tempting. Extremely tempting. Actually, though, I've got some news for you, although I'll take the croissants home for tomorrow's breakfast."

Bianca picked up a paper bag and tossed in a couple of croissants from one of the bins at the side. "What's up?"

"It's about the dinner at Tera's," I began.

Bianca grimaced. "That woman has caused more trouble in this town than any five residents I could name. And she only lived here a few months. She's even causing trouble post-mortem, which is quite a feat."

"We talked to Fowler this morning."

"Who's 'we'?"

"Me and Nate and Susa. Uncle Mike was there, too."

"Sounds like quite a party. Okay, what did the great stone face have to say?" She leaned against the work table.

I hid my grin. "A dozen guests came to Tera's dinner party, but six of them left after dinner was over. Fowler's people have checked with them, and none of them got sick. They're shaken up about Tera dying, but none of them had any of the symptoms Tera and the men at her place had."

Bianca narrowed her eyes. "Interesting. Very interesting. So what did the guys at the house eat the others didn't?"

Clearly I didn't need to spell things out for Bianca. "They had after-dinner drinks. But Fowler can't confirm the drinks were to blame until they get the results from the lab. Still, it doesn't look like our food was the source of the problem. I'd say tentatively we're all off the hook."

"Good for us." Bianca unfolded her arms. "I guess I'd better call Marcus to let him know. He's been pretty worried. And Sara's convinced they've lost business. But their business wasn't big to begin with since they're just starting out."

"Marcus already knows. I stopped by his shop on the way here."

"Good. That'll be one less thing he has to worry about, although I'm sure Sara will find a dozen more before the end of the day."

"Sara didn't seem too happy," I said cautiously. "I'm not sure she believed me."

"Don't take it personally. Sara never believes anyone. And she's always unhappy. I doubt you added anything she wasn't already feeling."

"If I hear anything more, I'll let you know. Fowler's not going to share the results of the analysis, though. We're lucky he told us the bit about the other guests."

Bianca shrugged. "He's more likely to share the results with you than with anybody else. He's sweet on you, as we used to say in my youth."

I raised my eyebrows almost to my hairline. "Nonsense. Fowler's not the type to be sweet on anybody, especially me. We're just sort of friends because of what we went through when Brett Holmes was killed."

Bianca grinned. "Have it your way, toots. I'm just glad you got the information, however you did it. You want these croissants?"

"Yes, ma'am. How much do I owe you?"

Bianca shook her head. "On the house. Thanks for the information."

I carried the croissants out to Main, walking toward the Made In Colorado store. I needed to talk to Annabelle, too, and the shop was the best place to find her since she didn't have her own store.

Fortunately for me, Annabelle was at Made In Colorado. She heard me out, then shrugged. "I wasn't worried. Pickles don't give people food poisoning unless you don't know what you're doing. I do know. Whatever caused it, I wasn't to blame."

As I drove home, I reviewed the situation and where we stood. It looked pretty good for Nate and me to be cleared of any suspicion as far as food poisoning was concerned. But there might be reporters interested in the details, since Tera was supposed to be a big deal in the Colorado financial industry. Wouldn't they want to know what had happened to her?

As I pulled into the farm, I found myself wondering why there hadn't been reporters around already. They'd certainly been interested in Brett Holmes's death, but that had obviously been murder and Tera's death might have been accidental.

I paused. Food poisoning would have been ruled accidental, although Nate and I might have paid a heavy professional price for having caused it. But since food poisoning had been ruled out, was murder more likely?

If Tera and her guests had been poisoned by the port, could that have been accidental? The only kind of bad alcohol I'd ever heard of had been the illegal kind—moonshine that had been poisoned by lead used in the distilling or Prohibition booze made with wood alcohol. I supposed it was possible for port to have been poisoned accidentally with tainted brandy, but that seemed very unlikely. And what were the odds Tera had the only bottle affected?

Which meant someone had probably put something into the port that had made everyone sick and killed Tera. And they'd done it deliberately.

I sat very still for a moment. My experience with actual murder had been limited to Brett Holmes. That didn't constitute enough experience to come to any conclusions about what had happened at Tera's place.

And I wasn't sure I wanted to. Staying out of the way in a situation like this and just letting the experts handle it made a lot of sense. One murder investigation was enough. I needed to focus my attention on my jam business.

I actually felt relieved I'd come to that conclusion. I'd become involved in the other investigation because some people in town thought I was responsible for Brett Holmes's death. Even when Fowler told me I wasn't a suspect, other people still thought I was. I spent a very uncomfortable month trying to find out who was responsible because my business was beginning to suffer. And then I'd stumbled over the murderer more or less by accident. I hadn't enjoyed the experience, and I didn't feel eager to do anything like it again.

I spent the afternoon experimenting with some new combinations of flavors. I'd had an idea for raspberry vinegar using some red wine vinegar I'd gotten from one of the wineries on the western slope. I wouldn't want to make much, but I'd discovered anything made with raspberries tended to sell like hotcakes, and I wanted something else to sell at the Winter Market. Not that I didn't have faith in my pumpkin butter, but, well, I wasn't as confident as I liked to be.

Fortunately, I had a large supply of frozen raspberries I'd put up from last summer's crop. I'd need some for jam, but I had enough left over to experiment. Also fortunately, fruit vinegar is easier to put up than other kinds of fruit products. It doesn't go bad, and it doesn't grow nasty microbes, both occasional problems for those of us in the home canning business. I'd bought a few cute bottles from one of my suppliers. If I could get the raspberry vinegar right, I'd decant it and then put the bottles in a dark place to age a bit before the Winter Market.

It would be ideal for salads and broiled chicken and poached pears you wanted to have a bit of a kick. The more I thought about it, the more excited I became.

I started happily measuring out frozen raspberries into a colander to let them thaw and drain. I could get a test batch of the vinegar going by late afternoon. It would have to sit and steep for a while before I could try it, but the recipe ideas were bubbling up in my mind as I worked. Maybe I'd even print out some recipe cards to attach to the bottles with ribbon (since I figured the first question a lot of customers would ask would be, "What do you do with raspberry vinegar"). The gift possibilities were great.

I was in the zone, packing drained frozen raspberries into a pint jar I would fill with red wine vinegar, when my phone rang. I really wanted to let it go to voice mail. I was in the middle of a creative spell, after all, and who knew how long it would last? Plus I wanted to get this vinegar steeping so I could see what it tasted like. I might need to add some sugar or some other sweetener if the raspberries were too tart. Although I'd probably add it to the raspberries before I made the vinegar.

The repeated ring of my phone reminded me I needed to pick up, but before I did, it went to voice mail and I heard Susa's voice. "Rox, where are you? I think I'm in trouble." Her voice trembled.

Well, crap. I could ignore a lot of people, but Susa wasn't one of them. I picked up the phone before she disconnected. "Hang on. I'll be there in a half hour or so."

Chapter Thirteen

Susa lived in what I thought of as Old Shavano, the part of town dating to the early twentieth century, with a few houses older than that. Most of the houses in the district have been renovated and are worth a hell of a lot more than the contemporary houses farther toward the edge of town. They're picturesque, and pictures of them have appeared in some high-end shelter magazines.

Susa's house is a renovated cabin. It's not quite as upscale as some of the others in her neighborhood, but it's a nice-looking place. Last summer she'd done some gardening around the house, but it looked like she hadn't done much this fall beyond some pots of mums on the front steps. Maybe she'd been too busy keeping up with Tera's demands to put in any work.

I knocked a couple of times and then walked in. Judging from how shaky Susa had sounded on the phone, I figured she'd want to dispense with ceremony.

Susa glanced up from her living room couch and gave me a wan smile.

She looked awful. So awful I felt guilty about taking a half hour to get there, but I had to finish with the raspberry vinegar before I left or I'd have had to throw it all out. Susa is a live wire usually, one of those people with so much extra energy she almost crackles with it. But right then she looked exhausted, complete with dark shadows under her eyes.

And she looked scared.

I dropped down beside her on the couch. "Hey, what's going on?"

"The chief was here. They got the results on the port. It was poisoned."

I stared at her. It wasn't a surprise. If the food hadn't been at fault—and thank God it wasn't—it pretty much had to be the port. And chances of the port going bad accidentally were nonexistent.

"Did he say what was used?"

She nodded. "I'd never heard of it before. Ipasomething."

I ran through my mental list of nasty substances. "Ipecac?"

She nodded again. "I guess so. That sounds right. What is it?"

"It's medicine people used to give kids to make them throw up when they'd swallowed something bad. But I don't think anybody uses it anymore. I mean, it's not a substance people have around the house these days." It also didn't seem like anything you'd choose to murder someone. "Was Tera allergic to it? I mean I don't think of it as a deadly poison."

Susa shook her head. "I don't know. He didn't say. All he said was the port had been tampered with, and somebody had added enough ipawhatever to make everybody sick. Everybody except me, that is." She raised her gaze to mine, biting her lip.

"So what? You explained about not liking port and why you didn't. Uncle Mike backed you up. Hell, I don't like dessert wines either, thanks to our adventures. Was Fowler giving you grief over that?"

"He asked me to explain it to him again. Then he asked me a bunch of questions. Like why hadn't I told Tera I didn't want any? Why didn't I just taste it, like take a sip to be friendly? Why did I stick around at all?" Her eyes were miserable. "I started sounding crazy even to me. I mean, I should have gone home. There was no good reason for me to stay. We weren't even friends. Just business acquaintances."

I reached over to take one of her hands. Her skin felt ice cold. "Okay, maybe it wasn't the smartest move you've ever made. It still would make sense to anybody who's ever been in that situation. You were trying to keep your relationship friendly so you could get paid. I understand it. Why wouldn't Fowler?"

"I don't know, but I don't think he did. I think I'm his number one suspect."

I drew myself up, ignoring the shiver slithering down my spine. "That doesn't make any sense. She owed you money. Now you may have a tough time collecting it from whoever her executor is. You're the last person who'd want to kill her."

"That's what I thought." Susa slumped on the couch. "I'm not sure I'll ever get paid now."

"He needs to look at the other people who were there," I said more forcefully. "I'll bet some of them had problems with Tera. And anybody could have put ipecac in the port." I paused as something occurred to me. "I mean, I think they could have. Was the bottle already open before Tera started pouring?"

"That's another thing the chief wanted to know. And I couldn't tell him. I know it was in a decanter, but I'm not sure when she poured it in there. Or even if she was the one who did it. And I wasn't there when Tera poured the glasses—I went to the bathroom. I'm not even sure she did any of the pouring herself. I mean, she might have asked one of the guys to do it."

"Well, you weren't there when the stuff was poured. You didn't give her the port. The only reason he has to suspect you is you didn't drink the stuff. And you already explained that. Plus you've got no motive. He can't consider you suspect number one, Suz. He needs to talk to the men who were there."

"There's another thing. I guess I'm the only one who heard her say the port was from someone special. It might make me sound more innocent if she'd told somebody else, but she didn't. Or at least she didn't tell any of the guys who stayed behind."

"Of course, she didn't. It's not the kind of thing you'd say to a bunch of men unless the 'someone special' was in the room. Did you get the feeling he was?"

"I don't know." Susa closed her eyes. "There's a whole shit ton of stuff I don't know. I wish to God I'd never gone to that dinner party, even though you and Nate did a great job on the food. I wish I'd just stayed home and had pizza."

I squeezed her hand. "I wish we'd stayed home, too, to tell you the truth. But it's all water under the bridge. Sooner or later Fowler will straighten it all out, and we can just return to normal."

Susa gave me a long look, like she was trying hard to believe me. "I don't know if this will ever return to normal, Rox. Remember how you felt when half the people in town believed you'd killed Brett Holmes? That's the way I feel now."

"Nobody thinks you killed Tera." Or they didn't

think so yet. At the moment, most people probably still thought Nate and I were responsible because of our unsafe cooking practices. But once word of the poisoned port got out—and I was pretty sure it would soon enough—they'd probably turn their attention to Suz. Which wouldn't be pleasant for anybody.

"Maybe they don't think it yet, but they will." Susa rubbed her eyes, leaning against the couch. "They may suspect one or two of the guys, too. But I'm the one who worked with her, and I'm the one they know. I'm the one they'll probably focus on."

The fact Susa had already deduced what I'd been thinking was unsettling. Clearly none of my comforting words were having much effect. "How well did you know Tera?"

"Not that well, I guess. I knew some things about her life in Denver, some things she'd said. But not a lot. We weren't buddies or anything."

Actually, I thought it was best they weren't buddies. If they weren't close, it would be harder to paint Susa as someone with a reason to kill her. "Had she been married?"

Susa nodded. "She said her ex-husband worked at some financial firm in Denver. I don't know how long they'd been divorced, but I got the idea she'd had a breakup before she moved here. Either her marriage or a relationship. She made a couple of references to Shavano being her 'fresh start.' I thought that referred to a guy."

"Not to her business?"

"I suppose it could have. But according to her, she was very successful at her consulting business. And other people in town said so, too. So I don't know why she'd need a fresh start. It was more like she just took her business from one location to another. Why do you want to know about her husband?"

"Well, if someone killed her, and it looks like someone did, it seems like it would either be for personal or professional reasons. And poisoning somebody strikes me as personal. I'd think a professional rival would just go after her customers or her reputation. Killing her seems extreme."

The corners of Susa's mouth edged up. At least I'd made her smile. "I think 'extreme' sums it up."

"The problem is, I don't know anything about Tera Bloomfield, except she was supposed to be rich and very good at her job. Maybe if I knew more about her, this whole thing would make more sense."

"Are you thinking about another investigation? Like we did when Brett Holmes was killed?" Susa's eyes widened.

"Maybe. Would that help you settle your mind?"

"Maybe." She smiled again, and I began to feel a little less worried about her. "I still have the file sharing site I set up for us when we were checking up on Brett."

"Who do you think we should talk to?"

Susa stared off into space, thinking. "I could talk to Alice. She used to be a mover and shaker in Denver business circles before she retired. She might know something about Tera's business."

I knew Alice Hoover slightly. She was a formidable old lady, and I could believe she'd been a big deal in Denver before settling in Shavano. "You mean Tera's business there or the one here?"

"Both, maybe. Alice gave me all kinds of advice before I set up my business. Other people in town have talked to her, too—she's an informal consultant. She still knows a lot about what's going on in the business world."

Susa was looking a little more energetic than before. Having something to do was apparently helping her deal with her worries.

"I could ask around among the people I know in the Denver restaurant world. If Tera was a big restaurant launch consultant, they should have heard of her at least. And they're great on gossip."

Susa nodded. "Okay, this could work. Get enough information so I'm not totally in the dark, so I'll know what I'm dealing with."

"Right. Do you want to come out to the farm? Stay over?" Under normal circumstances I might have volunteered to stay at her place, but I had a feeling we'd be better off outside Shavano, particularly if the news about Tera and the port dropped during the next few hours.

Susa sighed. "No. Thanks, but no. I'll be okay now I've got something to do. I mean, I had stuff to do before, but this is more on target."

"We can both get to work and then check back when we've got something to share. But honestly, Suz, I think this will blow over. There's no way Fowler could suspect you." Then again, if he had no other suspects, he might end up with Susa by default.

"Maybe, but I'm glad we're looking into this anyway. Even if it blows over, I'll feel better if I've got something to think about."

"Right. Think of it as a hobby. Something to do until they find the killer. Which they will any day now."

I hoped that was true, but I doubted it.

I decided to stop by Nate's place on the way home. The information about the port was something he needed to know. It let us off the hook, although it made life tougher for Suz.

Nate lived in an apartment over his mom's garage. It was a nice place—a large, single room with windows looking out on the spruces and cottonwood trees lining the back yard. Nate had had a heart attack a couple of years ago while he was working in Las Vegas, and Madge, his mom, had wanted him close. He was fully recovered now, and in a sense he was returning the favor, keeping an eye on his mom in case she needed his help, although Madge was a self-sufficient type.

I climbed the stairs to his front door and knocked a little tentatively. Normally, we spent a lot of time together. But I hadn't heard anything from him since we'd talked to Fowler, and I wasn't sure what he was doing. Nate and I had been pretty close for the past few months, but we hadn't made any commitments. It was always possible he was trying to cool things off a little.

The way he broke into a smile when he saw me standing on his doorstep made me feel more comfortable about coming over without calling first. "Hey, Rox, come on in. The place is a mess—sorry about that."

"No problem. You've seen my place when I've been in a jam-making frenzy."

The "mess" consisted mainly of a half dozen open books stacked around Nate's easy chair. I recognized Julia Child and Jacques Pepin and what I thought was an ancient copy of Escoffier. "Checking out recipes?"

He shrugged. "Putting together phantom menus for my phantom bistro, assuming the bistro isn't a fading mirage at this point." He gave me a bleak smile. "Business is still a little slower than usual at the café, and Bobby's still convinced it's because everyone thinks we poisoned Tera Bloomfield with our bistro food."

"Okay, I've got news that may help. It's why I came over."

Nate's excuse for a smile curved so it was a little closer to real. "What's up?"

I looked around for a place to sit, but Nate's easy chair and couch were both full of cookbooks at the moment. I decided to stay on my feet. "I just came from Susa's. Fowler was there earlier today—they found ipecac in the bottle of port."

"Ipecac?" Nate stared at me for a moment, then dropped onto his couch, pushing three or four books aside. "Sit. I definitely need more information."

I sat down beside him. "I don't have much more. The lab found ipecac in the decanter and the glasses. And Fowler grilled Susa about it, but she couldn't tell him anything she hadn't told him before. The only thing I don't remember her mentioning is that the port was in a decanter rather than a bottle, and she doesn't know who poured it out. Tera didn't tell anybody else about the bottle being from 'someone special.' "

Nate frowned. "Why would Fowler grill Susa?"

"Because she didn't drink the port. He's still obsessed with that, although Suz had no motive to kill Tera since the woman still owed her money." That was obvious to me and it was probably obvious to Fowler, too, or it would be once he considered it.

"But ipecac? That sounds more like a practical joke gone bad than an attempt to murder someone. I didn't know it was deadly. I just thought it made you throw up."

"I know. It's not like arsenic or strychnine. It's more like putting eye drops into someone's drink like they did in *Wedding Crashers.*" Something about that made me uneasy, but I couldn't quite put my finger on it. "Maybe it was meant as a mean practical joke, to ruin Tera's dinner, and it went too far. I don't know what ipecac is made of, but maybe Tera was allergic to its components."

"Hold on. We can find out." Nate pulled his laptop from the coffee table, typed in a few words, and then scanned the results. "Wikipedia says it's a syrup made from the *Carapichea ipecacuanha* root."

I leaned over to peer at his screen. "And what's that?"

"A plant. Looks like it's from Central America and Costa Rica. They describe it as 'a mild poison' once used an emetic but not anymore. Production was discontinued in 2010." He shook his head. "It's not the kind of thing you'd use if you were trying to kill somebody—even if Tera was allergic to this plant, that's probably not something she'd be aware of. She wouldn't have come across it."

I leaned against the couch. "But what does that mean? If it's not a poison why put it in her drink?"

Nate gave me speculative look. "It means the idea this was all a practical joke gone wrong makes more sense. Maybe somebody got hold of some ipecac and put it in the port to get back at Tera, to make her sick. Maybe it wasn't intended to kill her at all, just to ruin her party. Which means whoever gave it to her has got to be sweating. If he meant the port to be a sick joke, he's probably horrified it killed her."

"So the 'someone special' who gave her the port wanted to make her sick? And it was just a coincidence she served it to other people, and they got sick, too?" That sounded exceptionally nasty to me. In a way, though, it cleared the other people who were there since they'd all had the port and they'd all gotten very sick. You wouldn't drink the port if you knew it was laced with ipecac.

Like Susa. All of a sudden I understood why Fowler suspected her. *Oh, crap.*

"What's wrong, babe?" Nate took my hand, pulling me toward him. "You look like you're feeling sick yourself."

"It's Susa. I think I understand why Fowler suspects her. If she knew there was ipecac in the port, she wouldn't drink it. And the ipecac wasn't supposed to kill Tera, just make her sick. So maybe he thinks Suz was mad at Tera and gave her the port to mess with her. It's not an outrageous idea. Tera and Suz weren't getting along." I leaned against Nate's shoulder. "This is bad. This is very, very bad."

Nate put his arm around me. "I was there when all hell broke loose in the dining room. Susa was horrified. And then she tried to help. She didn't act like someone who knew what was going to happen."

"I don't know if Fowler would accept that as evidence of her innocence. Maybe he'd think she was horrified her practical joke went sideways." I closed my eyes for a moment. "So we'll have to find some evidence Susa didn't give Tera the port, something to get Susa out of Fowler's sights."

"What kind of evidence would that be?"

"We need to find out who the 'someone special' was who gave her the port. That's the person responsible for Tera's death." I grimaced. "But that's a lot easier said than done."

"Maybe Susa has some ideas. She knew more about Tera than either of us."

I shook my head. "I can't pass any of this on to Susa. She's already upset, and I convinced her things would get better. This doesn't qualify as *better*."

Nate pulled me closer. "It's okay. We'll help her. Your uncle will help her. All the people who know her will help her. Everybody loves Susa."

That was true, but I wasn't sure it was enough. All I could do was find out more about Tera Bloomfield. Surely Susa wasn't the only one who didn't like her much. And surely if we got a list of Tera's enemies, one of them would turn out to be the "someone special" with a taste for port and revenge.

Chapter Fourteen

While I decided how to start gathering information about Tera, I made more jam from frozen fruit and waited for my raspberry vinegar to mature. I was pretty sure it would be good, but I wouldn't make any more until I'd had a chance to taste it.

I finally decided to call my friend Lauren Ellinwood to ask about Tera's career as a restaurant backer in Denver. Lauren and I had gone to culinary school together and had been roommates in Denver until I'd gone home. She'd helped me out when I'd been trying to get information about Brett Holmes, and we'd actually hung out a couple of times since then when she'd come to Shavano.

Lauren was a friend. And she also liked my peach jam.

"Hey, Rox," she said when I called, "I was just thinking of coming up to Shavano again sometime this fall. What date's good?"

"We've got a winter market going on the second Saturday and Sunday in November. That's a good time to come up."

"Are you selling jam?"

"Yes, ma'am. Jam and some extras. Time for Christmas shopping."

"I'll be there, then. So what did you need today?"

I wished I could say I'd just called her to dish, but I

needed her help. "I need some information about a financial planner in Denver who backed some restaurants. Her name was Tera Bloomfield."

"*Was*? You're saying she's no longer around?"

"She died last week. It's a long story." One I didn't want to get into at the moment.

"Is the sheriff after you again? Geez, Roxy."

I sighed. "It was the chief of police, and no, I'm not under any suspicion. But my friend Susa is for some reason. I'd like to help her out."

"I remember Susa," Lauren said, her voice warming. "She was a sweetheart to Remi."

Remi was Lauren's nephew, a very nice kid who was so shy I don't think I ever got a complete sentence out of him. "That's Susa. She did some work for Tera. We're both trying to find out more about her."

"I'd like to help, but I don't think I've ever heard of her. Which restaurants did she invest in?"

"I don't know. She told Nate she had some experience in finding investors for restaurants in Denver. I don't think she ever gave him details."

"Nate's involved in this, too? What did this woman do anyway?" Lauren sounded more and more intrigued.

I finally gave up and supplied her with a quick summary of the whole Tera experience. Of course, even a quick summary took a while.

"Holy crap," Lauren said when I'd finished. "You guys dodged a bullet. If people went on thinking it was food poisoning, you'd both have been in deep shit."

"Yeah, we did. It's been a real mess." And I had an uneasy feeling our names would still be associated with Tera and her death. Yet another reason to get the whole thing cleared up.

"Anyway, I wish I could help, but I don't know a whole lot about the investment biz or about getting a restaurant started. I'm strictly back of the house."

She was actually a terrific line cook, but I'd been a line cook, too. And like her, I basically knew squat about how restaurants were financed. "Any ideas about who could fill me in?"

"Toby Sawyer might be able to help. He just opened his own place last year in LoHi. It's very popular. He could probably tell you what he went through to get financing."

Toby had gone to the same culinary school as Lauren and me, although he'd been a bit ahead of us. I'd known him a little. But the LoHi district in Denver is very popular—if he had a restaurant there, he was doing well. "Do you have his number?"

"Sure." Lauren gave it to me. "The name of his place is Bella Fortuna. You can tell him I said it was worth its rep."

"Okay. Thanks."

"And let me know what happens. For a jam maker in a small mountain town, you lead a more exciting life than I do."

"I will. And believe me, at this point I could do with a little less excitement."

I thought about calling Toby right then, but it was already late afternoon. His restaurant would probably be getting prepped to serve dinner, and he wouldn't be interested in having a long chat with me about restaurant finances. I decided I'd try calling him tomorrow morning and hope the place didn't serve breakfast.

Even though I hadn't gotten much information

from Lauren, I pulled up the file sharing app Susa had built for us when we'd been checking out Brett Holmes. Susa had bitched at me about not keeping accurate records, so I entered the little I'd gotten from Lauren to show I was making an effort.

Susa called me fifteen minutes later, as I was giving my raspberry vinegar a gentle shake. "I saw your notes."

"I'll call Toby tomorrow. I didn't want to bother him when he was probably getting set up to serve dinner at his place."

"That's fine. Look, do you want to come talk to Alice with me?"

"Alice Hoover?"

"Yeah. She said she'd give me some information about Tera, but she sounded a little annoyed. To tell you the truth, I'm nervous about talking to her. When she's irritated, she can be scary."

Alice was scary even when she wasn't irritated. But dealing with two people might keep her sarcasm within reasonable bounds. "Sure. When are you supposed to go over there?"

"Tomorrow afternoon. Two o'clock. Will that work for you?"

"That should be fine. I'll come to your place a little before."

"Great. Thanks, Roxy."

It was almost five. Time to start working on dinner, whatever we were having. I hadn't given it much thought yet. I checked the refrigerator and found some chicken breasts. I also had some leftover sour cream from an experimental batch of biscuits. It was looking like chicken paprikash again, a hearty perennial. At least Uncle Mike liked it, or he did usually.

Uncle Mike himself wandered in around five forty-five, followed by Herman. He paused, sniffing the air. "Paprikash?"

"Yep," I said, hoping he wouldn't point out I'd made it last week.

"Where's Nate?"

I stopped tearing up lettuce for a moment. "Nate's not here. Why did you think he was?"

"Because it's Friday. He's usually here for dinner on Friday."

I turned to stare at the calendar. "I lost track of the day. Maybe he did, too." Hard to believe I'd been so occupied with the Tera Bloomfield investigation I'd forgotten what day it was, but that was undoubtedly true.

Uncle Mike's forehead furrowed in concern. "Anything going on with you and Nate?"

"What do you mean 'going on'?"

"I mean are you two having a fight or something?"

"No. I don't think so anyway."

"But you're not sure?"

"I'm sure." This was not a discussion I felt like having. "Let's eat."

As I served up the chicken and noodles, I went over the last few days in my mind. Nate and I usually had Friday dinner together at the farm. He had to leave before ten because he worked breakfast on Saturday. Then I'd go to his place for Saturday dinner and stay over to have brunch and help out at the café. Nate was off on Monday so we usually came to the farm Sunday night to hang out and cook and talk and make love.

To be a couple, in other words.

We'd never spelled things out, but we'd fallen into the routine. We liked being together.

Or I did, anyway.

Now I wondered what I should do tomorrow. Was our standing weekend date not as standing as I'd thought?

I was quieter than usual during dinner as I mulled this over, which obviously worried Uncle Mike. "What's the matter, honey? Has that Robicheaux boy made trouble for you?"

I blinked at him, pulled to the present. "Nate? No. I'm thinking about Susa and the investigation into Tera's death." That was partly true, just not entirely.

"Why are you obsessing over that? Has something new happened?"

I realized I hadn't told him the latest, so I filled him in on the port and the ipecac and what it might mean for Susa.

"Fowler's after Susa now? Because he thinks she put ipecac in the port?"

"Apparently. I'm sure she's just one suspect, though. They still don't know who gave Tera the port, and I'd say he's a better suspect than Susa."

"How can they be sure whoever gave her the port put the ipecac in it? Couldn't it have been added by someone at the party?" Uncle Mike speared his last piece of chicken.

"I guess so. I wasn't out there when the port got served. That's one of the mysteries, how the port got from the bottle to the decanter Tera used to serve it. I suppose it's possible somebody put the ipecac into the port after it was poured into the decanter."

"Damn straight. Doesn't mean Susa did it. Doesn't

mean whoever gave her the port did it." Uncle Mike scowled in my direction.

"No it doesn't, but finding out who gave Tera the port is a logical place to start." I didn't think we were arguing, but we both sounded a little testy.

"That woman was trouble," Uncle Mike said. "I said so from the start. You and Nate should have steered clear of her."

"Right. We should have known she'd be poisoned and we'd be blamed. How could we have been so stupid? And how could Tera have been so careless as to get poisoned in the first place?"

Uncle Mike gave me his best don't-sass-your-elders glare. "Don't you get smart with me, missy."

"Then don't you start second-guessing what we should or shouldn't have done. Nate needed advice, and nobody in town knew what to tell him. Tera offered to give him information and help him find backers. Maybe in hindsight it wasn't a good idea to take her up on her offer, but it seemed good at the time. And the meal we served was excellent. Right up until somebody killed her."

All of a sudden I felt tears prickling my eyes. I bit my lip. This *so* wasn't the time to go all sniffly. "Come on, Uncle Mike, don't give me grief. It's been a tough week, and I'm very tired."

Uncle Mike's expression shifted from annoyed to concerned. "Aw, honey, you know I didn't mean to make things worse. Is there anything I can do to help Susa?"

That just about sent me over the top into genuine tears, but I bit them back. "I don't know. Right now we're just trying to gather information about Tera, trying to find out who her enemies were. Looking for other people who might have had reason to be upset with her."

"Doing what the police are doing, in other words." Uncle Mike gave me a dry smile.

"Doing what I *hope* the police are doing. I just hope they haven't decided Susa is their best suspect and stopped looking at other people."

"I don't think Fowler would do that. He strikes me as a competent cop. From what I hear he's kept control of his part of the investigation even though CBI is running all the forensic stuff. He's the one who knows the people around town. CBI is partnering with him instead of cutting him off, which they might do if they thought he wasn't up to the job."

I blinked at him. "You've got a police source?"

"I talk to people. And I listen to people. Having coffee at Bolger's can come in handy."

Bolger's was an old-fashioned diner on the edge of town where Uncle Mike and his friends went for their morning coffee break. Several cops picked up the occasional doughnut there, too. "Okay, that's something you can do. Keep track of what's going on with the investigation. Clearly your cop sources are better than mine."

Uncle Mike's grin turned smug. "I can do that. Easy."

I cleared the dinner dishes while Uncle Mike got ready to walk to the main house. "You want Herman?"

"He can stay. I can use the company."

Uncle Mike gave me another slightly concerned look, but he knew better than to ask me about Nate again. "Okay. See you tomorrow."

"See you," I repeated as he stepped through the door.

The evening spread before me, very empty. I could always follow Uncle Mike up to the main house and watch a movie. His TV was better than mine. On the other hand, he favored horror and action thrillers, which I wasn't in the mood for.

I decided I'd find something on my own, maybe some British detective series. Definitely *not* a rom com.

I'd just settled onto my couch, remote in hand, when someone knocked on my door.

Nate. I bounced to my feet and hurried over, ignoring the fact Nate usually knocked and then walked right in. I threw open the door and found Ethan Fowler on my front step, looking surprised.

At least he wasn't in uniform, but the jeans and flannel shirt he wore with his scuffed boots still looked official. "Hello?" I said, a little tentatively.

"Evening. Can I come in?" He raised an eyebrow, and I remembered my manners.

"Sure, yes." I stepped aside to let him pass.

Herman approached Fowler as soon as he stepped into the living room, his tail wagging happily. Apparently Fowler's repeated visits had turned him into Herman's definition of a friend. Fowler scratched his ears absently as he glanced around the room. "Boyfriend not here?"

"Nope. What's up?" No way was I going to discuss Nate with the chief.

"A couple more questions."

"Have a seat." I waved in the general direction of the easy chair opposite the couch. "Want a beer?"

One corner of his mouth hitched up. "Sure."

I had some craft beer in the refrigerator, so I brought him a can, along with one for me. I don't drink a lot of beer, but it seemed unsociable to let him drink alone. "Want a glass?"

He shook his head. "Let's rough it."

I sat down on the couch opposite, placing my beer on the coffee table. "What do you need?"

"We're still trying to work out the sequence of events with the port. When the bottle arrived, when it was decanted, who poured, all of that."

"I can't help you much. I was in the kitchen for most of the evening. I didn't see what was going on in the dining room or the other rooms in the house."

"What about when you walked in on your way to the kitchen? Did you see the decanter?"

I paused, trying to remember. "I know I saw the decanter at the end of the evening when everybody was sick—it was on a coffee table in the middle of the couch and chairs where Tera and her guests moved after dinner. It looked like a set—glasses and decanter that all went together. Maybe she had it sitting there as an accent piece." I stared down at the carpet trying to get my sluggish memory to oblige. I'd been trying to forget everything that happened that night. Now I had to dredge up what I remembered.

"Did you walk through the dining room on your way to the kitchen?"

I nodded. "I remember looking at the table setting, just to see how it was arranged."

"And the decanter?"

I closed my eyes, trying to visualize that side of the room—and trying to blot out the way it had looked later in the evening when it had become a horror show.

"I don't think it was there. I'm not a hundred percent certain, but I've got a memory of the table with some kind of flower arrangement. But you should ask Nate. He was out there more than I was."

I paused. Nate had called me out of the kitchen to take a bow. I'd forgotten all about that until now. So I'd walked by the couch and chairs on my way to the table. I stared down at the floor for a moment, organizing my thoughts. "I was out there again halfway through dinner. I came out just before dessert because Nate called me out to introduce me. I'm around ninety percent certain the decanter was on the table then."

Fowler nodded slowly. "Okay, that narrows it down a little. If it was full midway through the meal, it was probably full at the beginning. I can't see her leaving the table to fill the decanter while the dinner was going on."

"No, I can't see her doing that either." But that also meant the decanter was sitting there available for anyone to tamper with it for most of the evening.

I frowned, remembering my own questions. "Did Tera die from ipecac?"

Fowler's face went utterly blank. Clearly, I'd crossed a line.

"I thought that was something that just made people sick. I didn't think it could kill anyone." I kept my gaze riveted on his. No way was I backing down from getting an answer.

"That's something being investigated. Ipecac can kill in some circumstances."

Which was a wonderfully vague way of avoiding my question. "Not going to tell me, huh?"

He gave me another of those crooked smiles.

"Nope."

"So this is a one-way conversation, where I give you information and you keep quiet?"

"I'll pass along what I can. Obviously, there's a lot of information I have to keep confidential."

"Did the other guys go home from the hospital?"

Fowler nodded. "All okay. And nobody else at the party got sick. You can tell Robicheaux he's off the hook."

"You could tell him yourself. He saw a lot more than I did, and he might be able to confirm when the decanter was on the table."

"I'll do that." Fowler pushed himself to his feet. "Thanks for the beer."

"Sure." I started to say *any time* but thought better of it. "See you around."

He nodded, smiling his half-smile as he stepped through my door and into the night.

Chapter Fifteen

Nate called me just as I was getting ready for bed. "Hey, babe. Are you coming over tomorrow night?"

I thought about saying something like *Are you sure you want me to?* But I'm lousy at playing games. "Sure. Should I bring anything?"

"Just yourself. I missed you tonight."

"Was I supposed to be there?" I couldn't remember making any plans, but maybe I'd messed up.

"No, I was supposed to be at your place. Or anyway I thought I was supposed to be at your place. But I had another fight with Bobby, and I'm not fit company. I'm sorry—I should have called you earlier. But I was steaming. And I didn't want to take it out on you or Mike. Or Herman."

I considered asking him what the fight was about, but I already knew. Bobby was probably still bugged about the dinner at Tera's and the bistro plans and basically anything representing a change at the café. "Fowler was here earlier," I said by way of full disclosure.

There was a slight pause. "What did he want?"

"They're still trying to get the whole sequence of things with the port—when Tera got it, when it was poured into the decanter, and who poured it. I told him the little I remembered, but I wasn't out there much."

"Neither of us was. Susa's a better source than we

are—so are the other guests."

"Right, and I'm guessing they're questioning the other guests about what they saw when. But he's also going to ask you about it, what you remember about the decanter being on the table, and whether it was empty or full."

"I'll see what I can remember. Hell, I don't think I ever looked over toward the couch and chairs when I came out to talk to people."

"I know. It's hard to tell what's a real memory and what's something you only think you remember."

I caught myself yawning a bit on the last couple of words. I was tired, maybe more tired than usual.

"Okay, go to sleep," Nate said. "Come over tomorrow night. I'll make something special, assuming I can think of something."

"Don't knock yourself out. We can always order pizza."

"We can at that. Good night, babe."

I lay awake for a few more minutes, trying to get myself to relax. I had a lot on my mind, but most of it was stuff I didn't want to think about. After a few minutes of tossing and turning, I felt the bed sway under Herman's weight as he jumped up to drape himself across my feet. He does that when he thinks I need company.

"Okay, Herm. I'll drift off now." And I did.

The next day I called my chef friend, Toby Sawyer, at what seemed like a reasonable time—not so early I'd wake him if he'd had a late night at the restaurant or so late I'd cut into his lunch prep, assuming he was doing any. I was a little nervous about talking to him since I wasn't sure he remembered me.

But he did. "Hey, Roxy, I heard you'd moved into the hills and opened up a business."

"Yep, Luscious Delights. I make jam. And you opened a restaurant."

"That I did. Damn good one, too. What can I do for you?"

He sounded so chipper I almost hated to bring the conversation down to nasty details. "I'm trying to find some information about a woman who worked for an investment firm in Denver. She was supposed to have done some investing in restaurants, or she helped other people invest in restaurants. Her name was Tera Bloomfield. I thought maybe you'd heard of her."

"Doesn't ring a bell immediately." He paused. "You said her name *was* Tera Bloomfield. Is she dead?"

"Yeah. She died last week. It's possible she was poisoned."

Toby let out a slow whistle. "Wow. Not by jam, I hope?"

"No. My jam wasn't involved. But I was there, helping a friend cook dinner."

"Jesus, worse and worse. Food poisoning?" Toby sounded intrigued, and I remembered he'd always been into gossip at school. No wonder Lauren had recommended him.

"Not food poisoning," I said firmly. "It wasn't us. But we were there, and a lot of rumors are flying around. I'm trying to help a friend who's getting some bad press."

"Okay, let me think. Tera Bloomfield. Tera Bloomfield. Did she work for Fields and Dewhurst?"

"I don't know." I should have found out where Tera worked before I'd called Toby. "All I know about her is she worked in finance and claimed she'd helped connect restaurants with investors." I jotted down the name Toby had mentioned just in case it came up again.

"If she's the woman I'm thinking of, she worked for one of the bigger investment firms in town. And she did put together some groups of investors for a few restaurants, but she wasn't good at it. A couple of the places she backed went bust, and on one of them some investors pulled out before they could open, which screwed over the owners. I don't think she was someone who came highly recommended."

"So she wasn't a whiz kid when it came to getting restaurants up and running?"

"Not the ones I heard about. I guess it's possible she worked with others who were successful."

"Okay, that's a start. Thanks, Toby."

"No problem. So where are you located?"

"Shavano. Near the Collegiate Peaks."

"Right, high country. You got a website?"

I bit my lip. That was something I should work with Susa on. My website needed a better store before my episode of *Sweet Thing* was broadcast. "I've got one. It's a little rough and ready at the moment, but we're working on it."

"What's the URL? I'm always looking for Colorado brands to use at Bella Fortuna."

I gave it to him, promising myself I'd talk to Susa about the site today. I'd love to sell jam to Toby's restaurant, but I wasn't sure the current site would appeal to potential buyers.

Of course, I'd be seeing Susa later that day when we went to talk to Alice Hoover. I wondered if she knew where Tera had worked in Denver. Even if she worked at the firm Toby had mentioned, that didn't mean she was the one who'd screwed up on her restaurant investments, but it narrowed the odds quite a bit.

I drove to Susa's office around one. I figured we'd go to Alice's place together since I didn't want to walk in on Alice by myself. Carly was sitting in the outer office again, frowning at something on her computer screen. She grinned when she saw me. "Hi, Roxy. Did you bring anything for tasting?"

"Not this time. Is Susa in her office?"

Carly's smile faded to be replaced by a worried look. "She's there, but she's stressed right now. This thing with Tera has upset her."

"I can see that. It's upset me, too. Once the cops find out who did it, we can all breathe easier." Assuming they found the right person and didn't settle for the closest one.

I'd entered the information I'd gotten from Toby on our file sharing site, but I didn't know if Susa had seen it yet. I knocked on her office door, wearing the brightest smile I could manage. "Hey, Suz. Ready for Alice?"

Susa turned from her computer to glance at me and then at the clock over her desk. "Oh, yeah. I lost track of time. I'd better pull myself together."

"You've got some time. Don't rush." She still didn't look good. Her eyes were tired and showing those dark smudges underneath. She probably wasn't sleeping, not that I blamed her. "Sometime I need to talk to you about upgrading my website. I want to be ready in case I get more orders after the *Sweet Thing* episode is finally aired."

"Oh Lord, yes." Susa closed her eyes. "We talked about that, didn't we? I let it get away from me."

"It's all right. We can still get it done."

"This weekend." Susa nodded emphatically. "I'll come over tomorrow, and we'll work on it then."

"I'll be at Nate's until early afternoon. I usually help out with brunch at the café."

"Oh, well, maybe some other time." She seemed to deflate, all her determination disappearing as quickly as it had come.

I wanted to tell her to come tomorrow afternoon and stay for dinner, but I had a feeling she'd say no. I'd never seen her looking so defeated.

"Okay, let's go talk to Alice. Maybe she'll have some information to help."

"Maybe," Susa echoed. "It's possible." But she didn't look as if she believed it.

Alice lived in the same older part of town where Susa had her house, but Alice's place looked like a Craftsman cottage from the teens. It also looked like it had been renovated by people who knew what they were doing and did it well. The stained glass inserts around her front door gleamed in the autumn sunlight. "Nice place," I said as we climbed the wide front steps.

"It was her mother's. Alice had it fixed up before she moved in."

"Alice is from Shavano?" I'd always assumed she was from Denver.

"Shavano born and bred. She moved here when she retired." Susa rang the doorbell.

The door opened almost immediately, and Alice peered out at us. She turned to Susa. "Brought reinforcements, I see."

Susa gave her a tired smile. "You know Roxy. She was there that night at Tera's place."

"Well, I guess it's better to have multiple witnesses. Come in, both of you." Alice stalked away from us.

I wasn't sure how old Alice was, but I'd guess somewhere in her late seventies or early eighties. Unlike a lot of retired businesswomen, she didn't try to conceal her age. She kept her iron gray hair short, and it stood away from her face in spikes that might have been natural curls. She wore jeans and a button-down shirt that looked like oxford cloth, along with gold studs in her ears and no makeup. Her green eyes were as sharp as broken glass. She was a tough old broad, and she made no attempt to hide it.

She led us to her kitchen at the rear of the house, a large room with a planked pine floor and a round oak table at the center with matching chairs. The appliances were strictly modern, though, and very high end.

Alice waved at the table. "Sit down. I'll put on the water for tea. You want oolong or Darjeeling?"

The only kind of tea I drink is Twining's English breakfast, so I had no idea what to say.

"Oolong, please." Susa said.

Alice peered at me, and I worked up a thin smile. "That's fine with me, too."

She turned to fill her electric hot water kettle, then measured tea into the ceramic teapot. "Now, what's this all about? How did you get involved with a snake like Tera Bloomfield?"

Susa gave me a slightly startled look, then turned to Alice. "I did some work for her, putting together a website for her company. She invited me to that dinner party she gave last weekend, and Roxy and Nate Robicheaux did the cooking."

"Nate Robicheaux? That's Robert Robicheaux's boy?"

"Yes, ma'am," I said. "His younger son."

"Good cooks, all of them. Probably better than Bloomfield deserved. So tell me what happened."

Susa gave her a straightforward rundown of the evening's activities up to the moment when Tera and her gentleman friends had come to grief. She even included her pouring the port into a potted ficus.

Alice gave her a grim smile. "Normally, I'd say that was a waste of good port, but in this case I assume it turned out to be a good idea."

"Roxy knows more about that than I do."

"According to Chief Fowler, somebody put ipecac in the port. It's not clear when it happened, but there was enough to make everybody sick. Someone dosed the port deliberately."

"That fool woman died from ipecac?" Alice shook her head. "My mom treated my brothers with ipecac when she thought they'd swallowed something foul. It wasn't pleasant, but it wasn't fatal."

"I wondered if she was allergic to it. It's the only reason I can see she'd have died from it when no one else did."

Alice grimaced. "It's as good a theory as any, I suppose. All the men recovered?"

I nodded. "A couple of them had to stay overnight in the hospital, but they're all home and okay now."

"Which leads to the question, who would want to kill Tera Bloomfield?" Alice glanced between us. "Assuming that's what they wanted to do. Somebody might just have wanted to make her sick as a nasty joke, I suppose. Any candidates?"

"Not so far," I said. "The chief seems to think Susa is suspicious because she didn't drink the port. But that theory's not going to hold up when they look at it more closely."

Susa rapped her knuckles on the oak table. "Knock wood."

"But that's why you want to find out about Tera Bloomfield, I assume. To find out who else might have wanted to hurt her." Alice rose to her feet and brought the teapot to the table.

I nodded. "We want to know if there was anyone who might have had a grudge against her. Maybe somebody from her time in Denver."

Alice placed mugs in front of us. "And the answer is more difficult than you'd think. Countless people had grudges against her, some of them possibly murderous. The real question would be who among those countless people would follow her to Shavano and murder her with a child's medicine, possibly by accident?"

Susa and I both stared at her blankly. You had to hand it to Alice—she knew how to sell a punch line.

"Okay," Susa said finally. "Why did countless people have grudges against Tera? What exactly did she do?"

"To put it simply, she cheated those countless people out of a great deal of money. Either that or she was one of the most incompetent investment specialists I've ever encountered." Alice checked the teapot, then poured us both mugs of oolong. "Sugar? Milk?"

"Sugar please." I was almost afraid to take my gaze away from Alice's face. I didn't want to miss anything.

She placed the sugar bowl on the table in front of me, and I poured a teaspoonful into my tea. "I suppose you want details," she said.

"Yes, ma'am." Susa looked a little less tired than she had earlier.

"Tera Bloomfield worked for one of the better investment firms in Denver. How she got a job there, I've no idea, but she got one."

"Was it Fields and Dewhurst?" I asked.

Alice raised her eyebrows at me. "Yes, it was. Why do you ask?"

"It just confirms some other information I found out about her."

"Fields and Dewhurst is a well-respected firm in Denver," Alice said. "Or they used to be. I don't know if they've recovered yet from having Tera Bloomfield on staff. Her husband worked there, too, which is probably how she got hired in the first place."

"Is that her ex-husband?" Susa asked. "She said she'd been divorced."

Alice nodded. "She married Max Bloomfield when she first came to Denver. He was considerably older than she was—looking for a trophy wife, I suppose. After they divorced, he retired and moved out of town. I'm not sure where."

"Was this before or after she was involved in this financial problem?"

Alice went to the counter to pick up her own mug. "Before. The gossip at the time was she'd found someone else and Max had taken off in a huff, but I don't know any more about that. At any rate, he was long gone when she started pushing the Quicksilver Ranch."

Susa and I both looked blank. "What was that?"

"The Quicksilver Ranch was a large meadow acreage on the Western Slope, one of the largest undivided plots of land in the area. The family owning it had decided to sell. Tera Bloomfield offered her investors a chance to provide the cash for the sale at a decent rate of interest. The initial investment would not only pay off big when the purchaser developed it, the lenders would have the inside track on becoming part owners of the Quicksilver recreational development which would be subsequently built on the property." Alice leaned back to sip her tea.

"Was it a real property?" I asked.

"Oh, yes," Alice said. "The property existed. Several investors visited. The sale was being kept very quiet because the location was prime, and the developer who'd found it didn't want anybody else to snap it up. Tera assured the investors they'd realize a major return on their money as well as being positioned to make even more in the future. The purchase was being carried out by a front organization called Quicksilver Properties, so the ranch owners wouldn't realize the land was being sold to a major developer and jack up the price. The real purchaser's identity was kept secret."

"Scummy," Susa muttered.

Alice shrugged. "Not unusual. At any rate, Tera formed a group of investors, all of whom put in a sizeable amount of money to purchase the land. Which they did."

"And it wasn't worth as much as Tera said it was?" I was having trouble following all of this.

"It definitely would have been worth what the phantom buyer said it was worth except for one

166

problem: access."

Susa leaned back in her chair. "Meaning?"

"Meaning access to the property required cutting a road through a national forest. Tera claimed the buyer had inside information that the road approval would be automatic. The buyers could call in some favors, and the road would magically appear. It didn't. The Forest Service turned down the application." Alice sipped her tea with a Cheshire Cat smile.

I frowned. "How had the previous owners accessed the property?"

"Over a mountain road requiring all-wheel drive and a very strong stomach. They used the land mostly for pasture, so they didn't need roads much." Alice's smile widened. "The lenders had accessed the property using that road, but they'd been led to believe the development would have better access."

"Had they already bought the property?"

Alice nodded. "They'd bought the property with the borrowed money. When the Forest Service refused the road application, the whole thing became public. Nobody else wanted property that couldn't be developed easily, at least not at the price Bloomfield's investors had paid. Quicksilver Properties finally sold it at a considerable loss, then promptly went out of business. The lenders lost most of their investment."

"So Tera was a lousy business advisor," Susa said. "Was there more to it than that?"

Alice took her time pouring more tea. "This is where it gets interesting. After the debacle was over, rumors began to circulate that Quicksilver Properties hadn't had the same losses as the hard money lenders. That, in fact, the price for the property had been much lower than the lenders had been told and people behind Quicksilver, including Tera, had made a tidy profit. Nothing was ever proven, and the identity of the developer and his associates was never made public. There was enough outcry Fields and Dewhurst began an investigation. But they closed it down when Tera resigned and left Denver."

"And that's when she came up here?" Susa frowned as she sipped her tea.

"Around then. She may have made a few stops along the way, but moving to Shavano was her Next Big Thing."

I took some sugar for my second cup. "Did she have good severance from Fields and Dewhurst to help her buy her place up in the canyon?"

Alice snorted. "From what I understand, she was lucky to get away with the clothes on her back. She had whatever she'd made off her deal with Quicksilver and whatever kind of marriage settlement she got from Max, and that was about it."

"So you think she was operating on credit?" If Tera was operating on credit, a lot of people around town would be out a lot of money, including Susa and Nate.

"Possibly, although I don't know any institution fool enough to bankroll her in Shavano. Anyway, she came up here and set herself up as a financial guru. Some people even believed her. My guess is they wouldn't have believed her for long, not if they had any sense."

Susa sighed, pushing her mug away from her. "If she was operating on credit, I may never get paid what she owed me."

"Same here." And Nate hadn't even gotten any

investors out of the deal. I doubted any of the guests would want to put money into a restaurant that reminded them of one of the worst nights of their lives.

Alice shrugged. "That's the way it goes, kids. However, you should be able to give the chief a few more possibilities for people who'd like to see Tera Bloomfield dead. Or at least very uncomfortable."

"Did anybody ever find out who was behind Quicksilver Properties?"

"Not really. But I think it's safe to say Tera Bloomfield must have had a lover involved in it somehow. Otherwise, I'm not sure how she would have gotten so deeply involved herself."

"But you don't know who he was?"

"No idea. But you might find out who paid for her house in the canyon and her office downtown. That kind of real estate doesn't come cheap." Alice had her Cheshire Cat smile again. "When in doubt, follow the money. A rule to live by."

Chapter Sixteen

I wasn't sure what to tell Nate about Alice Hoover's story. Most of it wouldn't make any difference to him, except the part about Tera possibly not having much money when she'd come here and operating mostly on credit. Still, he'd made an investment in Tera and her activities, even if it was a small one. He needed to know what she'd been up to.

When I got to his place, he was in the kitchen, working on something that smelled heavenly. "I thought we were having pizza."

"I decided to do chicken noodle soup instead. Is that okay?"

"It's terrific. It smells like something that's been simmering all day."

Nate gave me a dry smile. "Amazing what you can do when you have access to fresh chicken broth and leftover roast chicken. And decent noodles."

"But you assembled them," I said loyally. "That makes a difference."

Nate's smile became a chuckle, and he turned to the stove. "I need to have you around more often. How was your visit with Alice Hoover?"

"Informative." I sat down at the dining table and gave him a brief summary of Alice's story while he worked on dinner.

He half-turned to listen to me. "So we've got one

or two powerful men making a lot of money off a deal everybody else got creamed on? And we don't know who they are, other than Tera had something going with one of them?"

"Yeah, I don't know if it helps much. But maybe you dodged a bullet by not having her invest in your bistro. Apparently people who invested with her ended up broke."

"This is getting weirder and weirder."

"There's something a little weirder still. According to Alice, Tera came up here on a shoestring. She didn't get any buyout from the firm where she worked, just *don't let the door hit your ass on your way out*."

"Not surprising if she really did screw over their customers. So what did she use to buy her house? And set up her office? Have you seen that place?"

I'd seen the outside of Tera's office in downtown Shavano. It was in one of the original buildings that had been renovated. All antique brick outside and stark white walls inside, with leather chairs and stained hardwood floors in the reception area. "It looked expensive."

"I'm sure it *was* expensive." Nate set a breadbasket on the table, along with a bottle of wine. "If you open that, I'll get the soup in the bowls."

I grabbed the waiter's corkscrew and got to work. "Alice said she was living on credit. Although Alice also said she couldn't think of any sane bank who'd loan her any money."

Nate set a bowl of chicken noodle soup in front of me. It smelled like Jewish grandmother heaven. "I'm with Alice. If what she says is true about what Tera did in Denver, even a rudimentary credit check would show she was a lousy risk for establishing a financial business. I don't know about her restaurant investments."

"I do. Sort of." I told him what Toby had said as Nate sat down beside me, noodle soup in hand.

He whistled softly. "Maybe you're right about dodging a bullet. Having her invest in the bistro could have been a disaster. Even having her put together a group of investors could have been bad news."

"Anyway, a lot of other people besides Susa could have it in for Tera. All the people in Denver who invested with her have terrific motives."

"True. Are you going to tell Fowler?"

"I don't know. He didn't react well the last time I got involved in one of his investigations. He might not be too happy with me if he found out I'd been asking questions."

"And that's a concern, him not being happy with you?" Nate's smile dimmed.

Oh for Pete's sake. "Not the way you're thinking it would be. I don't care how he feels about me personally. But if I want him to take this information about Tera seriously, and I do, I don't want to annoy him. Susa's still upset about being suspected, and I want to make sure Fowler considers other people as much as he considers her."

Nate sighed. "Okay, right. I understand why you're concerned. And Fowler needs to know what Alice knows. It might be good for him to talk to her directly."

"Agreed. Assuming Alice is willing to talk to him. She can be grumpy if she thinks people aren't worth her time."

I took a bite of the soup and then two more in

quick succession. The chicken broth was rich and savory, the noodles had a bit of bite, and the chunks of carrot and celery and roast chicken were lush and flavorful. "This is absolutely terrific."

Nate gave me a wan smile. "Like I said, access to good ingredients helps."

"So does knowing how to put those ingredients together. Come on, Nate, take the compliment. You deserve it."

"Sorry. Thank you. I'm just feeling played out right now. But I shouldn't take it out on you."

"Bobby?" I guessed.

He nodded. "He's been on a tear ever since that dinner. For a couple of days, he thought the number of customers was down, but I'm not sure he was right. And even if he was, there could be all kinds of reasons for that. But he was certain it was because of Tera, and because I'd cooked the dinner and people thought my food had killed her. Now, that's clearly not true and we're serving as many customers as we usually do, but he can't let go. For the last couple of days we've had big fights at the end of service. Shouting, throwing things, the whole bit. Mom had to step in today, or I swear I would have punched him." Nate rubbed a hand over his face. "It's bad. And it's getting worse."

I didn't know what to tell him. Bobby was being unreasonable, but Bobby was usually unreasonable. This sounded worse than usual, though.

"The thing is, I understand how he feels. He and Dad ran the restaurant together. And then he ran it mostly on his own after Dad died. I mean, Mom was there, but it took her a few months to pull herself together. And Coco and I were both off cooking in

173

different places."

"But you would have come if he'd asked. Wouldn't you?"

"If we'd thought he was having trouble, we'd have been here in a shot. As it is, we both came because of Mom. She wasn't happy with the desserts Bobby was serving, the commercial stuff, so she talked Coco into taking that over. Then I got sick and she hauled me up here, too. Bobby probably feels like we're horning in on his café that was doing just fine without us."

"But still. It's your family's place, not just Bobby's."

"That's true, and we all know it. But in his heart, I think Bobby still feels like it's his place and the rest of us are just interlopers. Particularly me." He took a couple more bites, then put down his spoon. "I don't know how much longer I can take it."

"What can you do?"

He took a sip of his wine. "The bistro was supposed to be one way out. I could concentrate there and leave the café to Bobby. But now I'm pretty sure that's over. At least for the time being."

"You could still find backers. Or even just talk to the bank about a loan."

Nate shook his head. "Nobody's going to want to invest in me right now. Not so soon after the thing with Tera. I know the news has spread our food wasn't at fault, but people are still going to remember I had something to do with what happened. Even after they forget our food didn't poison anyone, they'll still remember I was involved. It'll take a while for that association to die down. If it ever does."

"You can't give up. The bistro's a great idea. And

you're a great chef." Even as I was cheerleading, though, I had a feeling he was right.

"Thanks, babe. You've been golden all the way through this mess. You're one of the reasons I'm trying to work this out."

"One of the reasons…" I stared at him.

"The easiest way to get out from under all of this would be for me to leave Shavano, go to Vegas or just to Denver or Aspen. But I don't want to do that. You're a reason to stay. So is Shavano—I love this place. Two good reasons. I keep reminding myself of those two good reasons, every time I think about leaving." He reached across to cup my cheek in his hand, then leaned forward to kiss me gently.

My heart was pounding. Did I want him to say he loved me? I wasn't sure. I sort of did, but at the same time I sort of didn't. I'd never been in love before, and I was nervous about taking that final step.

I put my hand on his, hoping I didn't look as terrified as I felt. "I don't want you to go. You know that."

Nate gave me a very small smile. "I don't want me to go either. I'm going to do my best to work this out."

"Anything I can do to help, I will."

Nate leaned over and kissed me again. And very soon, we moved on to other, far more enjoyable things.

The next morning, I went to the café with Nate to help out with brunch. It was a routine we'd fallen into after we'd started spending the weekends together. Needless to say, the café didn't actually need my help, since the Robicheaux family had been functioning just fine without me. But they were still happy to have my unpaid labor making mimosas and Bloody Marys.

Or anyway, some of them were happy. Bobby was indifferent.

I'm no bartender, but breakfast drinks are mainly about proportions anyway. The café used a terrific Bloody Mary mix and mimosas are just a matter of being judicious with the champagne and orange juice. I also made sure the coffee kept flowing.

Usually Bobby at least said good morning before he withdrew to the flattop where he and Nate turned out the bushels of eggs and bacon and sausage and ham and flapjacks and French toast and just about anything else you can think of in the way of breakfast food. But this morning he walked across the kitchen, keeping his gaze locked on the flattop, and pretended I wasn't there.

I'm six feet tall and my Greek ancestors probably included a few Amazons. Ignoring me isn't easy. But Bobby did it. Pointedly. Nate looked like he was grinding his teeth.

"Roxy! How lovely to see you. And you're doing the drinks for us again. Thank you so much." Madge made up for Bobby's rudeness with more cordiality than I usually got from my own family.

"Hi, Madge. Lovely day."

"It is. It definitely is." Madge spread her smiles around the kitchen, although I saw her jaw tighten when her glance passed over her oldest son, currently glowering down at an innocent fried egg. "All right, everyone. The after-church crush is starting. Let's do our best."

She hustled out the kitchen door, leaving me alone with two simmering brothers and a few drink orders to fill.

"Are we having fun yet?"

I wasn't entirely alone. Coco stood at my elbow watching her brothers ignore each other.

"I'm just pouring drinks. Fun doesn't enter into it."

"Yeah, right. Thanks for doing this. If you weren't here, I'd be stuck doing double duty, and I've got another bunch of cinnamon buns due out of the oven in five minutes. I hear we're off the hook with the whole Tera Bloomfield thing."

Since Coco had made the fruit tart we'd served at Tera's, she'd been under suspicion, too, although probably not as much as Nate and me.

"I think we're good. It looks like the port was tampered with, and we had nothing to do with that." I poured some champagne into a glass, then added a splash of orange juice. I'm of the two parts sparkling wine to one part orange juice school. I also believe in adding the orange juice second.

"Any thoughts on who did the tampering?" Coco raised her eyebrows.

"Lots of candidates. The lady had quite a few enemies, as it turned out."

"No shit. Jealous wives and business associates at the front of the line."

I turned to look at her. "Jealous wives? Tera had a married boyfriend?"

"So they say." A timer dinged in Coco's part of the kitchen. "Oops, that's the cinnamon rolls. Gotta go."

I wondered if I'd get a chance to ask Coco for details before we finished service. This was the first I'd heard about Tera having a local boyfriend, but it made sense. She'd been carrying on with a married man in Denver, according to Alice, and someone was bankrolling her lifestyle.

Had he been at the house that night? Was he the "someone special" who'd given her the bottle of port laced with ipecac? I filed the information away for future use, particularly for when I talked to Fowler. The more possible suspects I could pass along, the better for Susa.

"Two bloodies and a mimosa," Bobby called, giving me a look that acknowledged my existence but just barely.

I grabbed the vodka and got to work. I'd process all the information later.

Once the brunch rush began to die down around one thirty, I took a moment to call Susa. I'd decided to invite her out to the farm to go over my website and then get her to stay for dinner. She still seemed stressed out. Dinner with the four of us (I included Herman, of course) might not be the best stress reliever there was, but it couldn't hurt.

Susa picked up after a few rings and I gave her my invitation in a rush since I'd just gotten an order for six mimosas. "I don't know. I don't want to crowd you and Nate."

"No crowding. Please, Suz. It'll give us a chance to talk about the site without anybody pressuring either of us."

"Well, okay. But let's have a code. If you say 'it sure is hot in here,' that'll be the signal for me to take off."

"Right." I rolled my eyes. "It's forty degrees outside, Suz."

"It just means you won't say it by accident. I'll come by around three."

I poured the six mimosas, wondering why the

customers didn't just buy a bottle of champagne, then wondering if maybe a pitcher of mimosas wouldn't be good to add to the menu. Then again, that might make people stay around longer when the idea was to move them out to make room for the next bunch. Plus making menu suggestions was way out of bounds—any changes in the menu made Bobby go ballistic.

Five Bloody Marys and a couple of mimosas later, Bobby called out, "That's it. Door's closed."

I stripped off my apron and dropped it in the laundry bag as Bobby and Nate exited from opposite ends of the flattop, carefully not looking at each other. The whole thing was ridiculous, but it was their family drama, and I wasn't about to get in the middle of it.

At least not on purpose.

The guy who cleaned up the café on weekends was already loading dishes in the dishwasher, and Coco stacked her empty baking tins on the end of her counter where he could reach them.

I screwed the top on the Bloody Mary mix and took it to the cooler. There was a little over a third of a bottle of champagne left, not enough to save since it would undoubtedly go flat before next Sunday. When I returned from the cooler, Bobby stood glowering down at the mostly empty bottle. "Another wasted half bottle."

The champagne the café bought for their brunch was far from expensive, and even so I didn't do lavish pours. "It just worked out that way."

Bobby gave me a searing look, then stalked toward the kitchen door. "Goddamn waste. We need to hire a professional," he muttered a little more loudly as he pushed through.

"Oh, for Christ's sake." Nate started after him.

I could see nothing good coming from a confrontation in front of customers. Actually, I could see nothing good coming from a confrontation, period. I grabbed his arm. "Nate, let it go. It's nothing. I'm okay."

Nate paused to look down at me. His face was flushed. "It's not nothing. It's today's version of whatever's been chapping his ass for the last week."

"What's the use of going after him? You won't change his opinion and you won't make him see reason. Let's just finish up and head for the farm." I *so* didn't want to deal with a shouting match between the brothers. And I *so* didn't want to ruin Madge's day.

"You'll probably make him madder if you *don't* go after him. He's probably waiting for you so he can throw some more crap your way." Coco gave him a dry smile. Nobody knows a sibling better than another sibling.

Nate's shoulders relaxed marginally. "You might have a point."

"I have an excellent point. In fact, I'd recommend you leave through the back door. That way if he's waiting for you out front, he's going to go on waiting a long time."

Nate gave her a slow grin. "You are a nasty woman."

"Thanks, I appreciate that." But I thought I saw Coco's smile fade as we walked out the back door.

Chapter Seventeen

I got Nate to help me put labels on my raspberry vinegar once we got to the farm. Winter Market was bearing down on me, and I had to make some final decisions about what I was going to sell. I was still on the fence about the pumpkin butter. Sometimes I thought it was a great idea and others I thought I was probably going to go down in flames. The raspberry vinegar seemed like a much surer bet.

The bottles I'd gotten from my supplier were half pint size, which meant customers wouldn't be taking on a lot of vinegar if they bought some. A half pint of vinegar was relatively easy to use up, and as gifts they didn't obligate the giftee to do a lot of exotic cooking. I'd had some rustic-looking labels printed up, along with a small recipe card I was attaching to the bottle neck with twine. Overall, the bottles screamed *hostess gift*, and I hoped they'd move quickly.

"Are you going to cook something with this vinegar so I can taste it?" Nate asked.

I paused in my task of attaching the recipe cards to the bottles. "I don't have anything planned. Do you want to taste it?"

"Sure. I like tasting your stuff."

I'd tasted the raspberry vinegar when I'd made the first batch, just to make sure it wasn't awful. But I hadn't done anything else with it. I'd been too busy clearing our names and trying to find a more likely suspect than Susa. "I've got a little left in the jug where I aged it. Maybe we can do a salad or something."

"Or something." Nate stepped to my refrigerator and retrieved the half-empty bottle of champagne he'd brought from the café. "We can make raspberry shrubs with this."

Shrubs are drinks where you mix flavored syrup with sparkling wine. I'd never tasted one. "With vinegar?"

He nodded. "And simple syrup. It's a standard recipe, particularly with fruit vinegar. It'll work."

"Okay. As soon as we finish labeling."

"Yes, boss," Nate muttered, but I was pretty sure he was kidding.

Susa got to the farm a little after three. I thought she looked less stressed but still not her normal cheerful self. We spent a relaxed hour on my laptop, studying my website and figuring out what to do to make it ready for the onslaught of customers I hoped would show up.

Susa shook her head. "This needs to be updated. Why did I let it go for so long without doing renovations?"

I knew, of course. Tera Bloomfield had arrived and taken all of Susa's time so the rest of us had had to settle for Carly and Kip.

Susa's cheeks flushed. "I'm sorry, Roxy. I should have paid more attention."

"It's okay. We'll fix it now and I'll be ready for whatever happens after that *Sweet Thing* episode airs."

"We will. We'll be ready in plenty of time. In fact, if I can get Kip to do the coding, I can get a new version up next week."

"Kip?" I tried not to sound dubious.

"He's actually very good at his job. He just needs supervision. Something I haven't been able to give him for a few weeks."

There were lots of things I could say about that, but I kept my peace. "I can't wait to see it."

Nate had been puttering around in the kitchen while we worked, and now he emerged with three wine glasses filled with faintly pink liquid.

"What's that?" Susa asked.

"Shrubs." Nate grinned. "Give it a try. I've been experimenting."

"Shrubs?" Susa's eyebrows went up. "Made with viburnum or something?"

Nate gave her a long-suffering look. "No. Shrub is the name of a drink. Dates back a couple hundred years. Champagne is involved. So is Roxy's raspberry vinegar. Just taste it."

Susa took a glass, sipping a little tentatively, then with more enthusiasm.

I took a taste of my own, not quite sure what to expect. It tasted a little fruity, a little sweet, a little acid—completely unique. I took another swallow. "Wow. Is it too late to add this recipe to the cards on the vinegar bottles?"

Nate shrugged. "You know your printer better than I do."

"I'm going to try to get some made up ASAP. This is unique."

"What's unique?" Uncle Mike stepped into the room, followed, inevitably, by Herman who was ecstatic to discover Susa was there.

She held her glass above her head to keep it out of

Herman's immediate range. "This drink. This shrub."

Uncle Mike looked confused. "Shrub? What shrub?"

This led to another long explanation, which led to Uncle Mike wanting a shrub of his own, which led to Nate discovering he'd run out of champagne, which led to Uncle Mike returning to the main house to snag a bottle of prosecco he was pretty sure he had, which led to…well, you get the idea. We all had a couple of shrubs and pronounced them hits. Then we had a couple of frozen pizzas for dinner, doctored up a bit with some spare salami and a handful of mozzarella and black olives. It was a great dinner, with a lot of laughter and not a single mention of Tera Bloomfield.

Around nine, Susa pushed herself to her feet. "I'd better get home. I've got a lot of work to catch up on tomorrow, including your website, Rox."

"Yeah, I imagine Herman and I had better take our leave, too." Uncle Mike stood up, gesturing to Herman, who decided to obey for once.

Susa gave me a quick hug. "Thanks, Roxy. I needed this."

"We all needed this. It's been a bad couple of weeks."

"It has. But we're through it now. It should get better from here on in."

I felt a little like rapping my knuckles on the wooden table, but I didn't.

Monday afternoon I took some jars of jam to Bianca's shop, along with a few jars of pumpkin butter. I wanted to test the waters with the pumpkin butter. If it sold at Bianca's, aided by the powerful marketing influence of her bread, maybe I'd increase the number of jars I'd planned to take to the Winter Market.

The aspen trees on the mountainside were still colorful, although the leaves had begun to fall. I wondered if we'd had the usual influx of leaf lookers, tourists who came up to take pictures of the autumn colors. They provided a little extra money during the fall season when tourism was usually down. Downtown was full of Halloween decorations, complete with an annoying cackling witch near the drugstore. Bianca had confined herself to a few pumpkins and some autumn leaves scattered around her display windows.

Inside, the same bored teenager was behind the counter, still obsessed with whatever was on his phone. He glanced up at me briefly.

"Bianca?"

"In back." He returned to his phone.

I found Bianca in her bakery workroom, turning out several loaves of rustic bread onto the cooling racks. I explained about the pumpkin butter, and she recommended putting out a little bowl for sampling along with some cubed whole wheat she was trying to move. The conversation evolved into a discussion of her son's unhelpful wife. I didn't have much to say about Sara, but I could at least be a sympathetic listener. Once again Tera Bloomfield's name never slid into the conversation.

I was beginning to think maybe we'd turned the corner and the whole unpleasant episode would slide beneath the town's radar, always provided Fowler didn't decide to charge Susa with murder.

I headed into the shop with Bianca to set up the pumpkin butter and bread. As I spooned the butter into a bowl and Bianca chopped up a mini-loaf of whole wheat, I noticed another customer checking out the cookie case. He was older, maybe in his early sixties His clothes were casual but they also looked expensive—I recognized the plaid flannel shirt from the last LL Bean catalog.

He also looked vaguely familiar in the way a lot of Shavano residents did, but I couldn't put a name to his face. Something about him pricked at my memory, though, something that made me feel uneasy.

He glanced up at me, then paused, eyes widening. And I recognized him—the man I'd given water to the night of Tera's death, the one who'd asked me what we'd put in his food. My shoulders tensed. Apparently, I wasn't as over the whole Tera Bloomfield experience as I'd hoped.

He was staring at me a little nervously, as if he wasn't entirely sure how to react. I wasn't sure myself, but I thought I'd dive in and give it a try. "Hi. I'm glad to see you're back on your feet."

His smile became a little more definite. "Oh, yeah. They let me go home later that night. I never got to thank you for helping me out."

"That's okay. I'm just glad you're all right."

"Me, too." He extended his hand to me. "We never got introduced, I guess. I'm Tom Everett."

"Nice to meet you, Tom." I shook his hand. "I'm Roxy Constantine."

He nodded. "I know. I remember when they introduced you. That was a great dinner you guys served. Well, up until…" He paused.

"Yeah. Up until then. You know about the port, right?"

"I heard something about it. I know your food

didn't make me sick."

"No, it didn't. I think they're still trying to figure out exactly what happened, but our food wasn't involved."

"Glad to hear it. That was an excellent meal." Everett glanced around the shop quickly. "Can I buy you a cup of coffee? To make up for implying your food made me sick that night?"

I started to tell him he didn't need to, but that seemed ungracious. Plus this struck me as a time to pick up a little more information. "Sure. Bianca's coffee is great."

A few minutes later we had coffee and a couple of peanut butter cookies and were seated at one of the tables lining the front windows.

"How did you know Tera?" I asked. That seemed like a neutral way to start.

"I didn't know her before that night. Phil Duncan and his wife invited me. Two or three of us were there because of him. He wanted to introduce us to her."

"Did he use her investment services?"

"Maybe. I'm not sure. He wanted me to talk to her about what she was doing because he thought it was interesting. I didn't get much chance. Too many people. Maybe that's why she invited me and Tony to stay after dinner to sample her port. We were both there to find out about her company."

"Tony?"

"Tony Aldo. He runs an insurance agency here in town. I'm with First Federal myself. I think that's why Phil wanted me to come. Not that I'd be representing the bank, you understand," he added hastily.

"No, of course not. I guess Tera's company was

successful. A lot of people were talking about it."

Everett's expression became guarded. "There was a lot of talk. I don't know much about what she was trying to do, though."

"Who else did she ask to stay?"

"Four of us and Susa Sondergaard. But I only knew Tony. One of the others was a guy named Allison from Vail. I guess he had something to do with the ski area, but I didn't get a chance to talk to him much. And there was Fred Hoekstra, who just bought the Blankenship house on Third Street."

"The Blankenship house?" I dug through my memory of Shavano mansions. "Is that the one with all the flowers?"

Everett nodded. "He just moved in last month. I've talked to him a couple of times, but I can't say I know him. We didn't get much time to talk before everybody got sick as dogs."

His affable smile slid into a grimace, and I was sorry to remind him of unpleasant stuff. It wasn't his fault, after all. Or probably it wasn't—I needed to keep an open mind about guilt and innocence.

"Did you ever find out anything about Tera's business?"

"Not really. Phil was working with her, I think. She kept turning to him at dinner whenever the subject of her company came up. But Phil wouldn't talk business while we were eating. Maybe we were supposed to talk about her business once dinner was over."

That made sense. Everett and Aldo were likely part of Shavano's rather small privileged class. And the Blankenship house was a Victorian mansion with a huge, landscaped garden. Anyone who owned it was probably a good bet for an investor. "So Tera was going to explain it all after dinner?"

"I guess. Frankly, she didn't look too good. I wondered if she'd eaten something that disagreed with her." He paused as we both thought about that. If she'd eaten something that disagreed with her, nobody else had. At least not until they'd sampled the port. Maybe Tera had had a glass of port before dinner.

"I'm sorry to make you talk about this. It's just…Nate and I are still trying to figure everything out."

Everett raised his eyebrows. "Nate?"

"Nate Robicheaux. He was the chef who cooked the dinner. I helped him out."

"Right, right." Everett nodded. "I remember now. I knew his dad. Plus I've had coffee and pie at that café more times than I can count. Does he make the pie?"

"That's his sister, Coco. She does most of their pastries. She did the fruit tart you had for dessert at Tera's."

I finished the last bit of my cookie. "Nate was showing what he could do at that dinner. He'd like to open a restaurant of his own sometime, and he wanted people to know what kind of cooking he did."

"That was a real shame. Like I said before, it was a great meal. You and Robicheaux did a good job, but then you got roped into this just because you were there. Whoever decided to make Tera Bloomfield sick didn't care if he messed up a lot of other people, too."

"That's true. We've bounced back. The café's still doing a good business, and I haven't noticed any slacking off in my jam sales. But it may be a while before people forget we were there that night. It's definitely a bummer."

"It is at that. I got a trip to the hospital out of it and you guys got accused of food poisoning. Whoever did this doesn't seem bothered by collateral damage." He took a last sip of coffee. "I hope Fowler finds this jerk before he can do anything else. He's not someone we want running around."

"Definitely not," I agreed. "I'm sure the chief is working on it."

"Right." Everett gave me another smile as he got to his feet. "Well, thanks again for your help that night. It made a difference."

"You're welcome. And I'm glad you're all right."

"Me, too. Say hello to your uncle for me. We're both in the Merchants Association." Everett smiled at me, nodded at Bianca, and turned on his way.

Bianca narrowed her eyes as I stood up again. "What was that all about?"

"Mr. Everett was at Tera's the night of the dinner party. He was one of the ones who got sick. I gave him some water and sat with him until the ambulance got there. He was thanking me."

Bianca's lips edged up in a dry smile. "Do you also pull thorns out of lions' paws?"

"Not lately. Why?"

"Because Tom Everett is the chairman of the board at First Federal. He's a good man to have on your side."

I blew out a long breath. "Good to know. Thanks for the information."

Before I drove to the farm, I took out my notebook and jotted down the names Everett had mentioned: Tony Aldo, Fred Hoekstra, and Allison, the last with a question mark since I had no idea what his first name was or what he did in Vail, assuming Everett's memory was accurate. It wouldn't hurt to do a little investigating about the other men who'd been there, although since all of them had been throwing up after the ipecac, I doubted any of them had doctored the bottle of port.

In that regard, Phil Duncan struck me as a much better bet. He'd invited Everett and Aldo, after all. And for all I knew, he'd invited Allison and Hoekstra, too. Then he'd left while the others had all stayed. Maybe he'd actually had a good reason for going home. Or maybe he'd left before Tera could pour him a glass of port.

In that case, he was either very smart or very lucky.

Chapter Eighteen

I called Bianca the next afternoon to check on the success of the pumpkin butter. "It was interesting. The people who liked it *really* liked it. We sold all the jars you left and it helped move the whole wheat bread, too. For which I thank you. But some people took one bite and tossed the rest in the trash. Not as many as the lovers, mind you, but still some. I guess it's one of those polarizing things, like fig jam and seven-grain bread. Either they'll love it or they'll hate it."

Unfortunately, that didn't help make up my mind about how many jars to bring to the Winter Market. "Thanks, Bianca. I'm glad we moved some whole wheat bread."

"Me, too, sweetie. Bring some more jars by later this week, okay?"

Susa made good on her promise to get the new version of my website up and running by the end of the week. Unfortunately, that meant I had to spend a lot of time on the phone with Kip, getting my new online store ready. Kip was apparently quite fluent in whatever coding language they were using to put the site together, but his English fluency was limited.

"Well, like, if I did, like…um…a drop down with a rollover that popped up the graphics, would that be what you want?" There was a lot of that.

In the end, though, the site looked great and Kip

assured me I'd be able to populate the store fairly easily. I admit the idea of my "populating" anything brought forth a series of very risqué images, but I was pretty sure I knew what he meant.

On Wednesday, I took a load of jam to the Made In Colorado store. It was a lovely late October day, lots of sunshine and bits of remaining color on the mountainsides. The Collegiate Peaks were sharp against the bright blue sky, sprinkled with lines of snowfields. We often have lots of rain in October since it's still monsoon season, but at least this day was clear.

Halloween decorations were everywhere in downtown Shavano, and I could also see some in the front yards of houses. I decided to take the long way to my truck by strolling through Old Town. The residents frequently decorated their houses, and most of them had enough money to do it up right.

I passed piles of fantastical jack-o-lanterns, some carved and some painted, along with a broad array of tombstones, some with zombie hands emerging from the dirt nearby. Skeletons hung in fiberglass cobwebs, along with a few artificial king-size spiders that gave even me chills. Some of the houses had gone with inflatable décor, several of which were uninflated and lying in sad little puddles on the lawns. But most of the Old Town residents had gone for more imaginative decorations, as befitting a part of town where some of the houses looked a lot like the Addams family mansion.

I turned a corner, thoroughly enjoying the crisp fall weather and the extravaganza of scary artifacts, and saw one house with no Halloween at all. But their gardens made up for the missing jack-o-lanterns. Where the other houses had the occasional pot of mums on the front steps, here giant urns of mums marched alongside the house and bordered the front walk. Scarlet Virginia creepers spilled over the fences, and baskets of brighter flowers hung along the porch.

I paused to take it all in—the Victorian architecture and the riot of flowers so unusual for fall in the Rockies. It took me a minute to realize I was staring at the Blankenship house Tom Everett had mentioned when I'd talked to him at Bianca's. I tried to remember the name of the man who lived there.

Fred something. And he'd moved in only recently.

As if I'd summoned him with ESP, a man in baggy gardening pants and a broad straw hat emerged from the side of the house carrying a watering pot. He paused when he saw me staring at his house. Then I got another version of the expression Tom Everett had had, the dawning recognition of someone who'd been there for an extremely unpleasant moment in his life. But where Everett's look of consternation had transformed into a smile, Fred whatever's consternation transformed into something closer to suspicion.

"Can I help you?" he said finally.

I tried for a friendly smile. "I was just admiring your yard. It's lovely."

"Thanks." He was younger than I'd realized, maybe late forties or early fifties, with dark hair beginning to gray and deep-set gray eyes. "You're the woman from the dinner at Tera's, right?"

I nodded. "I'm Roxanne Constantine. I helped with the cooking."

He paused, then seemed to come to an internal decision. "Fred Hoekstra." He held out his hand and I shook it briefly. "I guess they've decided it wasn't anything to do with your food."

"No. Apparently someone tampered with the port you guys drank."

Hoekstra's jaw tensed. That probably wasn't a pleasant memory.

"This is such a great house," I said. "The gardens have always been first rate."

"Thanks. We're trying to keep them up." Hoekstra relaxed a little. Maybe he was the main gardener in the family.

"It's beautiful year round, a real showstopper." I fumbled through my memories of the Blankenship house, trying to come up with something relevant. "In the spring the lilac bushes are gorgeous, and the tulips and daffodils and iris."

"We kept the iris. The tulips and daffodils don't always do well at this altitude."

"Right. The lilies of the valley were always nice, too."

His face went blank. "I guess we got here too late to see those."

"Oh, well you've got lots of them over on the far side of the yard." I tried to think of other flowers I'd seen around the house. Hoekstra was frowning at me, except not exactly at me. More like over my shoulder.

At which point I heard a short bleep from a police siren. I turned to see Fowler pulling his patrol car to the curb, looking stonier than usual. "Got a minute?" he said.

"I...guess so?" I said.

He leaned across and opened the passenger door. "Get in."

195

There didn't seem to be any way to refuse. Plus I was curious what this was about. I turned to Hoekstra. "I'm glad to see you're all right now. Enjoy your garden."

He nodded at me, his expression almost as stony as Fowler's. I seemed to be charming the multitudes today. I climbed into Fowler's patrol car, pulling the door closed. "What's up?"

He stared straight ahead instead of answering, pulling away from the curb. "Where's your truck parked?"

"On Second. A couple of blocks down from Robicheaux's." I'd planned on stopping to see Nate on my way. Now I wondered if I'd end up in a cell.

"I'll drop you off. After we have a chat." Fowler pulled to the curb a few blocks down from Blankenship's.

I folded my arms. "What are we going to chat about?"

"We are going to chat about you staying the hell out of my investigation. I shouldn't have to tell you this. You should remember from the last time our paths crossed."

I drew myself up, although it was hard to do when the roof of the patrol car was so low. I prefer pickup trucks. "I'm not interfering in your investigation. You all but accused my best friend of murder. I wanted to find all the other people who might have had reason to kill Tera Bloomfield before you decided to lock Susa away."

"I didn't accuse Susa Sondergaard. I haven't accused anybody. And you have no business looking up people associated with the case."

"I talked to two people about Tera, mostly to get information about her. Neither of them were associated with the case in the way you mean. I don't even know who you've talked to, and Lord knows I've got no access to the forensic information you've got. Why are you so pissed with me anyway?"

"You talked to two of the men who were victims, Everett and Hoekstra. You've got to know that crosses the line." Fowler's jaw looked like granite.

Weirdly enough, I could see his point, but only because he didn't have all the facts. "I didn't search out either of those men. Tom Everett happened to walk into Bianca Jordan's bakery while I was there, and he offered to buy me a cup of coffee as a thank you because I stayed with him when he was sick at Tera's. And Fred Hoekstra just walked out while I was admiring his garden. Which was all we talked about."

"Hoekstra just happened to walk by while you happened to be admiring his yard?" Fowler gave me the kind of glacial look that probably reduced guilty prisoners to jelly.

Only I wasn't guilty, and I wasn't a prisoner. I gave him my best steely-eyed stare. "It's the truth."

He raised his eyebrows, as if he was weighing my story. "All right, leave it. Who else have you talked to?"

"Alice Hoover and a friend of mine in Denver who knew a little about Tera's track record investing in restaurants. I know you haven't talked to Toby, because you've never heard of him. And I'd guess you haven't talked to Alice because it wouldn't occur to you. She doesn't talk to a lot of people, and you're still new in town."

I was working up a good hit of righteous anger. Who knew how many people had seen me being bundled into Fowler's patrol car? The gossip mill might be working overtime by the end of the day.

Fowler leaned back in his seat, eyebrows still up. "Okay, I don't know who Alice Hoover is. Why should I talk to her?"

"Because she knows a lot about Tera Bloomfield's business in Denver, and why she ended up in Shavano with her tail between her legs. Before she retired up here, Alice was a big deal in Denver financial circles. She knew most of the details of what Tera did when she worked in Denver. But maybe you know all that already." I widened my eyes at Fowler, giving my best imitation of guileless innocence.

Fowler's lips flattened, letting me know my guileless innocence imitation needed work. "Why don't you just tell me what she told you and save me a trip?"

It was in everybody's best interests for Fowler to know as much about Tera's background as possible. If he knew what kind of person she was, he might be less likely to assume Susa had killed her with a misplaced practical joke. "I don't have my notes with me so I don't have all the names, but I can give you the gist."

"Do that."

"Okay. Tera worked for a big, prestigious financial firm in Denver. I don't know how successful she was overall, but she had some weaknesses."

"Such as?" Fowler folded his arms.

"Such as she tried putting together some groups of investors for restaurants in Denver, but a lot of them went bust. That's what I found out from my other friend in Denver who owns a restaurant there."

"I thought restaurants were tricky investments—they go bust more often than not."

"True. But a good broker knows what to look for. Apparently, Tera didn't. She also got involved in a large-scale real estate deal that turned out to be shady. A lot of people lost a lot of money. But there were rumors Tera and a couple of big investors actually came out ahead."

"Big investors from Denver?"

"I don't know. Their names never got out, according to Alice. But there was a lot of suspicion related to Tera. The investment firm fired her, and she came up here. Alice was pretty sure they didn't give her much severance. Which leaves you with the question of how she could afford the move. That house in the canyon wasn't cheap. And she had an office in a historic building downtown that went for big bucks. So either some bank was dumb enough to loan her money…"

"Unlikely. At least in Shavano."

"Or she got the money from somebody else. The point is she may not have had much of her own." I folded my arms again, ready for round two.

Fowler frowned. "She have a husband?"

"Divorced. I don't know how long ago, but Alice said he'd moved away from Denver."

"You know his name?"

"Max Bloomfield." I paused, wondering just how much gossip I should include. "According to Alice, Tera may have had a rich boyfriend. A married rich boyfriend. Maybe he bankrolled her setting up in Shavano. Or maybe he just paid her to leave Denver. Either way he might have provided her with enough money to set up her business here. Whatever her business was."

He gave me one of those half-smiles that meant he wasn't telling me squat. "We're figuring that out. Your friend Susa might have some information."

"Susa just put Tera's website together. She didn't have anything to do with her business beyond that."

Fowler stared out at the street in front of his patrol car. "But putting together a website would require her to know something about the business. Bloomfield would have had to explain what she wanted on her website and why."

"Maybe." I still wasn't convinced. "Can I leave now?"

He raised his chin. "You understand about not interfering?"

"I'm not interfering. You understand about there being a lot of people who might have wanted to hurt Tera Bloomfield?"

Fowler sighed. "Yes, ma'am. I understand that." He leaned across me, pushing the door open. "Thanks for your time."

"Like I had a choice," I muttered as I climbed out. I was still pissed about being picked up by a patrol car. Shavano isn't a small town, but it's not a large city either. Chances were somebody I knew had seen me sitting with Fowler, and the news would definitely get around.

As it happened the news got around a lot faster than I expected. Nate was standing on the street next to my truck as Fowler drove off. He didn't look happy. "What was that all about?"

"We had a disagreement about who I was and

wasn't supposed to be talking to. I think I convinced him a lot of people besides Susa didn't like Tera." I kissed Nate on the cheek, hoping it would at least earn a smile.

He put an arm around my waist, sighing. "I still don't understand why you feel like you have to spend so much time with Fowler."

"It wasn't my idea to spend time with him. He picked me up downtown."

"He picked you up?"

I resisted rolling my eyes. "He requested I join him in his patrol car so he could yell at me for interfering in his case. Except I haven't been interfering in his case. And I told him so. I think he's doing an investigation of Tera's background, which is good since all those people in Denver who lost money with her have got to be pissed. Although I don't know how he'd deduce which one might have poisoned the port." I tried for a winsome look. "I'm hungry. I didn't have any lunch. Have you got anything left over at the café?"

Nate sighed again. "Come on. I'll fix you a sandwich."

I followed him down the street to Robicheaux's. Our crisis had apparently been averted, but I needed to convince Nate there was nothing between Fowler and me.

I was pretty sure there wasn't. And the part that wasn't sure, I could and would ignore.

Chapter Nineteen

Halloween fell on Friday this time around, so I invited Nate to the farm for a Halloween dinner. What that would consist of, I wasn't entirely sure, but I'd think of something suitable. Something without pumpkin spice, which I'd had more than enough of.

We live far out in the country, so we rarely get trick or treaters. Occasionally one of the neighborhood families will take their kids around to the other farms, but they usually let us know they're coming. Otherwise, the pickings might be slim since few of us bother to stock up.

Uncle Mike is indifferent to Halloween, and I must have inherited my attitude from him. I like the Halloween decorations I see around town, but I never get into the spirit of the thing myself.

I finally decided to fix shepherd's pie since it had a certain mysterious quality—you never know what's hiding under those mashed potatoes. For a split second I considered putting carrot slices on the top like tombstones, but the impulse passed quickly.

Uncle Mike arrived at the house while I was chopping vegetables and frying the hamburger (no ground lamb, no matter how authentic it might be, and yes, I know it's technically cottage pie).

"What did you do yesterday to get picked up by a cop?" he asked.

I gritted my teeth. I'd hoped that news of my ride in Fowler's patrol car hadn't made it around town, but obviously it had. "Fowler wanted to talk to me, and when he found me, I was looking at the decorations in Old Town. He gave me a ride to my truck." The sanitized version.

"What did he want to talk to you about?"

"Tera. What else have we been talking about lately? I passed on what Alice told me about Tera's life before she came up here."

"And that was all he wanted?" Uncle Mike gave me the look he'd used when I was a kid trying to convince him I hadn't messed up a math test. It worked then, and it sort of worked now.

"He had some misconceptions. I cleared them up for him."

"Misconceptions concerning…"

Well, crap. I wasn't going to get out of this without telling him the whole story. I gave him a quick summary of my adventures with Tom Everett and Fred Hoekstra and explained why Fowler was annoyed. Groundlessly, of course.

Uncle Mike watched me mash the potatoes for the shepherd's pie topping. "I know Tom Everett. Nice guy for a banker. Honest man, so far as I know. Never heard of Hoekstra. Bought the Blankenship place, you say?"

I nodded. "When did the Blankenships sell it?"

"Beats me. No Blankenships have lived there all the time I've been in Shavano. I think they moved out in the thirties."

"Then why is it still the Blankenship house?"

"They built it. In the nineteenth century. He was some kind of rich guy, probably a son of a bitch like they mostly were. It was the biggest house in town. It's on the National Historic Register, for what that's worth. But several other houses in Old Town are on the register, too."

"Looks like it's in good shape. Must have cost a lot."

"Must have. You could always check online."

I could, but I doubted I'd go to the trouble. The bottom line was Hoekstra must be loaded. Another rich guy Tera was trying to entice into her web, whatever her web might have been. The guys she'd asked to stay for port must have been the ones she wanted to impress. "Do you know Tony Aldo?"

"I know who he is. I've probably said hello to him a few times—he's in the Merchants Association."

"What does he do?"

"Insurance. Mostly commercial. He owns the Collegiate Peaks agency downtown. Probably the biggest in Shavano, but I don't know that for sure."

"So Tera invited a big-time banker, the most successful insurance agent in town, and the guy who bought the Blankenship house. Along with somebody named Allison from Vail, where there are a lot of billionaires running around during the season. Sounds like she was trying to pull some top tier people into whatever scheme she was running."

I poured the vegetables and meat into the casserole dish, along with the pan gravy, then began spooning the mashed potatoes over the top. "I wonder if the other guests were rich people, too."

"Probably. If she was running a scam, and she most likely was, why waste time running a scam on people who didn't have enough money to make it worthwhile?"

"True enough." I put the shepherd's pie into the oven to brown up and dug out a couple of bottles of fine Colorado lager for Uncle Mike and me.

"Nate coming over?"

I nodded. "He'll have to go home afterward since he works tomorrow morning, but he's coming for dinner. You should ask Madge over sometime."

Uncle Mike's ears turned bright pink. "Oh. Well…maybe sometime." He took a quick swallow of beer and looked out the window at the setting sun.

Nate arrived a few minutes later. I gave him a beer of his own and he took a seat next to Uncle Mike at my kitchen table. "It's already nuts in town. The merchants are doing the Halloween Trick Or Treat Walk up and down Main, even though it's raining. They've got it all blocked off and the place is full of kids."

"Good publicity," Uncle Mike said. "The farmers market should have set something up."

"They're concentrating on Winter Market right now," I said. "It's coming up, remember?"

Uncle Mike nodded. "Yeah. I sold what winter squash we've got to Aram Pergosian so he could sell it at his stand. Lean pickings this time of year."

"For the farmers. Those of us who sell prepared stuff are building up inventory for the Christmas rush."

"Raspberry vinegar for Christmas?" Uncle Mike gave me a dubious look.

"With any luck." I rapped my knuckles on the oak dining room table.

"It's good stuff," Nate said loyally. "Remember those shrubs? Mom said you made her one."

"Ah, yes." Uncle Mike's eyes grew dreamy.

"Those were great. Raspberry vinegar has its uses."

His ears turned pink again, and I turned toward the stove. "Time to eat."

The shepherd's pie was fine. We each had another beer and talked about Halloweens past and the Winter Market and Nate's attempts at recreating his father's cornbread dressing for their upcoming pre-Thanksgiving special.

"It's the cornbread. I can't get it right. I know he wouldn't use sugar because he probably got the recipe from our Louisiana ancestors, and they wouldn't have used sugar."

"He might have started with a mix and then fiddled with it," Uncle Mike said. "I remember he liked to do stuff like that."

Nate paused, staring at my uncle. "You're right. I forgot about that. Yeah, he probably started with a commercial mix and then added something to give it some tang."

"Buttermilk," I said. "Nothing better for tang."

We tossed ideas around for a while until I got up to bring over the mint chocolate chip ice cream that wasn't particularly Halloween-oriented but was all I had in the way of dessert.

"Oh," said Nate. "I almost forgot. I brought dessert. We had some leftover pumpkin pie."

I gave him my best phony smile. I'd had so much pumpkin lately I'd lost my enthusiasm for more, even Coco's pie. "Great."

"Don't worry. I brought lots of whipped cream, too."

Coco's pie was tasty, but I admit I pretty much smothered it in whipped cream.

Uncle Mike leaned back in his chair. "Well, a great meal. Thanks, Roxanne."

"You're welcome." It had worked out very well, and once again Tera Bloomfield's name hadn't been mentioned. Neither had Fowler's.

"Let me help with the dishes." Nate pushed to his feet.

"I should probably go to the main house." Uncle Mike usually withdraws discreetly when Nate is visiting. "C'mon, Herman."

Across the room, Herman's head came up. But he wasn't looking at Uncle Mike. He made a sound low in his throat.

"Herman?"

Herman's growl became louder. He came to his feet quickly, stalking toward the door. And then he started to bark.

Herman's normally a very relaxed dog, although he's a very large relaxed dog. He seldom barks at things unless it's something unusual. Now he was barking his head off, stalking toward my front door as he did.

"Herman, shut up," Uncle Mike snapped.

"What going on, dog? It can't be trick-or-treaters." I started across the room toward him, and a dark shape moved across the front window as I did.

"There's something out there." As soon as I opened the front door, Herman shot by me into the rain-sodden yard.

"Herman, damn it, get back here," Uncle Mike yelled. "Now he's going to get all muddy."

I was more concerned about the person I thought I'd seen going by the window. I started out the door after Herman, but Nate grabbed my arm. "Let me go first."

I stood aside to let him get by, then followed him out onto the front porch. "I don't see anyone," Nate said.

I looked around the yard, rubbing my arms against the cool air. "I don't either. But somebody was at the front window. I saw them move away when I got to the living room."

"Well, there's nobody here now. Herman," Uncle Mike yelled, "come on back."

I stared out into the darkness, trying to decide if I'd actually seen something or if I'd gotten spooked by an animal or a bird. We do get deer at night sometimes, and occasionally coyotes and raccoons. I thought I heard a car driving away on the main road, but it was a county highway. Cars went by regularly.

Herman finally padded up, thoroughly wet and muddy. "Damn it, dog," Uncle Mike muttered, "now I've got to take you up to the house and hose you off."

Nate stepped into the house and then re-emerged with the flashlight I kept near the door. "Let me check the window."

I followed him out into the light drizzle. He played the flashlight across the muddy ground near the window, then paused. "Footprints. There."

I looked where he was pointing and saw two distinct footprints in front of my window. I shivered with a sudden chill.

"What the hell?" Uncle Mike squinted in the darkness. "Who'd come out here at this time of night?"

"Prowler?" Nate asked. "I can't think of any legitimate reason for a person to be standing out here when we were inside."

"Why would a prowler come here? There's nothing to see."

"There's you," Nate said flatly. "He could be looking for you."

A moment of silence stretched after that. My heart was pounding so loudly I was amazed they didn't hear it.

"Call the cops," Uncle Mike said. "Get somebody out here. At least it'll go on record we had a prowler. If he comes again, they'll know we've had a problem."

That didn't reassure me one bit. "Okay, I'll call. But it's Halloween. My guess is they'll consider a prowler pretty low on their radar."

The police dispatcher I talked to was polite but unimpressed. He said he'd send someone out if they had anyone to spare, but he suggested taking pictures of the footprints and bringing them in tomorrow when things were a little more settled downtown. That made sense to me, and I took some shots on my cell phone.

Nate was playing the flashlight across the grass leading to the gravel driveway. "There may be more traces here. I can't tell in the darkness."

"We can look at it tomorrow," Uncle Mike said. "Come on, Herman." He grabbed hold of the dog's collar, pausing to look at me before going up to the main house. "You want to come stay at the big house tonight? I'd feel better if you did."

I might have felt better, too. But Nate stepped to my side. "I'll stay. Rox shouldn't be by herself tonight."

"I agree." Uncle nodded at Nate and me. "Good night, then."

I took a breath as we stepped into my house. "You

don't have to stay. I know you have to work breakfast tomorrow."

"I can get up early and get there in time." He stopped, putting his arms around me and pulling me close. "I don't know what's going on here, Rox, but I don't want you staying by yourself. And you're coming to my place tomorrow night, right?"

"Right."

"Okay." He steered me toward the kitchen. "Since I'm staying, we can have another beer."

"Right again."

It was maybe an hour later, while we were cuddled on the couch watching *Dracula* (hey, it was Halloween), when I heard a car turn in on the gravel drive leading to the house. "Who's that?"

It was almost ten, way too late for casual visitors this far out in the country. Nate stood up while I paused the movie. "It might be the cops."

"They're busy keeping track of the kids at the Halloween Walk. Or they should be."

"It's over by now. Close to it, anyway."

The car stopped outside my house, which meant Nate was probably right. I started for the door, but he put a hand on my arm. "Let me open it, okay?"

I started to tell him that no prowler in his right mind would arrive in a car, but then I let it go. Sometimes you let yourself be protected.

Nate opened the door and stepped out on the porch.

"Evening," Chief Fowler said. "Roxy around?"

Nate stepped aside, his expression carefully blank, and I stepped forward. "Evening, chief. What brings you out here?"

"You reported a prowler?"

"Somebody was looking in the front window earlier tonight. Herman started barking and scared him off. But he left some footprints beneath the window." I reached inside and grabbed the flashlight again.

Fowler followed us to the window beside the porch, then studied the footprints in the mud, or studied them as much as he could during a dark night. "Looks like he took off up the drive when Herman started barking. Did you get a good look at him?"

I shook my head. "I saw someone moving outside the window when I went to quiet Herman, but it was just an impression. I couldn't even tell if it was a man or woman."

Fowler turned to Nate. "What about you? Were you here?"

"Yeah. But I was still in the kitchen with Mike. We were too late to see anyone."

"Did you hear a car? It's too far out here for somebody to walk. Plus it was raining."

"I might have heard one. But it was on the county road, and there's traffic up there. I couldn't swear it wasn't just a passing car."

Fowler sighed. "Okay, there's not much here we can do anything about, but I'll put in a report. That way if you have more problems, we'll have a record of this."

"Thanks for coming out," I said. "I would have thought things were too busy downtown for anyone to come until tomorrow."

"The patrol guys are all busy. I wasn't. Plus I was curious since you've had some problems lately." He glanced between Nate and me. "Any ideas about who this might be?"

"Not a clue."

"Okay. If anybody bothers you—either of you—let us know."

"We'll do that." I felt a lot more uneasy all of a sudden.

Nate and I stood in the doorway, watching the taillights of Fowler's patrol car disappear up the road to town. "What do you think he was talking about? Who might bother us?"

Nate shook his head. "Don't know. I suppose people who hadn't heard it wasn't food poisoning with Tera might be harassing us, but he made it sound personal."

"He did." I bit my lip. "I don't like this."

"I don't like it much myself." Nate put his arm around my shoulders. "Want to finish *Dracula*?"

"Unless you're really interested in what happens to Jonathan and Mina—and if you are, I can give you a quick summary—I think I'd rather switch to *Ghostbusters.*"

"Works for me," Nate muttered. "Definitely works for me."

Chapter Twenty

I went to Nate's house Saturday night, and he came to stay with me again on Sunday. Both of us kept watch for suspicious characters or unexplained visitors, but nothing happened. On Monday night, Uncle Mike insisted I come and stay with him in the big house. Honestly, it didn't take much persuading to get me to go.

But on Tuesday I decided enough was enough. The Winter Market was being held on the upcoming Saturday and Sunday, and I needed to get my stock in order, which included putting the custom labels on the two cases of pumpkin butter I'd be taking with me in a cooler. I needed to be where I could keep working until midnight if I needed to.

Uncle Mike reluctantly agreed. But he still came down to my place for dinner every night and stayed suspiciously long into the evening, helping me load jars or watching TV when I was doing something he couldn't help with, like stirring up a pot of extra pear butter just to make sure I had enough.

He also left Herman with me full time, which simultaneously reassuring and scary since Herman was one of those dogs who kept coming to full alert at odd times, apparently reacting to phantom calls from beyond my puny human range. Still it was nice to have him stretched across the foot of my bed, more than willing to leap into action at the drop of a footprint.

Around midweek, the good weather finally gave way to November, and we had a cold rain that quickly became snow. There was no accumulation to speak of since the ground was still fairly warm, but it was a harbinger of things to come. The daytime temperature plummeted into the low forties, and the nights were freezing. I dug out my fleece vest and my winter parka, ready for whatever the weather gods decided to throw at us.

Winter Market was held all day on Saturday and on Sunday afternoon. The location rotated annually between a gym at one of the high schools and the exhibition hall at the fairgrounds, depending on what space was available when. This year it was being held in the gymnasium of the high school where I did mentoring, which meant I could get a good parking space with my part-time faculty hangtag.

They gave us Friday afternoon to set up. Since I didn't need an electrical connection, my booth was at the side, near one of the hall entrances. Usually the halls were closed off to keep people from wandering around the classroom area, but this one led to the restrooms so it was kept open. I decided this was a good thing since people going to and from the restroom would pass by my stuff.

I had constructed a kind of modified version of my farmers market booth with plastic walls at the sides and a backing that read Luscious Delights. I also had a table drape that read *Mmmm for the Holidays*, which was totally my idea. I was very proud of it. I'm lousy at marketing, so when I actually have inspiration, I hang on like death.

There was space behind the backing to stack cases of jam, enough so I wouldn't be running to the truck every half hour. I'd put the cooler with the pumpkin butter next to my chair so I could replenish the stock when I needed to.

Nate had volunteered to be my runner, but the café did a big business on Saturdays, particularly Saturdays like this one when scads of tourists would be in town. Winter Market attracted a lot of people, not just from Shavano but from several other towns in the high country. I'd be on my own until mid-afternoon at least, so I planned on stacking as many cases behind the backing as I could.

Other people besides the farmers market merchants were also setting up booths. I saw several jewelry artisans, along with some soap and lotion people, clothing designers, wood workers, and toy makers. Even some service providers like the local cell phone company and an insurance agency. Susa had a booth, too.

I walked over to check her decorations. She was carefully fastening Styrofoam snowflakes along the wooden frame in front. "What exactly are you selling?" I asked. Computer services didn't seem like anything you'd give for Christmas.

She nodded toward the display card she had propped at the front of the booth. "It's Kip's idea."

Have trouble setting up that new game system or smart TV? Call on the pros! We'll connect those Christmas gifts and have you up and running in no time.

"That's brilliant. But you're going to have a huge run on Christmas Eve."

"It's more likely to be Christmas day or the day after. Kip says he's willing to work both, but we're going to charge a premium for Christmas day."

"Very clever. And I assume you're also offering your usual stuff."

Susa waved toward a pile of classy brochures touting the expertise of her crew. "We've caught up on all the stuff I let slide while I was working on Tera's site. But I could use a few new customers to make up for a couple who dropped out."

I gave her a commiserating smile. She still hadn't been paid for Tera's site, and she'd lost more than a couple of other clients because she hadn't been able to keep up with everyone else. "You want some coffee? They've got a pot set up in the break room."

"Maybe later. Believe it or not I've got more decorating to do." She picked up another snowflake and her glue gun.

I returned to my own booth to do some final checking. Everything seemed to be in place. I had a small pyramid of jam jars and a stack of empty bowls behind the counter ready to be filled with samples tomorrow morning. I also had a few boxes of crackers to place alongside the tasting bowls. They wouldn't be as great as Bianca's whole wheat, but they'd do, and they wouldn't dry out the way bread cubes would. I checked around the rest of the table with the nagging feeling I was missing something.

And then it hit me. Raspberry vinegar. I didn't have the raspberry vinegar set up. In fact, I was pretty sure I'd forgotten to bring the boxes of raspberry vinegar I'd had sitting next to the door ready to be loaded that morning.

I closed my eyes and resisted screaming in frustration.

I could wait until tomorrow and hope I had enough time to get the bottles of vinegar set up before the customers started flowing through the door. But I knew from experience the organizers would probably jump the gun and open early. Chances were I wouldn't have enough time to construct a nice display. I could call Uncle Mike and see if he could bring one of the boxes to the gym. But I knew he was out in the fields with Donnie. Even if he was within cell phone range, it would be an imposition to expect him to drop everything and bring me a case of vinegar.

Which left the only real alternative: I needed to drive to the farm and grab the vinegar. It would be a thirty-minute round trip, more or less, plus maybe fifteen minutes to get the vinegar. *Which means you'd better get started. It's your problem and your responsibility to fix it.*

I headed out toward my truck, careful not to run inside the gym since the floor was full of decorating paraphernalia but hitting a trot as soon as I was in the parking lot. Fortunately, there wasn't a lot of traffic on the county road, and I made it to the farm in a little over ten minutes. I grabbed the boxes of vinegar and hoisted them into the rear of the truck, slamming the cover shut over them.

I made it to the gym twenty minutes later, thanks to a super slow tractor moving from one field to another. It was around four, and a lot of the other people had already left. I carried a couple of boxes of vinegar to my booth and spent a few minutes arranging the bottles in a sort of artistic grouping. Design isn't my forte, but

I did the best I could. I started to carry the empty box to the truck but paused to think about it.

I'd been drinking coffee most of the afternoon, and I needed a rest stop before I took off again. I put the box in front of my booth and turned down the hall to the restroom.

Once I got away from the gymnasium, the halls were surprisingly deserted. School was out, and the students hadn't lingered. The janitorial staff must have already cleaned the halls around the gym because the lights had been turned out. The only illumination came from the winter sunlight leaking through the windows above the lockers lining the hall.

I quickened my pace slightly and turned in at the restroom. Fortunately, the lights were motion activated so I didn't have to pee in the darkness. I washed my hands and opened the door into the darkened hall again. Going from lights into dimness, it took my eyes a moment to adjust. The shadows had deepened during the time I was in the ladies room—it was a lot darker.

I was walking swiftly toward the booth area when I heard footsteps echoing in the empty halls behind me. At first they seemed distant, but then they were a lot closer. I increased my speed, not bothering to look back. It was probably a janitor or one of the other exhibitors, but I didn't want to take the time to check. Just then I felt like I needed to hurry toward the light.

I had almost reached the point where the hall turned toward the gym when a hand fastened onto my shoulder from behind. And the next thing I knew, I was slammed up against the lockers.

For a moment, I was so shocked I didn't respond. The person who'd pushed me seemed to be wearing a hoodie pulled up over his head and something across his face. I didn't recognize him.

As soon as I got over my shock, I blurted, "What the hell are you doing?" as I tried to pull away. I pushed hard against his chest, but I was off balance.

And then his hands moved quickly from my shoulders to my throat.

That, of course, got all my attention. Thank God, my flash of terror expressed itself as a need to fight with everything I could. I grabbed at his hands, trying to pry them loose as they tightened. I was having a hard time breathing, but by then adrenaline had kicked in.

I kicked out at him, trying to aim at his crotch as I dug my fingernails into his hands to force him to let go. I heard him curse, and then he let go long enough to slap me hard across my face. I saw stars, but I didn't stop. I turned my head enough to bite down on the thumb near my face.

"Bitch," he growled and slapped me again, but at last one of my feet connected with his knee.

He stepped away then, fumbling in his pocket, and I staggered away from him toward the gym, trying to run. My legs weren't working the way they should, and I was coughing from the pressure he'd put on my throat. He grabbed hold of one of my feet, pulling me to my knees. I looked back and saw something flash in his hand. And I knew I couldn't let him drag me into the darkness.

I yelled "Help" as loud as I could, yanking my foot free and scrambling toward the turn in the hall. I kept yelling, trying to get to my feet, to get away, to find someone. My voice was hoarse and my throat felt raw, but I made as much noise as possible.

"Roxy?" someone said.

I looked up and saw Susa standing at the turn in the hall, staring down at me.

"Get help," I yelled or tried to. My throat felt ragged and my yells were more like croaks. "Call the cops. He's trying to kill me."

"Who?" Susa asked.

I turned, but the man in the hoodie was gone. Footsteps echoed down the hall, but it was too late to go after him.

Not that I had any intention of doing that.

I collapsed onto all fours, trying to get my breath. And then I started to sob, great wracking gasps that made my throat hurt even worse.

Susa dropped to her knees beside me. "My God, Rox, what happened? Who did this?"

I shook my head. "I don't know. Call the cops, Suz. Just please call the cops."

The patrol car was there within ten minutes. By then Susa had helped me to the gym and found me a place to sit. I was surrounded by concerned exhibitors, none of whom could agree on what they should do. I was handed multiple cups of water and coffee and dampened paper towels. Some of the exhibitors checked the hall but said they couldn't find anybody, which didn't surprise me. A campus security guard showed up, but he seemed as helpless as everybody else. I was almost ready to give up and drive home when the doors across the gym burst open and Fowler strode in, followed by a couple of awed patrolmen.

He stopped when he saw me, his eyes widening. "Who did this?"

"I don't know. He had something over his face, and

he wore a hoodie covering his head. He was male. That's all I can say."

Fowler glanced around at the crowd, apparently noticing them for the first time. "Y'all can move on now. We'll take care of things."

Most of the people began to drift away. There weren't many left since it was so late in the afternoon. Maybe that's what the guy in the hall had been counting on.

"Go check the halls," Fowler said to the patrolmen. "See if there's anyone around who saw anything. Look for anyone who doesn't seem to belong here."

The patrolmen jogged off in opposite directions, covering the two halls off the gymnasium. I doubted they'd find anyone either way, but I was just as glad they weren't hovering around Fowler.

Susa maintained her position behind me, her hand on my shoulder. "I'm not moving. Roxy needs me."

Fowler raised his eyebrows, but he didn't make her leave, for which I was thankful. She was right—I did need her. He grabbed a folding chair from another booth and sat down beside me.

"Okay, tell me what happened. And then I'll take you home."

"I can drive myself," I mumbled.

"Nope. Nonnegotiable. So what happened?"

I told him. The footsteps in the hall, the hand grabbing my shoulder, the hands on my throat. And how I'd fought or tried to. I was pretty sure Susa had saved my life. If she hadn't come to see what I was yelling about... That wasn't something I wanted to consider. Although I was pretty sure I'd be dreaming about it that night.

"So you think he pulled a knife?" Fowler asked when I paused for breath.

"Maybe. He had something in his hand he'd pulled out of his pocket."

Fowler nodded. "Strangling someone is a lot harder than people think. He must have decided you were too tough to choke."

Susa gasped. "Geez, could you be any more insensitive? Someone just tried to kill her."

"Yeah, they did. My guess is it was a spur of the moment thing. He didn't think it through, and he sure as hell didn't understand what he was taking on when he went after Roxy. You gave as good as you got."

Susa's hands tightened on my shoulders. "Got that right."

"Can I go home now? I feel like I need to be home." What I really needed was Uncle Mike. And Herman. And Nate. I really needed Nate.

"Do you want to clean up some before you go?"

I hadn't thought about that. I probably looked pretty bad, given the amount of time I'd spent fighting and the amount of punishment I'd taken. But the thought of going to that restroom to wash my face made me tremble. I shook my head.

"Okay, don't take this the wrong way, but I need to take some pictures of you for evidence. And I need to take any tissue underneath your nails."

My shoulders tightened. I didn't want to get my picture taken when I was a wreck. And the thought I might have "tissue" from the guy under my nails turned my stomach. But that was stupid. When they caught the guy, they were going to need evidence of what he'd done. And I was the best evidence they had at the moment.

Fowler put a piece of paper on the table, then used his pocketknife to scrape my nails. I did my best not to look at what he collected and put in an evidence bag. Then I sat still while he took several shots with his cell phone. The only time it bothered me was when he had me raise my chin so he could take shots of the bruises on my neck.

"Son of a bitch," Susa muttered. "Lousy son of a bitch."

"I agree," Fowler said.

The patrolmen returned then. They hadn't found anybody in the halls except for a janitor who hadn't seen anything and was way too old and arthritic to have been my attacker. They did find an open door a short distance away from where I'd been attacked. The guy in the hoodie had apparently pushed his way out and taken off.

And one of the patrolmen had had the presence of mind to check a trash can near the open door. He held up a gray hoodie and what looked like a ski mask. "Was this what he was wearing?"

I nodded. "Looks like it."

Fowler sighed. "Put it down and go get an evidence bag. There might be some DNA." Unfortunately, some of that DNA would probably come from the patrolman who'd picked it up. He turned to me. "You need to go to the hospital to be checked out. You may have injuries you're not aware of."

I shook my head again. "I'm not injured. I just want to go home."

"Roxy..." he began.

"Please," I grated. "Please just let me go home." I

closed my eyes tight. I was a lot closer to the edge than I'd realized.

Fowler sighed after a moment. "Okay. This is against my better judgement, but okay."

"I can drive her to the farm," Susa said.

Fowler paused. "I want to talk to Mike."

"What about my truck?" I'd decided I was willing to be driven, since I felt way too shaky to drive myself.

"Leave it in the parking lot," Fowler said. "I'll tell patrol to keep an eye on it. They're going to be watching the school tonight anyway."

That seemed to settle everything, and I was more than ready to leave. Susa walked with us to Fowler's patrol car. "You want me to come with you?"

I shook my head. "No, no. I'll be okay. Uncle Mike will look after me." Uncle Mike would be worried enough as it was.

The drive to the farm was blessedly silent. I'd been a little afraid Fowler might want to ask me more questions, but he seemed content to concentrate on driving. I leaned my head against the window and tried my best to forget the past couple of hours.

Finally, we turned down the drive to my cabin. Fowler pulled up outside and turned to me. "Do you want to be here or up at the big house?"

"Here, I guess. Uncle Mike will come down here anyway."

Fowler stared up at the big house at the end of the drive. "Yeah, I want to talk to him. I need to ask you some more questions, so we can figure out who did this. But I'll wait until tomorrow, after you've had a chance to rest."

I started to nod then paused. "I'll be at Winter

Market tomorrow. Probably not much time to talk."

"You're going back to that gym tomorrow? Seriously?"

"It's the biggest sales day I'll have until the farmers market opens again in May. I can't afford to miss it."

"Maybe somebody else could run your booth. It would probably be best if you stayed home." Fowler looked incredulous.

"I can't stay home. And I don't want somebody else to run my booth. There'll be loads of people around. I'll be fine."

"I don't think…" Fowler began.

But at that point, Uncle Mike arrived and got a good look at my face. "Jesus H. Christ, Roxanne, what happened now?"

Chapter Twenty-One

Fowler gave Uncle Mike a quick summary of my afternoon, which I appreciated since I felt too tired to explain it myself. I climbed out of the car, but Uncle Mike insisted on helping me into the cabin, all the while muttering I should go up to the main house where Carmen could take care of me.

Right then I didn't want anyone to take care of me, even Carmen.

Fowler finally left after he and Uncle Mike had had a whispered conference probably concerning my plans for the Winter Market. Whatever. I was so tired all I wanted to do was stretch out. But I needed to check out what everybody else was so horrified about, so I stepped to the bathroom.

Once I got there, I stared at myself in the mirror, wondering if I could go to the Winter Market looking like this. One side of my face was a deep reddish purple from where I'd been slapped. It looked like I might get a black eye, although I might be able to prevent that with an ice pack. My upper lip was swollen and bloody, and my hair looked like I'd been rolling in dirt, which was close to the truth.

In short, I was a mess. I needed to call Nate, but I also needed to take a shower and swallow a dozen ibuprofen. I limped into the living room to get my cell phone.

"Who are you calling?" Uncle Mike asked.

"Nate. I need to let him know what happened."

"My guess is he already knows." He pointed out the window, and I saw Nate's car rolling down the drive at a speed that wasn't great for gravel.

"Okay, well, good," I mumbled.

Nate didn't bother knocking. He just marched in, then stood staring at me. "Ah, Rox," he said. And then he put his arms around me.

I wanted to cry on his shoulder, but I was afraid if I started I might not be able to stop. "I'm okay. Honest. I'm okay."

"Susa called. She told me what happened. This whole thing is nuts." He rubbed a hand down my back, which unfortunately reminded me I'd been slammed into some lockers.

"It is that." I pressed my face against his shoulder. "I was going to call you. I just got here."

"Why don't you sit down? I'll bring you a beer. Or maybe something stronger."

"I want a beer, and maybe some nachos or something. But I need to take a shower first. I really, really want to get out of these clothes." And probably burn them.

"Go ahead," Nate said. "I'll fix us something to eat. Mike went to get Herman."

I had a feeling Herman's reaction would be like Uncle Mike's, which meant I needed to get cleaned up before he got there. "Okay, I won't be long."

"Take as long as you want. Seriously. Stay in there until you feel up to facing us."

I gave him a quick hug. I needed to wash up before I tried any kissing. And even then, my lip might be a problem.

The shower revealed all sorts of bruises I hadn't known about. Actually, I'd known about them in the sense my body ached all over, but now I had confirmation. I only hoped the other guy was suffering too.

I paused to think about that. I'd dug my nails into his hands and bitten his thumb. And I'd kicked him hard in the knee, along with some other punches and kicks. With any luck, he should be having some problems himself. I wondered if he had a spouse or a live-in, someone who might notice those strange marks on his hands. If so, I hoped they'd remember when the news of the attack got around town, as I was sure it would.

When I finally emerged from my shower, cleaner and somewhat refreshed, Uncle Mike returned with Herman, who came toward me whimpering. "It's okay, Herm. I'm okay." I knelt down and rubbed his ears, while he licked my face and tried to put a paw on my shoulder.

Something smelled terrific and I glanced at the kitchen. Nate was chopping up a couple of tomatoes. "Nachos. Coming right up. Fortunately, Mike had tortilla chips."

"Wonderful. Just what I wanted." I grabbed a beer out of the refrigerator and sank down on the couch with Herman stretched out beside me on the floor. Uncle Mike looked as if he wanted to whisk me up to the big house and pack me in cotton. "Did you get a beer?"

He raised his bottle to show me.

"Good." That seemed to end the conversation. I took another deep swallow.

"I'm coming with you tomorrow," Uncle Mike said. "I'd take Herman, too, but they've got that no dogs policy in the high school gym."

"Yeah, they do." I wished they had a no over-protective uncles policy, too. Uncle Mike frequently glowered at my customers, which dampened sales. "We can talk about it tomorrow."

"No, Roxanne." Uncle Mike's jaw was clenched. "I'm not letting you go there by yourself."

"She won't be by herself." Nate carried a platter so loaded with nachos I was afraid some would go skating across the room. "I'll take her." He set the platter on the coffee table, then went for plates and napkins.

"You have to work," I pointed out.

"I've already discussed it with Mom. Bobby and Coco can cover both meals. I'll work Sunday brunch."

"I'm not sure what you two think is going to happen to me. The Winter Market is always packed. No chance for somebody to jump me. The only reason this guy tried it today was because I was in a deserted area. Fowler thought it was probably a spur of the moment thing. Nobody would try to do something like that in the midst of hundreds of people."

Uncle Mike and Nate both looked unimpressed. I concentrated on the nachos, which were terrific.

"You don't know what this guy is capable of," Nate said, "because you don't know who he is. He might be a total nutjob, which could mean he'd come after you no matter who's around. He's got a reason to resent you now. You got away."

I admit—that idea sent a chill down my spine. But I wasn't giving in. "I don't think he's a nutjob. He ran away when Susa came down the hall; he cares about being seen. As long as I'm surrounded by people, I should be fine."

"What about when you have to go to the truck to get another case of jam? What about when you need to take a bio break? Hell, what about when you get there bright and early in the morning, or when you leave after it gets dark in the afternoon? He doesn't seem like the kind of asshole who's scared off easily." Uncle Mike regarded me as he munched another nacho.

"Okay, maybe you've both got a point. You can take it in shifts. Uncle Mike can be there in the morning and Nate can be there in the afternoon. That way I won't be screwing up the café's schedule and neither of you will have to be there all day."

"Unlike you." Uncle Mike sniffed. "I'll be down here at seven tomorrow morning. The chief said you left your truck at the high school, so I'll drive you down. And I'll pick up your jam during the morning when you need it. And…"

I think he was trying to figure out a way to accompany me to the restroom. I decided to nip that in the bud. "That'll be fine, thanks."

"Okay, I'm glad we got that settled." He pushed himself to his feet. "Now Nate's here, I'll go home. You're staying, right?"

"Right." Nate nodded emphatically.

"Good enough. Great nachos. See you in the morning. Come on, Herman." He and his faithful hound headed out my door.

Nate grabbed a nacho of his own, then sat down beside me. "I can do the whole day, Rox. It's okay. Bobby and Coco won't mind."

"I'll mind. I don't want you to have to sit there in

my booth all day and be bored to tears. Although I'll be delighted to have you for the after-lunch shift."

"Okay. I'll be there as soon as lunch is over. I might even bring Coco so she can take you to the restroom when you need to go."

"Trust me, I can handle that. I've been going to the restroom by myself since I was three or so." But I was glad to know I'd have company at the booth tomorrow.

We spent the evening watching British comedies on Britbox and carefully avoiding any discussion of the elephant in the room. But after a while, I noticed Nate seemed distracted, staring at the TV without paying attention.

Finally I turned to him. "Okay, what's on your mind?"

He blew out a long breath, then turned to look at me. "This has got to be related to Tera Bloomfield's murder, right?"

I nodded. "Most likely. Unless the guy was some random attacker."

"So the question is, why would anybody attack you over that? You couldn't have seen anything. You were in the kitchen almost all night. Hell, I'm more likely to have seen something sketchy than you were."

"Did you see something sketchy?"

"You know what it was like. Crazy. We were working every minute. None of us had time to notice anything except whether they were ready for the next course."

"Right. The only people I saw besides you were Alex and Siggi." I paused. In considering all the other stuff, I'd forgotten all about the two people who'd been in the kitchen with us.

And who'd both handled the food.

Nate frowned. "Could Alex have been the guy in the hall today?"

"Well, it sure as hell wasn't Siggi. I'm a head taller than she is in my bare feet." That was meant to be a joke, but it didn't feel funny. Could Alex have attacked me? I tried to think back, which made my whole body tense.

Nate put his arm around my shoulders, pulling me close. "I'm sorry, babe. Just let it go. I shouldn't have brought it up."

"No, I need to think about it. And I need to talk about it. If I don't I'll probably end up dreaming about it, and that'll be worse." I'd probably end up dreaming about it anyway. But I did need to go over what had happened, if only to get my own thoughts straight.

Nate sighed. "Okay, then. Could Alex have been the one who attacked you this afternoon?"

I thought about Alex and Siggi carrying plates in and out of the kitchen. "He might be the right size. But I couldn't see this guy well. His head and his face were covered."

"How strong was he?"

I thought about those hands on my throat and shuddered. Nate pulled me against his chest. "It's okay, babe."

It wasn't. But I needed to work through my feelings so I could move beyond them. "The guy who grabbed me was fairly strong, but not strong enough. When he tried to choke me, I got my hands on his wrists and dug in my nails until he let go. If he'd been stronger, I wouldn't have been able to do that."

My voice trembled on the last few words, and Nate

kissed my hair. I dropped my head onto his chest again.

"Did you tell Fowler all that?"

I nodded. "He even cleaned under my fingernails in case I had some of the guy's skin." My stomach churned a little over that, but I ignored it.

"Good. Maybe they can get some DNA. And I hope he's checking all the suspects in Tera's murder to see if they've got scratches on their wrists."

"Right." I paused. "I bit him, too, on his thumb. But I may not have broken the skin."

Nate gave me a shaky grin. "If attacking you was a spur of the moment idea, I'll bet he's sorry he tried it. You showed him he shouldn't take on a kickass woman."

I blew out a long breath. "I don't feel kickass right now. I'm just glad I got away from him."

"I'm glad, too. I'd like to show you how glad I am, if you're up to it."

I paused to think. Was I up to it? I was pretty battered, and the painkiller I'd taken was making me a little woozy.

"If we can take it easy. I've got a banged-up lip and some other bruises to deal with."

"We can take it however you want it. Easy suits me fine." He stood up, reaching a hand to help me to my feet. "Come on, sweetheart. Let's get you to bed."

I stood up beside him and then let him lead me down the hall to the bedroom. His plan sounded great to me. I couldn't think of a better way to chase the bogey man away.

At least until tomorrow when the bogey man might show up to see if I recognized him. I hoped I would. I didn't want to take the risk of running into him again some other dark night.

Chapter Twenty-Two

Nate left early the next morning, so he could get to the café to cook breakfast. I'd slept all night in his arms, and it seemed to help. When the nightmares came—as we both knew they would—he was there to hold me, and gradually I moved into a deep sleep with no dreams to speak of.

Uncle Mike showed up at seven as promised. He sat sipping his coffee as I tried to decide what to do about my face. Putting makeup over my bruises made me look like a clown, plus the makeup didn't cover the bruises that well. Fortunately, I hadn't developed the black eye I'd feared, but I wouldn't be wearing dark eye shadow. In the end, I decided not to try covering anything up. Instead I put on some light eye makeup and combed my hair down on my shoulders so it covered part of my cheeks.

If little kids pointed and stared, I'd stare right back.

The parking lot at the gym was already partly full at eight-fifteen, at least the section toward the front where the exhibitors had their cars. My truck was still where I'd left it. Before going inside, I opened the cover and checked my extra cases to see if they'd been tampered with, but they looked okay.

I took a deep breath and followed Uncle Mike into the gym, carrying the cooler with the pumpkin butter.

I hadn't expected to have much reaction when I got

inside. I'm not the dramatic type. I just go with the flow. But the flow that Saturday was like a set of Class Five rapids.

My stomach dropped as I stepped into the room. Suddenly I remembered everything that had happened to me. I remembered staggering into the gym, being surrounded by anxious people all trying to help, and then seeing Fowler and his men striding through like the Seventh Cavalry. *Can I do this? Do I want to do this?*

The answer to the second question was a definite yes. The answer to the first was a little more iffy. Uncle Mike glanced at me, then extended his hand. "Show me where your booth is, Roxanne."

I took his hand, and the warmth of his palm took some of the chill off my soul. I guided him through the crowd of exhibitors to my booth at the side.

He stood for a moment, studying my setup. "Not bad," he said finally. "*Mmm for the Holidays.* Cute."

"Yeah, I like it." I fiddled around a little more with the arrangement of bottles and jars, putting a couple of jars of pumpkin butter in place, while Uncle Mike went off to find an extra chair. I checked my watch. The doors would open in another ten minutes, and I decided I was ready for them. Or even if I wasn't, I was ready to give it my very best shot.

Saturday morning at the market was usually family time—parents and kids looking for special Christmas stuff. I filled my sample bowls then hid the half-empty jars in a box on the floor, knowing they'd probably need refilling within the first twenty minutes. Moms and kids flowed by, some of them people I vaguely remembered from the summer farmers market. I got a few curious glances but nothing like the kind of horrified fascination I'd pictured. A lot of people tried the pumpkin butter, and the reactions were the same as the ones at Bianca's. I sold three jars quickly, but I also had people who surreptitiously dropped the remains of their cracker and pumpkin butter into the nearest trash can.

Oh, well. I'd only brought two cases. I still hoped I'd get enough people to sell out.

Several customers asked me about the raspberry vinegar. I hadn't put any out to taste because it's tough to taste vinegar straight. People were intrigued by the shrub recipe, and I sold more vinegar than pumpkin butter. About what I'd expected.

And I sold a lot of my standard jams, usually in multiples. Uncle Mike returned about ten minutes after the doors opened, carrying a folding chair. Getting him behind the table required some shifting around, which I tried to do without upsetting the people in the booth next door, a Palisade winery I didn't recognize.

Uncle Mike had brought his copy of the Shavano paper, along with a couple of magazines, and he'd picked up a cup of coffee from the break room. He moved his chair to the rear of the booth so he was out of my way, and I ignored him, hoping he'd concentrate on his reading rather than glowering at people.

Midway through the morning, I saw a familiar face. Marcus Jordan paused to check out the pumpkin butter, trying a minute sample on a cracker. "That's different."

"I think it's kind of a love it or hate it thing," I said, although I'd sold a little over a half case so far.

Marcus stared meditatively at the ceiling. "Be nice

with pork. Or ham. You might even be able to do something with smoked turkey. Guess I'll take a jar to Sara to see what she can do with it."

I had a sneaking suspicion Sara would trash it, but that wasn't my problem. I found myself looking at his hands, even though I knew there was absolutely no way Marcus was involved in Tera's murder. Predictably, I saw nothing like the marks of my nails on his wrists. I took his money and smiled him on his way.

Susa stopped by around eleven. "How's it going?"

Behind me, Uncle Mike put down his paper and leaned forward to give her a hug. Susa grinned at us both, her smile fading a little when she saw my bruises.

"It's been busy," I said quickly, hoping to stave off any expressions of outrage. "Better than last year, I think."

"I wasn't here last year, but we're doing okay. We've sold a lot of Christmas installation packages, and I've given away a lot of pamphlets about everything else. Bianca's got her booth a little down from me, and she's been sending me referrals all morning, bless her heart."

"Good for her."

"Yeah, I've got to get back. Kip's on his own and Lord knows what he'll agree to. Talk to you later." She turned and walked toward the main entrance where her booth was located.

"What can she sell?" Uncle Mike asked.

"A lot of services take part in the Winter Market, too. They're trying to raise awareness and get people interested in what they offer. We've got some cell phone companies, home repair contractors, insurance agencies, day spas. They're trying to pass out information about what they do."

"Insurance agencies. Like Collegiate Peaks? Tony Aldo?"

My shoulders tensed, but I shifted to loosen them. "I guess. I don't even know what Tony Aldo looks like."

"Big guy. Beefy. Played football in college."

Right. Like my attacker but not exactly. I didn't think the guy who'd had his hands around my throat was that strong. Fortunately.

I sold a few more jars of pumpkin butter, and a lot more raspberry vinegar. I was glad I had another case in the truck, but I'd probably sell all I'd made by the end of the weekend. I might do another batch before Christmas just so I'd have some to offer on the website.

"Hey, Roxy," someone said brightly. I glanced up to see Siggi, the bartender from Tera's party, dipping a cracker into my raspberry jam.

"Hey, yourself." I kept my voice casual. "How's it going?"

"Fine. I'm over at the Magpie Grill now, working the bar from five until closing."

"That's a nice restaurant. Gets a lot of customers." I didn't suspect Siggi of anything she was way too short to have been my attacker, and she'd seemed honestly distraught the night of the dinner. Still, I found myself checking her wrists. They were absolutely clean.

"Yeah, it's a living. I may move on after Christmas. Go up to Breckenridge or Aspen for the ski season. Have you seen Alex lately?"

"Alex? No. Not since the...dinner." When they'd both walked out and left Nate and me to deal with the police. "Is he still in town?"

"Far as I know. Well, good to see you." Siggi gave me another bright smile and dived into the moving crowd.

"Who was that?" Uncle Mike asked.

"She's a bartender. She was working at Tera's the night everything went sideways."

"Oh." Uncle Mike craned his neck, trying to see Siggi in the crowd.

After that I found myself watching the people who came by a little more closely. Would Alex show up? Would it mean anything if he didn't? I wasn't even sure he was still in Shavano, although the chief might have told him to stick around.

A few minutes later, I saw another vaguely familiar face, although this one was easier to place: Tom Everett, the banker. He smiled at me. "Hey there. Got any of that peach jam with the chilies?"

"Pepper peach? Sure." I reached into the jars on the table and handed him one.

As he took it from me, I noticed a nasty scratch along the back of his hand. My shoulders tensed again, although I was pretty sure the damage I'd done to my attacker had been to the wrists and thumb, not the back of his hand. "That looks painful."

His grin turned rueful. "Yeah. My own stupid fault. I reached under a barbed wire fence instead of over it."

"Ouch." The scratch looked like one you could get from barbed wire. Which didn't necessarily mean that was how he got it, of course. Tom set down his jar of pepper peach to try some of the pumpkin butter. He paused, chewing.

"That's…unique," he said.

"It's kind of a specialized taste. I won't be

offended if you pitch it."

He grinned at me. "Okay. But I'll take the pepper peach and a bottle of the raspberry vinegar. My wife will probably love it when she gets back from visiting our daughter."

I was aware of Uncle Mike looming at my shoulder. "Have you met my uncle, Mike Constantine?"

"Sure. We're in the Merchants Association together, right?" Tom extended his hand, and Uncle Mike shook it. He wasn't smiling but he wasn't snarling either. "Good to see you."

"Just here to support my niece."

I might have been the only one who heard it, but he sounded a little like a cop getting ready to say *move along*. I resisted standing on his toes.

Tom was oblivious to the undercurrents. "Your niece makes some of the best jam I've ever tasted."

I handed him a bag with the jam and the vinegar, and he smiled again. "Talk to you later, Roxy."

"Sure." I wasn't sure what we were going to talk about, but it seemed friendly.

Uncle Mike watched him walk away. "You think it was him?"

I shook my head emphatically. "No. He didn't have any marks on his wrists, and he's the wrong size."

"Had that scratch on his hand, though."

"I didn't touch the back of the guy's hand. It wasn't him, Uncle Mike."

Uncle Mike raised his eyebrows but returned to his newspaper.

Nothing much happened for an hour or so after that. I sent Uncle Mike out to the truck to get more jam and vinegar. I sold the rest of the pepper peach I'd brought with me. Several people took the cards that had my website address, which meant they might order from me in the future.

Uncle Mike brought me a burrito for lunch from one of the food stands. I munched between selling jam and pushing pumpkin butter. If I could sell the last two jars, I'd be well set up to clear it out on Sunday afternoon. At the moment, I was rating the pumpkin butter a qualified success. Not so successful I'd try it again, but it did give me some ideas for the future.

Nate walked in at two, looking fairly well put together for a guy who'd gotten up at five and worked two meal shifts since then. "How's it going?"

"Fine. Sold out pepper peach, down to the last few jars of raspberry. Vinegar's selling well. Even the pumpkin butter is moving."

Uncle Mike pushed to his feet. "Everything quiet so far. Everett came by, but Rox said he was clean."

I rolled my eyes. "He definitely didn't have any nail marks, and I doubt the one who does is going to be here. If I were him, I'd be lying low."

Uncle Mike gave me a severe look. "You can't count on that, Roxanne. You need to be on your guard. You never know who's likely to show up here."

I wished I could say he was wrong. "Okay. I'll keep my eyes open for anything sketchy."

"And I'll be checking everybody out," Nate said. "That's my primary purpose here."

Uncle Mike nodded at us both. "If anything happens or you need any help, give me a call."

The flow of customers slowed a bit after lunch. The families had taken off to watch football or go on to other errands, so we were down to couples and groups of friends who'd decided to spend a Saturday afternoon checking out the pre-Christmas goodies. Fortunately for me, they were more adventurous in their tastes, and I sold off the last of the pumpkin butter, along with the raspberry vinegar. I began to wonder if I'd sell out of everything and have to close early. I could have sent Nate out to the truck to grab a few more boxes, but I didn't want to cut into my Sunday supplies.

And I didn't particularly want to be sitting there alone.

A few minutes later, I saw another familiar face. "Hey, y'all," Alex said, "just like old times."

His smile was half-hearted, like he hadn't expected to see us again. I hadn't expected to see him either, but as long as he was there, I could take advantage.

"Have some peach jam." I motioned toward the sample bowl. "I didn't know if you were still around Shavano. Siggi thought you'd left."

"Nope. I'm still waiting tables at High Country. I may take off in a couple of months, though. I think I'm ready to move on." He reached for a cracker, dipping it into the peach jam, and I realized he was wearing gloves.

There was nothing suspicious about that. The temperature was still in the forties outside, and most people were wearing winter coats. And they were nice leather driving gloves, the kind you could wear indoors without looking weird. Still, it gave me a quick chill.

Nate leaned forward, extending his hand. "Good to see you again, Alex."

I watched to see whether Alex would take off his gloves. After a moment's pause he shook Nate's hand. Without removing his glove. "Likewise. Good jam.

Hope you sell out." He turned and walked down the corridor to the other booths.

"Well, damn." I rubbed my hands across my face. Had Alex been wearing gloves to conceal the marks of my teeth and nails? Or was he just cold?

"What do you think?" Nate asked.

"I don't know. He's the right size, but that's about all I can tell you. It wasn't like we had a conversation."

Nate frowned as he watched Alex's retreating back. "Did Alex seem like the type to brazen it out if he attacked you?"

"I don't even know what that type would look like." I slumped in my chair. "I think I'm more tired than I realized."

Nate rubbed my back. "Why don't you go home? I can close up here when the market is done for the day."

"I'll stay until I sell out. But I'm not going to worry about getting refills. When we're out, that's it."

"Sounds sensible. Do you want to come over to my place? We can skip brunch tomorrow and sleep in. Or you can, and I'll go take care of the flattop."

"That sounds good. I need to be here by eleven tomorrow morning." The feeling of his hand on my back was almost mesmerizing. I closed my eyes, leaning my head forward so he could reach my neck. In another few minutes, I could fall asleep.

"Afternoon, all. How's the jam business?"

My eyes snapped open to see Fowler leaning negligently on my counter.

Chapter Twenty-Three

I sighed as Nate dropped his hand from my back. "I'm doing okay. How's the police business? Catch any murderers?"

Fowler gave me a half-smile. "Not yet. Anybody suspicious been hanging around here?"

I glanced at Nate, then shook my head. "No more than usual, I guess. I can clear Tom Everett—he stopped by to buy some jam and his wrists didn't have any claw marks."

Fowler nodded absently. "That's helpful. Have you seen any of the other people who were at Bloomfield's that night."

"Alex the waiter stopped by, but he was wearing gloves. I couldn't tell anything one way or the other."

"Okay, I'll see if one of my men can find him here and check him out." Fowler scanned the room again. "How about Tony Aldo?"

"I don't even know who he is. I can't see a total stranger trying to kill me, although I guess it's possible."

"It's possible. If you're curious, that's him over there." He nodded toward a couple of men at the end of the row. One of them fit Uncle Mike's description of Aldo as a former football player—thick through the chest and gut, but he looked like it had been a while since he'd been on the field.

"I don't suppose you recognize him," Fowler said.

"I may have seen him at Tera's, but I don't remember him. And I'm pretty sure I haven't seen him since."

Fowler nodded. "Okay. Who's left?"

"I guess there's Fred Hoekstra. I might have seen him sometime today. It's hard to say with the crowds, but I think he sidled by." I tried to remember if he'd seemed to be the right size to be my attacker, but it was hard to tell in the crowd.

"He's here," Fowler said. "In fact, he's right over there."

I craned my neck to see around him. Fred Hoekstra was standing in front of one of the winery booths, sipping something from a plastic cup and talking to the man standing next to him. Like Alex, he was wearing gloves.

"What do you think?" Nate murmured.

I sighed. "I don't know. Maybe he's the right size. I guess he's as tall as I am. It's hard to tell unless I'm standing next to him."

Fowler paused, and I was afraid he might ask me to go stand next to Hoekstra. Nate sold a couple of jars of peach jam as I stared. After a moment Hoekstra put the plastic cup down, and I noticed something. His fingers were curved around the cup but his thumb stuck straight out.

I leaned forward, watching him more closely.

The woman behind the booth poured him another sample of wine. Hoekstra reached for it, then paused and switched hands. He wrapped the fingers and thumb of his left hand around the cup and tasted. The fingers of his right hand were slightly clenched, but he held the thumb straight out.

As if it hurt to bend it.

My shoulders pulled tight, and my hands drew into fists. "Son of a bitch," I whispered.

Nate glanced at me, frowning. "What?"

"His thumb. He can't bend his right thumb."

Fowler pushed himself upright, staring at Hoekstra's hand. "That the one you bit?"

"Yes, sir," I said. "I do believe it is."

Fowler started to work his way through the crowd, careful not to cause any commotion. Nate stepped from behind the booth to stand beside me. Both of us gave Hoekstra our undivided attention.

Fowler was drawing closer to the wine booth when Hoekstra looked up and saw him. His expression shifted from a grin to something more guarded. Fowler gave him a smile that wasn't much more than a few stretched muscles. He was almost next to him by then, and he looked like he was drawing himself up to his full height. Hoekstra tensed, turning away from the man who was talking to him to place his cup on the counter.

And then he ran, hitting Fowler so hard with his shoulder he staggered into the winery booth, catching hold of the front strut to keep from falling. The people around Hoekstra started in amazement, and someone screamed as he pushed bodies out of his way in his rush toward the exit.

He was running straight for my booth, although I doubt he was aware of it. His head was down, and he was plowing through the crowd, looking like another former football player with a lot more determination and a lot less flab than Aldo. Another minute and he'd be to the main entrance and out into the parking lot, although I didn't know where he thought he could go.

And then abruptly he hit the floor in front of my booth, face first.

Nate was on top of him almost before I was aware he'd stepped away from the booth. I didn't know for sure what he'd done to bring Hoekstra down, only that it had worked. He put his knee in the middle of Hoekstra's back to hold him against the floor and leaned down so only Hoekstra could hear him. Well, Hoekstra and me, because I was kneeling beside him by then.

"Lie still, you bastard," Nate said. "You tried to kill the woman I love, and I will wring your freakin' neck with pleasure."

I stared at him, wide-eyed and open-mouthed. I'd never had a second-hand declaration of love before. Hell, I'd never had a *first-hand* declaration of love.

A moment later, Fowler was leaning over Nate, a pair of handcuffs in his hand. "Thanks, Robicheaux, I'll take it from here."

Nate moved aside and Fowler grabbed Hoekstra's wrists, clicking the handcuffs into place. Then he pulled him to his feet. Hoekstra looked around the room a little wildly, then caught sight of me. If looks could kill, I would probably have been a pile of rubble.

I was still pretty confused. What had I done to earn that kind of hatred?

"Fred Hoekstra, you are under arrest for attempted assault, with other charges to be determined later." Fowler pushed him forward none too gently, and I heard him repeating the Miranda rights as they moved through the wide-eyed crowd.

I put my hand on Nate's shoulder. "Are you okay?"

"I'm fine. Better than fine. I got to see that son of a bitch in handcuffs. That's going to make my week." He looked up at me and smiled.

All kinds of questions racketed around my brain. I still had no idea why Fred Hoekstra wanted to kill me. I wasn't sure he was the one who'd killed Tera, although that seemed likely. If that was true, then that was another question I needed answered: Why kill her? And what did I have to do with it? I was just the cook, for Pete's sake.

But I had a hard time thinking about any of that. Nate had said he loved me. He hadn't said it *to* me, but he'd said it.

Nate was beginning to look a little concerned. "How about you? Are you okay?"

I nodded. "Sure. I didn't do anything except stand here." And then I sat down abruptly. Because as it turned out, I wasn't okay. I was pretty shaken up. It was one thing to be attacked by an unknown person, but it was something else to be attacked by someone you knew, to see something like hatred in his eyes, and to have no idea why he felt that way.

Nate knelt beside me, holding my hand. "It's not your fault, babe. You know that, right?"

I nodded, suddenly not at all sure I could talk without bursting into tears. "I need to go home," I managed finally. "Uncle Mike might hear about this from one of his friends, and I need to get there and talk to him before he does."

"Right, I can see that." Nate stood up, offering me his hand. "I can stay here and run the booth until you sell out."

I shook my head. "No. Let's just pack up and go. I

don't have much left to sell, and it's almost closing time anyway."

It was actually about an hour before closing, but I didn't want to think about it anymore. And I wanted Nate with me, wherever I went.

We packed up the few remaining jars of jam and my cash box and walked out. I decided to leave my truck in the parking lot for another night rather than try to drive in my current state. Uncle Mike could help me bring the rest of my jam tomorrow. Not that I couldn't have driven, mind you, but, well, I didn't want to.

"So I guess that's it," I said, as Nate pulled out of the parking lot. "Hoekstra killed Tera with the ipecac and then decided to kill me for reasons unknown."

Nate frowned, turning onto the highway toward the farm. "I guess. Although if he poisoned the port, why did he drink it himself? He had to know it would make him sick."

"You'd think so." I leaned my head against the seat. "And did he know the ipecac would kill her, or did he just mean to make her sick as some kind of practical joke?"

"Lousy kind of practical joker if he got caught up in it, too."

We didn't say much more, but I still had a whole heap of questions. A lot more questions than answers.

Chapter Twenty-Four

Uncle Mike had a few questions of his own, after we'd explained what had happened and he'd had a chance to fulminate a little. He hadn't taken the news about Hoekstra well. "Why would he try to kill you, Roxanne? Did you even talk to him?"

"Not that night. The only time I've ever spoken to him was when I walked by his house and told him his garden looked nice. So far as I know, anyway."

"So was he crazy?" Uncle Mike asked. "Did he get fixated on you or something?"

I shuddered a little at the thought of Fred Hoekstra becoming my stalker. "I don't know. Maybe Fowler will tell us after he's had a chance to question him."

"Assuming Hoekstra feels like telling anybody anything," Uncle Mike said darkly. "If he's crazy, he may clam up."

"I don't think he's crazy. He'll probably have some high-powered legal help who'll tell him to keep quiet, though. I mean, if he owns the Blankenship house, he must be rich. And maybe he knew Tera from her time in Denver since he moved here from there and she invited him to her house. Maybe he was one of the people she cheated. Or maybe they had some other dealings he wanted her not to tell anyone about."

"Why don't you think he's nuts?" Uncle Mike asked.

"He probably had a motive to kill her. It wasn't just some crazy impulse."

"That makes sense," Nate said. "Whoever killed her had to have done some advance planning, at least enough to bring the ipecac to her house and put it in her port. But that doesn't explain why he went after you. Unless he thought you were involved with Tera's newest venture, which makes no sense at all."

"Maybe he thought I was up to something else with Tera."

Nate shook his head. "You hardly knew her. He would never have seen you together before that night."

I grimaced. "Okay, there's no obvious reason for him to attack me. But he did. Could we order pizza?"

Uncle Mike flushed, then cleared his throat. "Well, actually I've got a pizza on the way."

"Delivery?"

"A dinner guest." He stared out the front window. "She's bringing pizza."

"Susa?" Nate looked confused, but then the penny dropped. His eyes widened. "Mom?"

"We thought you'd be back in town. But I called her and asked her to bring two pizzas instead of one."

"We can go back," Nate said. "If we take Roxy's jam with us, we can go to my place and then I can take her to the gym tomorrow."

"Too late." Uncle Mike gave him a sour grin as Madge's car pulled up outside the cabin.

When Madge walked in, Herman padded over to her as if she were an old friend, nudging her hand until she petted him. She grinned. "Hello, there, Herman. I should have brought you a bone."

Okay, so Madge had been here before.

She was clearly determined this situation wasn't going to be awkward. Not if she had anything to say about it. She hugged me and patted my cheek, after expressing her outrage about what Fred Hoekstra had done to my poor face. Then she had Nate go to the car and get the two large Fratelli's pizza boxes. Soon we were far too busy finding plates and napkins and wine and wineglasses to think about how weird it was that Nate's mom and my surrogate dad were having dinner together along with us in my jam-making cabin.

Madge had us go through the story again so she could get the details she hadn't gotten from Uncle Mike. She didn't have any better explanations to offer than we'd already come up with, though. "Fred Hoekstra hasn't even been in town that long. I mean, I've seen him a couple of times. But his wife just got here a week or so ago. She wasn't happy about moving. They held onto their house in Denver."

"Maybe they're just using the Shavano place as a vacation house," Nate suggested.

"The Blankenship house?" Madge raised her eyebrows. "That thing has at least nine bedrooms. And a pool. And a greenhouse. Some vacation place."

"Lifestyles of the rich and larcenous?" Nate grinned at his mom, who grinned back.

"It still doesn't make any sense, but I'm not going to worry about it," I said. "Maybe Fowler will tell us what Hoekstra's motive was, assuming he ever finds out."

"I'm sure he'll do his best," Madge said. "He's a nice man."

Nate looked like he was gritting his teeth, but he didn't say anything.

After dinner, Madge insisted on helping me load the dishwasher, while Nate and Uncle Mike cleared the table. When we walked into the living room, Uncle Mike was leaning against the front door jamb, looking deceptively casual. "Want to see the main house, Madge?"

Madge's cheeks flushed, but her smile was carefully calibrated. "Why, yes. That sounds nice. Let's drive my car up there so I won't be blocking Roxy's door."

Her car wasn't anywhere near my door, but I understood why she didn't want to leave her car out front where Nate and I could keep track of her comings and goings. Nate watched his mother's car turn up the road to the Uncle Mike's house, looking bemused. "I guess I need to start thinking of my mom as a person with a private life."

"Yeah. She's a big girl now. And he's a big boy." Like Nate, I was feeling a little unsettled. If Uncle Mike had had other girlfriends—and I was certain that he had—I hadn't known about them. On the other hand, I really liked Madge. They could both do a lot worse.

Nate seemed to share my opinion. "I like Mike a lot. He's a great guy."

"He is. And Madge is wonderful."

"She is." Nate gave me a rueful smile. "So why does this feel so weird?"

"Because we're letting ourselves think about stuff that's none of our business." I stepped forward, pulling the curtains across the main window. "Okay, now we'll have no idea who's where. So we can relax and enjoy ourselves."

"That," said Nate, "sounds like a very good idea."

He started toward me just as the phone rang. I considered letting it go to voice mail, but there were several people I needed to hear from, with Fowler at the top of the list.

It wasn't Fowler, though, it was Susa. "I just heard they picked up Hoekstra. Does that take care of everything, then?"

I felt guilty about not calling her. I'd gotten swept away with dinner and Madge and everything. I settled into my chair. "Yeah, Hoekstra's under arrest for attacking me. I assume that means he was also the one who killed Tera, but I don't know for sure."

Of course, Susa needed to know if Tera's killer had been found since she was one of several people who'd be freed from suspicion if he was.

"I just wanted some confirmation. Is Nate there?"

"Yep."

"Then I won't keep you. At least both of us can sleep easier tonight."

"That we can." But I reflected I'd sleep a lot easier if I knew exactly why Fred Hoekstra thought I needed to be killed.

I went into town with Nate the next morning. He had to cook brunch at the café, and I had to open my booth at the gym for the afternoon sales. Neither of us checked the main house to see if Madge's car was still there. Which is to say, both of us checked, but Madge had either gone home or she'd parked where we couldn't see.

Brunch didn't start until ten, and Nate figured he could be a few minutes late. He helped me unload my cases of jam and vinegar and stack them under the counter. I also had a half case of pumpkin butter packed in the cooler.

I washed out my sample bowls in the ladies room, telling myself I had no reason to be nervous about being there. A lot more people were around, along with a lot more traffic in and out of the ladies room. Still, I found myself checking all sides, including behind me, as I walked down the hall to the gym. It would take me a while to get back on my game when it came to walking around on my own, even in places I knew were safe. And when I thought about that, about the fact I was nervous even when I didn't need to be, I wished Nate had punched Fred Hoekstra a little harder.

The Sunday crowds were a mixture of families and couples, mostly people looking for Christmas gifts. I sold out of raspberry vinegar fairly quickly, although the pumpkin butter was moving more slowly. A few people wanted to talk about Fred Hoekstra, but I didn't have a lot to say. Most wanted to know why he'd gone after me and were disappointed when I had to admit I didn't know.

Nate had told me he'd come over after he finished with brunch, but that probably meant two or three in the afternoon since he had to clean up and do a little prep work for Tuesday. I didn't mind. I hadn't been alone at my booth since I'd set up on Thursday, and I wanted to enjoy it a little. Also I wanted to prove I didn't need a guard. I was still capable of looking after myself as I usually did.

I told myself I felt fine, and I mostly believed it.

Several people who'd bought my stuff at the summer farmers market stopped by to stock up on peach and raspberry jams. Pepper peach had a loyal following, too, and I sold out the two cases I'd brought with me within a couple of hours. Of course, now I could tell people who wanted pepper peach or any of the other flavors that they could order more on my website. Thank you, Susa.

Susa herself showed up around twelve thirty. "Carly's running the booth with me today. We've basically sold out of our Christmas installation specials because we don't have enough people to cover the demand. If I'd realized it was going to be so popular, I would have hired a few high school computer whizzes as temps. I may still do that. Carly and Kip both think we should add electronics installation as one of our services."

"Sit down. You can help me sell what jam I have left."

"Still trying to get rid of the pumpkin butter?" Susa took the same chair Nate and Uncle Mike had used.

"It's developed a following," I said a little defensively. "I've only got three jars left."

"You'll sell it all. People know your stuff is quality." Susa leaned back in her chair, half closing her eyes. "I shouldn't have come in today. I was out with Wilson until three."

Wilson Krebs was Susa's latest conquest. He was a nice enough guy, although he seemed a little dim to me, maybe because I was dazzled by his muscles. Susa had recovered from any heartbreak at losing Sean to Tera. Assuming that heartbreak had ever existed. "Where did you go?"

"His place." Susa gave me a lazy smile, and I found myself grinning back.

Someone cleared his throat, and I turned to the front of the booth a little guiltily. I was supposed to be selling jam, after all.

Phil Duncan, the real estate magnate, stood with his legs wide apart, regarding me with a guarded expression. He was a relatively small man, given his importance around town. His white hair was close cropped, and he wore aviator sunglasses that concealed his eyes. I happened to know his massive parka retailed for a couple thousand. Unfortunately, it looked as if his parka was swallowing him whole.

"Hi, can I help you?" I'd never spoken to Duncan before, not even at Tera's.

Duncan surveyed the jars of jam I had arrayed in front of me, all the varieties I had left. "Pumpkin butter?" He raised an eyebrow.

"It's a specialty product. Made for the holidays." I gave him my professional smile. "An unusual taste. Try a sample?" I nodded at the sample bowl.

Duncan picked up a cracker and took a minuscule dip of pumpkin butter. He chewed slowly, as if he was weighing the relative merits of the pumpkin butter as his morning spread of choice. "Unique," he said finally.

"Thanks."

He looked at Susa for a long moment, and she gave him a slightly uncertain smile. Then he looked at me again. "I'm in the market for some particular merchandise. I understand you have it in your possession. How much are you asking?" He spoke without raising his gaze from the jars.

"For the pumpkin butter?" That struck me as an odd way to put it.

He grimaced. "If that's the way you want to describe it. How much for everything you've got?" His expression seemed somewhere between angry and amused. I was absolutely sure he was asking me for something other than what was on the counter.

"Are you asking the price for all the jam I have left?" I wanted him to spell things out.

He looked at Susa again, and then at me. His smile was close to a sneer. "Sure, let's go with that."

I blinked, then glanced at Susa, who looked as mystified as I was. She shrugged and I dug my calculator out of my purse. "Hang on a minute."

I checked the number of cases and jars I had left. "I'll help." Susa entered the figures into the calculator as I gave them to her, then handed it to me. I turned to Duncan. "In round numbers, two hundred seventy-five."

Now it was Duncan's turn to blink. "Two hundred seventy-five thousand?"

I heard Susa gasp, and I kept my jaw from dropping. "No, Mr. Duncan. Two hundred and seventy five dollars. Plus tax. That's for everything I have here."

He stared at me. I stared at him. *What we've got here is a failure to communicate.*

He turned to Susa again. "Is that everything? Are you sure?"

"It's Roxy's stuff. I've got nothing to do with it. If she says that's all, that's all there is."

He gave her another long look, as if he was trying to read something more into what she'd just said. Then he reached into his pocket and pulled out his wallet. He dropped three hundred-dollar bills on the counter in front of me. "Keep the change. Now where is it?"

Weirder and weirder. I pulled aside the curtain at the back of the booth and pushed the remaining cases in front of me. "This plus what's on the table. That's it."

Duncan's expression went suddenly blank. "That's jam."

I bit back a whole variety of responses. "Yes, sir. That's what I sell. These three cases, and I'll put the rest of the jars in an empty box."

He stared at me for a moment longer, as if he was waiting for me to say something else. But I had no idea what he wanted me to say. Then he sighed. He turned and made a quick gesture. A moment later a large man in a significantly less expensive parka appeared at his side. "Pack up all this jam and take it to the car," Duncan said.

The man, his assistant or bodyguard or whatever, balanced the three cases of jam I had left, along with a box containing the three jars of pumpkin butter and the miscellaneous jars left on the counter, and tottered toward the main entrance. Duncan glanced after him, then turned to the two of us again. "And this is all, correct? No more after this. I won't be hearing from you?"

Once again I was apparently supposed to know what he was talking about but absolutely didn't. Plus I was getting very tired of this conversation. "If you're asking me if I intend to go on making jam, I do. If you're asking me if this is my entire inventory, it isn't. What exactly *are* you asking me, Mr. Duncan?"

Duncan drew himself up, his expression carefully blank. "Nothing. Good afternoon, Ms. Constantine, Ms. Sondergaard."

"Good afternoon. Thanks for the sale." I watched him stride toward the main entrance where his minion had disappeared with my jam.

Chapter Twenty-Five

Susa turned to me. "What the everlasting hell?"

"I don't know." I had a feeling whatever had just happened was significant. And weird. It wasn't unusual to have someone offer to buy up what I had left at the end of the day so I didn't have to take it home, but they usually made an offer or bargained with my price. The idea Duncan had seemed ready—not happy but ready—to pay me two hundred seventy-five thousand dollars for some jam absolutely did not compute.

"I think we need to talk to Fowler. I think he needs to hear about this."

"You think he'll be at work? It's Sunday." Susa's frown switched to an incredulous look.

"Maybe. It's worth checking anyway." I stood up and grabbed my coat and purse, along with my cash box. "I need to text Nate to meet me later. And you need to grab your coat and tell Carly."

"Right." Susa took off at a trot.

I parked in the city parking lot. Most of the city buildings were closed and locked for the weekend, but the police station wasn't. I gave the desk sergeant our names and told him we needed to speak to Chief Fowler. He looked skeptical, but after he got Fowler on the phone, he turned, eyebrows raised. "He'll be right out."

And he was. At least Fowler wasn't in uniform. He

wore his usual off-duty jeans and flannel shirt, but he still looked official as hell. He gestured us down the hall to his office.

He sat at his desk and we sat in front of it. "Now, what can I do for you?"

"Something very strange just happened, and we wondered if it might be related to Fred Hoekstra and maybe even Tera Bloomfield," I said.

Fowler leaned back in his chair. "Okay, you've got my attention. What happened?"

I explained about Phil Duncan and the jam and his odd reaction when I'd given him the price.

Fowler frowned, holding up a hand. "He asked if you wanted two hundred and seventy-five *thousand*? For jam?"

I nodded. "Except I don't think he thought it was jam he was buying. It was…weird."

"That's putting it mildly. Is there more?"

"Yeah. After he had his assistant take all the jam away, he turned to Susa and said something like 'That's all, right? No more?' "

Fowler tapped his fingers on the desk for a moment. Then he turned to Susa. "What did you say?"

"I said it was Roxy's stuff and I had nothing to do with it. He looked like he didn't believe me, but he asked her the same thing."

Fowler frowned at me. "And you said…"

"I asked him what he was talking about. He said 'Nothing' and left."

Fowler stared at us silently, and I wondered if I'd over-reacted. Maybe we should have waited until Monday to tell him about this. Or maybe we should have skipped the whole thing. But after another moment, Fowler leaned back again, staring at the ceiling.

"It sounds like Mr. Duncan is looking for something."

"Maybe. But why would he think I have what he wants? Or Susa? I'm pretty sure I've never spoken to him before today, not even at Tera's dinner. I just knew who he was because he's big stuff around Shavano."

Fowler glanced at Susa. "Did you talk to him at that dinner?"

She shook her head. "Not that I recall. I might have asked him to pass the salt or something."

Fowler turned to me. "What about Hoekstra? You said you'd only spoken to him once, right?"

"So far as I know, I only talked to him one time when I saw him in his yard. The time you picked me up in your squad car." I narrowed my eyes.

Fowler stared down at his desk for a moment, drumming his fingers again. Then he looked up at me. "I'm going to tell you something not many people know. And I'd prefer it stayed that way." He gave me a long look.

"I won't broadcast anything that would endanger your case."

Fowler nodded. "When we brought Hoekstra in, he lawyered up with the speed of light, but it took his lawyer some time to get here. Not that he could do much. We've got Hoekstra dead to rights, all in all. Your nail marks were all over his hands and the skin you had under your nails will match his DNA if we can ever get a sample. Plus your teeth marks are on his thumb. But anyway, while we were sitting in the interview room waiting for the lawyer to arrive, I asked

Hoekstra why he'd attacked you."

"I thought you weren't supposed to ask anybody anything after they'd called for a lawyer." That's what they always said on TV.

Fowler shrugged. "Anything he said might not be admissible in court, but I figured what the hell, chances were he wasn't going to answer anyway."

"And did he?" Susa asked.

"Yeah, he did. He said, and I quote, 'Ask her. She knows.' " Fowler stared at me again for a very long moment.

"Ask *her*?" I said. "Me?"

Fowler nodded. "Must be. Can't ask Tera Bloomfield much of anything. And he didn't seem interested in Ms. Sondergaard."

"But I *don't* know. None of this makes any sense. None of it at all." Frustration was making me angry. Worse, I felt like I was on the verge of tears.

"Tell me what you and Hoekstra talked about. Everything you remember."

I blew out a long breath, trying to sort through my recollections. "It was about his yard. You know, the gardens. The Blankenship House has terrific seasonal gardens. Like right now he's got mums out the wazoo."

Fowler looked like he was fighting a smile. "What else?"

"I think he said they were trying to keep the gardens up, I guess maybe him and his wife."

"Yeah, she just moved in. What else?"

I closed my eyes, recreating the conversation. "I told him they were beautiful year-round, that the spring flowers were great." I paused. "He got stiff after that, like maybe I'd insulted him or something."

"By saying his spring gardens were beautiful? What exactly did you say?"

"I think he said he hadn't seen the spring flowers yet, so I sort of listed them. I said they had great daffodils and tulips, and a great border of lilies of the valley."

Fowler straightened, suddenly very focused.

I stared at him, trying to make the connection. And then I did. "Oh, God. They're poisonous, aren't they? Lilies of the valley, I mean."

"Now how would you know that?"

"Because I grew up on a farm with lots of dogs. If dogs eat lilies of the valley, it can kill them. I always wanted to grow them at the farm, but I couldn't." I was remembering Hoekstra's face now, the blank look, the way he'd seemed to cut off the conversation. "You're saying that was it? The fact I mentioned he had lilies of the valley in his garden."

Fowler's expression closed, and I had the feeling he was backtracking swiftly. "Maybe."

"But they were poisoned with ipecac, Tera and the others," Susa said. "And Hoekstra was one of the ones poisoned. Where would lilies of the valley come in? Why would he think Roxy knew anything about Tera's death?"

Fowler stared down at his hands again, weighing how much he could tell us without screwing over his whole case. "Ipecac isn't fatal," he said finally. "It makes people sick, but it doesn't kill them. It's an emetic."

"Tera wasn't killed with ipecac?" Susa looked confused. "Was the ipecac mixed with something else? Why was Tera the only one affected?"

"She was the only one affected because she was the only one poisoned. By the time she drank the port, Tera Bloomfield was already in dire straits." He sighed. "No, she wasn't killed by the ipecac."

"Lilies of the valley?" I asked.

Fowler nodded. "We'd been thinking maybe monk's hood, which grows wild around here. But lilies of the valley were a strong possibility."

"Hoekstra fed her lilies of the valley? Not while I was there." Susa still looked confused.

Fowler rubbed his eyes. "Lilies of the valley are nasty flowers. Virtually all parts of them are poisonous. If you put a bunch in a vase of water, even the water becomes poisonous. Hoekstra or somebody else could have come up with a concoction to add to her food or wine."

"Why would he want to?"

"We're working on that. Bloomfield's house was owned by a corporation. They also paid for the lease on her office downtown. I had Alice Hoover do a little checking for me. It's the same corporation that bought the Quicksilver Ranch."

"The front group." Susa leaned forward. "Was Hoekstra behind it?"

"Possibly. According to the talk when the Quicksilver Ranch deal went south, there was a consortium behind it, but Alice thought it could be one or two people. The corporate records are a maze. Finding out who was behind Quicksilver could take quite a while. Hoekstra may have been one of the people involved, but there's nothing to prove it. CBI has Bloomfield's computers but so far they haven't turned up any evidence related to the people who were supplying the money. And Hoekstra isn't talking. Yet."

"You think Tera had proof that Hoekstra was involved? That she was blackmailing him? What about Duncan?"

Fowler shrugged. "She might have some kind of documents that implicated Hoekstra and maybe Duncan, too. If we could find them, that would be a big step forward."

"She'd want to keep any proof close by, wouldn't she?" I asked. "Maybe in her house?"

"I've been through her house and her office, including her wall safes in both places. We've been over every place associated with her, but we haven't found anything relating to Quicksilver or to Hoekstra. CBI is going through her computers, like I said. Maybe they'll turn up something, but they haven't yet."

"Could Phil Duncan be the other man behind Quicksilver?"

"You've got me wondering if he is. Maybe he thinks one of you has Tera's files." He gave us one of his half-smiles. "I don't suppose he's right by any chance?"

"Like I've said repeatedly, I only met Tera Bloomfield a few times." I drew myself up. "I never had a conversation with her. And the only time I was in her house was the night she died, when I was way too busy to have searched for anything."

Fowler nodded. "And we now know Hoekstra went after you because he misunderstood something you said."

"Plus you loaded me into a squad car right after that." I wasn't letting him off the hook on that one.

"So where does Duncan come into this?" Susa

asked.

Fowler leaned back in his chair, staring at the ceiling again. "Let's say Hoekstra calls Duncan after the conversation with Roxy and tells him you're onto them. Maybe he even tells Duncan he's going to take care of you. But then he flubs it."

"For which I'm sure we're all very grateful," Susa said acidly.

Fowler nodded. "Right. But maybe that makes Duncan think he needs to step in. Like Hoekstra, he thinks you know more than you know, that you've got Tera's files that would implicate the two of them. Only unlike Hoekstra he prefers to pay you off instead of killing you since he doesn't want to end up sharing Hoekstra's cell. And when he sees the two of you together, he figures maybe you're both in on it. He's ready to meet your price. Two hundred and seventy-five thousand and you'll give him whatever Bloomfield had to connect him to Quicksilver."

I blew out a long breath. "Only it was two hundred and seventy-five dollars, and I gave him three and a half cases of jam. Talk about your failure to communicate."

"But did Duncan help kill Tera?" Susa asked.

Fowler shrugged. "Don't know. One of many things I don't know. One of many things I'll be asking Mr. Hoekstra, although I doubt I'll get an answer."

"One of them must have given Tera the port," I said. "Have you checked at the liquor stores to see who bought it?"

"I sent one of my men to do that, but we didn't have any suspects then. Maybe we'll try it again with some pictures."

"One of them poisoned Tera, and one of them poisoned everybody else with ipecac." Susa paused. "Which makes no sense."

"Sure it does." Fowler leaned forward again. "The ipecac was a distraction. If the pathologist hadn't found another poison in her system, we'd have assumed all the victims were poisoned with the port. And that included Hoekstra. It gave him an alibi, and it misdirected the investigation."

"I wonder if Hoekstra knew about the ipecac. Maybe that was Duncan's idea. Hoekstra puts the lily of the valley decoction in Tera's food when she isn't looking. But Duncan's given her the port laced with ipecac to have after dinner as a distraction. And Duncan doesn't drink it, but Hoekstra does."

"I can imagine what Hoekstra had to say about that later." Susa shook her head. "This is all speculation. You've got Hoekstra for attacking Roxy, but you've got nothing on Duncan. And you'll never be able to nail him unless you find Tera's files."

"You worked with her, right? Did you ever see anything suspicious in her office?" He gave her a half-smile. "Like an invisible wall safe?"

"I didn't spend that much time there. When I came in, we mostly looked at the website so she could tell me what she wanted. I did most of my work remotely."

"What about Carly and Kip?" I asked. "Could they have seen anything?"

"They didn't do any work for her. She wouldn't let anyone else near the site except for me. The two of us were the only ones who had access." Susa's voice trailed off, and she stared into space for a moment. "Just us two."

"Suz?"

"An invisible wall safe." She extended a hand to Fowler. "Let me see your laptop."

He frowned. "Why?"

Susa gave him an impatient grimace. "Give it here."

Fowler looked dubious, but he handed it over.

Susa brought up a list of files on the screen.

"What are you looking for?" I asked.

"The website. Tera's site. It's online for testing, but it's password protected. Tera and I were the only ones who could upload anything. I did most of the uploading, but Tera uploaded some data, some files she wanted me to use."

She scrolled down the list of files, as Fowler and I watched her. "We worked on this for months, literally months. I kept expecting it to be done, but she kept finding new things she wanted. It was a nightmare assignment. Maybe literally."

She went back to scrolling silently. After a few moments, she whistled. "Ladies and gentlemen, we may have a winner." She clicked on a file folder then scrolled down the list of files inside. "This isn't a folder I created, and these documents don't have anything to do with the site so far as I can tell. Of course, none of them is named 'Incriminating Documents' either. Tera uploaded this folder at some point. I have no idea what's in it."

"Let me see." Fowler leaned over her shoulder. "Can you open that one?"

Susa clicked on the file. I couldn't see what was in it, but I could see Fowler's face. He looked like a bird dog that had just gotten a strong scent. Then he gave a low whistle. "She hid it on the website. All the files. In this folder."

"Looks like it. Nobody had access to the site except her and me, and I was way too busy making all the changes she wanted to look for extra files. It was hiding in plain sight. Your invisible wall safe."

"You wouldn't notice spare files?" I asked.

"Not likely. I would have checked for extra files before we went live, but we weren't ready to go live yet. And as it turned out, we never were, and we might never have been. If she had finally decided to let the site go live, she could have moved the files somewhere else or hidden them in another folder. Like I said, she had upload and download access."

"Why didn't CBI find it?" Fowler asked.

"It wasn't on Tera's computer. It was online, just not accessible to anyone but the two of us."

"Can you download that folder onto my computer?"

"Yep." Susa tapped a few more keys.

I sank down again, staring at Fowler. "If this turns out to be the files proving Duncan and Hoekstra were behind Quicksilver, you owe us a beer."

"If these files are the ones we need, I owe you more than that. Maybe a margarita." His smile was closer to genuine this time.

Susa closed the laptop and handed it to Fowler. "So I guess we're done here."

"I guess you are. But it looks like I've got work to do." He opened his laptop and began scrolling through the files again.

I stood up, and Susa followed. "See you, chief."

He nodded without looking up. "See you."

As we stepped through his door, Susa turned. "Just so you know—I don't forget promises of margaritas."

Fowler glanced up, deadpan again. "I'll bear that in mind."

"See that you do." She closed the door behind her.

Chapter Twenty-Six

I headed to the gym so I could pack up my booth and meet Nate at Dirty Pete's. Only when we got to the booth, I found Nate sitting behind the counter.

He gave us a concerned look. "What's wrong? Why did you go to the cops?"

"I'm okay, but I've got a long, involved story to tell you. Only could we do it over beer and chips?" I wanted to break down the booth and get going. It was always possible Duncan would realize what a dumb thing he'd done and come looking for me. Not that I gave refunds.

With the three of us working together, I got the booth down in record time and stowed the pieces in the now-empty truck. Susa drove her own car, and Nate rode with me. We parked outside Dirty Pete's.

Harry grinned as he saw us enter. "And there she is. Looking a little worse for wear, but still smokin' hot."

I blinked at him. *Worse for wear?* What did he mean? And then it struck me. It was Sunday. Fred Hoekstra had attacked me on Friday. I probably still looked like hell, but Fred was in the slammer. "Thanks, Harry," I said and meant it.

We ended up at a table in the corner with room to expand in case anyone else showed up. I thought Fowler might drop by, but Uncle Mike and Madge strolled in a few minutes later. "Evening, all," Madge said. "Can we join you?"

"Sure." I slid over closer to Nate. "We were going to have some chips and beer."

"Sounds good," Uncle Mike said. "A couple of pitchers and maybe some nachos."

We decided to go for super nachos since there were so many of us. "Keep 'em coming, Caroline," Uncle Mike said when he put in the order. "I'm famished. Now, what's up? Hondo Carrick said you two were at the police station."

I'd forgotten about Uncle Mike's police sources. "Okay, this all began this afternoon when Phil Duncan bought the rest of my stock for three hundred dollars. Including the pumpkin butter."

I ran through everything that had happened since then. Well, most of it, anyway. I left out the speculation about Hoekstra and Duncan both being part of Tera's murder and the very interesting but very classified files Susa had found on the website. I might tell Nate about it later, but I didn't want to do it in an open setting like Dirty Pete's.

"Tera Bloomfield was involved with both Duncan and Hoekstra?" Madge asked.

"I don't know about Duncan. She definitely had some kind of hold over Hoekstra." I reached for a cheese and guacamole laden chip. "He probably moved up here because of her. He was either mad about her or she had him by the short hairs."

"And since he probably killed her, I'd guess it was the latter." Nate reached for a nacho of his own.

"Have I mentioned how glad I am you tackled that SOB?" Uncle Mike said. "Not somebody we want running around loose."

Under the table, I squeezed Nate's hand. We still needed to talk about the whole "woman I love" thing if I could find a way to ask about it. Which might be several months from now.

"So what was Duncan trying to pay you off for?" Nate asked. "I mean, your jam is terrific, but I'm assuming he was after more than just a treat."

That led to a discussion of just how involved Duncan had probably been, which produced a lot of wild speculation but no hard answers because, of course, nobody knew anything. Well, Susa and I did, but we weren't sharing.

"Hey," I said finally, "I got three hundred dollars out of the deal. I'm not sure what Duncan thought he was buying, but he got some great jam. And if he was doing anything else with Tera Bloomfield, one of the many investigations currently going on will find it. Win/win."

"Is Fowler sure it was Hoekstra who killed Tera?" Madge asked. "I mean, is that why he went after you?"

"Apparently." I told them about the lilies of the valley.

There was a long pause after I'd finished. "That," said Nate, "is nuts. The guy must have had a guilty conscience to think a random reference to lilies of the valley meant you were on to him."

"Well I did get into a police car immediately afterward. That might have sent him into suspicion overdrive."

"Lilies of the valley are very pretty," Susa said. "And I will never plant them in my yard after this."

"He poisoned himself with ipecac just to divert

suspicion?" Uncle Mike shook his head. "The guy is mental."

Susa shrugged. "The port diverted suspicion, at least at first. I was the chief suspect because I hadn't had any of the damn port."

"No you weren't."

We all turned toward the voice. Fowler stood next to the table, giving Susa an exasperated look. "You were never a serious suspect."

"Could have fooled me," she replied. "For the first couple of days everybody in town thought I'd killed her."

"Then they were idiots," Fowler said flatly. "I owe both of you margaritas. Do you want them now?"

Susa and I both stared at him. He gave us a smile which I took to mean the files she'd downloaded had panned out.

Susa held up her glass. "I'm drinking beer. You can pay up some other time."

Uncle Mike and Madge looked curious. Nate looked suspicious.

"Sit down, Ethan," Madge said. "Have a nacho. And a beer. Or a margarita if that's what you're into." Unsurprisingly, Madge was on a first name basis with Fowler. Madge was on a first name basis with everybody.

Fowler pulled out a chair next to Susa. "You were the only one who didn't drink the port. I had to talk to you about that. But nobody suspected you."

Susa frowned. "Why not? Didn't you think I was capable of murdering her?"

Fowler sighed. "Let me get this straight: first, you were angry because you thought we suspected you, and now you're angry because we *didn't* suspect you?"

"I'm not angry. Just curious. Why not me?"

"Motive?" Fowler said dryly. "You had opportunity, but I'm not sure you had means. Although I guess anybody can distill poison from plants that grow around here. Then there was the fact you were freaked out at the scene, according to the EMTs. That could be acting, but I was inclined to think not."

Susa took a breath to object, but then she subsided. "Okay, but I wasn't *that* freaked out."

She turned to me, and I shrugged. "You were. I was, too. It was hard not to be with all the…stuff happening." A lot of people vomiting more or less simultaneously was enough to freak anybody out.

"Okay, I forgive you. At least you didn't throw me in handcuffs." She gave Fowler one of those smiles that usually reduced men to gibbering. No male was ever unimpressed with Susa.

Fowler raised an eyebrow. "Maybe next time." He reached for a nacho as Caroline brought him his beer.

Oh, this was going to be fun. Susa regarded him through narrowed eyes, probably deciding how much of a challenge he'd be. *Game on, chief.*

After that, the conversation slid into more general topics—the town's Christmas decorations, the Santa Claus parade, what we were fixing for Thanksgiving.

"I want you and Roxy to come to our place," Madge said to Uncle Mike. "We have dinner at the café because we can cook a couple of turkeys there, along with a ham. All the staff comes, and some of the restaurant people in town. It's usually a crush."

Uncle Mike glanced at me, maybe for confirmation or permission. "That sounds great."

"Let me know what I can bring," I said. "Besides jam."

"You should come, too," Madge said, glancing down the table at Susa and Fowler. "Unless you've got other plans."

"Love to," Susa said. "I do great creamed onions."

Fowler looked a little shocked, but then he gave Madge one of his rare smiles. "Thanks, I'd like that. I don't cook, though."

Madge waved a dismissive hand. "Trust me, we've got enough cooks for this event."

"What are you fixing?" I asked Nate.

He shrugged. "Dressing, potatoes, veggies, you name it. Bobby does the turkey."

"We can split it up. I do a mean Brussels sprouts gratin."

Nate smiled, and my heart sped up slightly. I really needed to talk to him about the *woman I love* thing.

Dirty Pete's began to fill up with the dinner crowd then, mostly young but fairly eclectic. When one group sailed in the door I was surprised to see Tom Everett bringing up the rear. I would have assumed Dirty Pete's was too lowbrow for a bank executive, but apparently not.

He paused by our table. "Madge, good to see you."

"Hi, Tom," Madge said. "Lois not back yet?"

"Next week. I'm more than ready for her to be home, believe me."

"Tom's got a new grandchild," Madge informed the table. "His wife's been helping out."

"I've been on my own for three weeks." Everett glanced at Nate and me. "In fact, I've been thinking..." He pulled out another chair and sat down opposite

Madge. Susa scooted closer to Fowler to accommodate him, which didn't seem to bother Fowler much.

"Thinking about what?" Madge asked. Her expression had morphed smoothly into professional.

"I'd like to have a party to welcome Lois." He turned to Nate. "And I'd like you to cater it."

Nate frowned. "Cater it?"

"Like you did at Tera Bloomfield's. That was a terrific meal." Everett grimaced. "I mean before everyone got sick. But that wasn't your fault."

Nate was still frowning. "But we don't…"

"What kind of meal did you have in mind?" Madge said smoothly. "Formal, informal, buffet?"

"Probably a buffet." Everett stared at the ceiling while he thought. "Maybe around twenty-five guests. Appetizers, main course and sides, desserts. You know, the works." He grinned at Madge and Nate. "I've been missing Lois. Let's give her a meal to remember."

"Absolutely, we can do that. Why don't I email you some sample menus and prices and you can let us know what you need." Madge's smile was very bright.

"Great, I'll look forward to it. Nice to see you all." Everett pushed himself to his feet and walked off to join the rest of his group.

Nate turned to his mother. "Since when do we cater?"

"Since five minutes ago. Although to tell you the truth, I've been thinking about starting a catering sideline for a while."

Nate looked confused. "Why?"

"Because we can always use some new sources of income. And because the caterers in this town suck."

Down the table, Fowler choked on his beer. Susa

thumped his back with enthusiasm.

Madge warmed to her subject. "Georgia Cummings has been in business for thirty years and she's still serving chicken Marbella and beef stroganoff. Blanchette's Barbecue is great if you want barbecue, but not so much if you want something a little more classy. Some of the others just do specialty items like Guisado's fajita dinners. There's a real opportunity here, Nathan."

"I'll take your word for it."

"Good, because you'll be in charge."

Nate's eyes widened to deer in the headlights. "Me? Why me?"

"Do you still want your bistro?"

"Yeah. Once the whole Tera Bloomfield thing dies down, I thought I'd see if I could find investors again."

"This will be faster." Madge's eyes took on a determined gleam. "We'll set aside part of the profits to fund the renovations. Having a second kitchen for the catering business will be an advantage. I think even Bobby would agree."

Nate looked skeptical, but he didn't interrupt.

"And having a catering business will give you a chance to reach potential customers for the bistro. Once people know your cooking from the catered meals, they'll be enthusiastic about a restaurant you're running. The catering business can be a showcase for your cooking."

Nate looked closer to interested now. "We could do some pop-ups, too."

"Absolutely," Madge agreed. "The bistro can be operating before it has a physical space. That's a great idea, Nathan. I like it a lot."

"I do too." Nate sounded a bit surprised.

"Good. Come up with sample menus I can send to Tom Everett. Maybe Roxy can give you some suggestions."

I saw straight through her bland smile. If I liked the idea, I might get Nate totally on board. I gave her a bland smile of my own. I wouldn't pressure him into anything he didn't want.

"I'll think about it," Nate said. "I'll see what I can do."

The rest of the dinner focused on other topics, but I noticed Nate seemed quieter than usual. As we walked down Main to find my truck afterward, he stayed silent, staring down at the sidewalk.

"Do you hate the idea of catering?"

He shook his head. "I don't have anything against it. I just never thought about it before. I'm thinking about it now."

"Do you want to talk about it?"

Nate sighed. "Maybe. But let's wait until we're at your place."

I thought about what I ought to say all the way to the farm. Madge's plan sounded good. It gave Nate a way to finance the renovations that would also help their restaurant business. And it got Nate out of the café, which might stop the constant fights with Bobby. If Nate wanted his own business without undercutting the family, this struck me as a good way to get it.

But I didn't want to pressure him. Even though I liked the idea, Nate might not. And I was on his side. Always.

Inside my cabin, I found a bottle of wine and a couple of glasses. We'd each had a beer with the nachos, but a serious discussion called for wine. "Now," I said, "talk to me. What are you thinking?"

Nate leaned back in his chair. "Catering has a lot to recommend it. I'm inclined to give it a try."

I felt like cheering, but I didn't. "Good. I think it's interesting."

"But it can't be a one-man operation," he continued. "I'm going to need at least an assistant. Maybe a waiter."

"I hear Alex and Siggi are available." And if I never saw them again, it would be too soon.

Nate gave me a dry smile. "I'll pass. What I need is somebody in the kitchen with me. Somebody I trust." He paused, sipping his wine. Then he looked at me again. "Somebody like you. Having you in the kitchen at Tera's made a huge difference."

Of course, it had had a big effect on my life, too. But I decided not to point that out. "Do you mean someone *like* me or me?"

"You. If you're interested."

"I could be. But my business comes first. If I start getting a lot of orders from the new website, I may not have much time available."

"Understood. But I'd like to have you in the kitchen with me. I'd like to be with you, period."

His eyes were more brown than green in the shadows around my kitchen table, and I felt a slight sizzle in the air, a feeling of electricity passing between us. "I want to be with you, too. When you tackled Hoekstra…" I paused, gathering my courage.

Nate watched me. "Yeah?"

"What you said. About me. Was that…accurate?" *So* the wrong word, but my brain was too addled to think of the right one.

The corners of his mouth crept up. "You mean was I telling the truth? I wasn't lying."

"So…" I took a breath, trying to figure out how to stumble out of this.

"I love you, Roxy. I think I fell in love with you when you took pity on me and loaned me an extension cord the first time I saw you at the farmers market." He reached across the table, running his index finger along my cheekbone. "And I loved you more when you stood by me in this chaos. I got you into it, but you stood your ground. You helped get us out."

I swallowed hard to push down the lump in my throat. "I love you, too. And I'm not just saying that because you said you loved me. And incidentally I've never said that to anyone I wasn't related to before."

Nate grinned. "Me neither. It's been quite a ride, Rox. The last six weeks, I mean."

I nodded. "It has. Maybe now we can relax."

Nate took hold of my hand, pulling me over to sit on his lap. "Relax tonight. Tomorrow we start planning for Thanksgiving dinner. And the menus for Everett. No more relaxing for the rest of the month."

I smiled down at him, watching the way the shadows made his face even more mysterious. Even more lovely. "Tonight works for me. I'll take it."

And we did.

A word about the author…

Meg Benjamin is an award-winning author of romance. Along with her Luscious Delights series for Wild Rose Press, she's also the author of the Konigsburg, Salt Box and Brewing Love series. Along with these contemporary romances, Meg is also the author of the paranormal Ramos Family trilogy and the Folk series. Meg's books have won numerous awards, including an EPIC Award, a Romantic Times Reviewers' Choice Award, the Holt Medallion from Virginia Romance Writers, the Beanpot Award from the New England Romance Writers, and the Award of Excellence from Colorado Romance Writers.

Meg's Web site is http://www.MegBenjamin.com. You can follow her on Facebook (http://www.facebook.com/meg.benjamin1), Pinterest (http://pinterest.com/megbenjamin/), Twitter (http://twitter.com/megbenj1) and Instagram (meg_benjamin). Meg loves to hear from readers—contact her at meg@megbenjamin.com. http://www.MegBenjamin.com

Thank you for purchasing
this publication of The Wild Rose Press, Inc.

For questions or more information
contact us at
info@thewildrosepress.com.

The Wild Rose Press, Inc.
www.thewildrosepress.com

www.ingramcontent.com/pod-product-compliance
Lightning Source LLC
Chambersburg PA
CBHW070059030726

47506CB00002B/516